A Brilliant Convergence

A Brilliant Convergence

A Sparkling Regency Mystery

RACHEL GATES

WordCrafts Press

A Brilliant Convergence, while a novel, is inspired by actual events. The author has endeavored to be respectful to all persons, places, and events presented in this novel, and attempted to be as accurate as possible. Still, this is a novel, and all references to persons, places and events are fictitious or used fictitiously.

Hardback ISBN: 978-1-962218-51-1
Paperback ISBN: 978-1-962218-52-8

A Brilliant Convergence
Copyright © 2025
Rachel Gates

All rights reserved. No part of this book may be reproduced, stored in a retrieval system, or transmitted in any form or by any means—electronic, mechanical, photocopy, recording or otherwise—without the prior written permission of the publisher. The only exception is brief quotations for review purposes.

Published by WordCrafts Press
Cody, Wyoming 82414
www.wordcrafts.net

Mom: Thank you for teaching me not only how to read, but also how to love reading. In giving me books, you gave me the world.

Chapter 1

Provence, France

October 1824

With another stunning Provincial sunset setting the sky ablaze, Henry Rockcliff piled the last of the branches he was trimming from the grapevines into a narrow wooden cart, cleverly designed to fit between the rows of vines. Wiping his brow, he took off his straw hat and climbed into the back of the cart for a drink of water, gazing at the orange-pink masterpiece framing the rolling hills of southern France. Henry's younger brother, Charles, would have grinned at the painted sky and spouted the old "sailors delight" rhyme. The local villagers said the red sky heralded the coming mistral winds, a sharp northerly wind which could blow for days and drive a man half-crazy.

Maybe that was why he was feeling so restless today. The mistral would explain it. And yet...this uneasiness was a feeling he'd felt often during his two years of service while fighting Bonaparte's army—a prickling at the back of his neck, a pressure right between his eyes. Henry had been little more than a boy during the war, but he'd always had the uncanny ability to sense when danger was near. This somewhat macabre talent exposed him to no end of teasing by his fellow soldiers—the toff who needed spectacles to read but could sense death like a parlor-room mystic, they said. But after he saved their lives more than once, Henry had quickly earned their respect—though he suspected his ability to keep a level head under pressure had much more to do with the situation than any so-called sixth sense.

But this feeling—this restlessness—was different. He was safe at his maternal grandmother's vineyard, just as he had been for the past nine years. Despite his status in England as a Viscount's son, here he was little more than a farmhand, browned from laboring in the field with his cousins. It suited him. He had never been as happy in his boyhood home as he was here in the French countryside, tending grapes to turn into wine as pink as the sunset, and enjoying long, lingering meals with his grandmere and French side of the family.

No, there was no danger. Here, all was quiet. Could it be too quiet? Perhaps he was missing the action of the war. Henry chuckled at the thought. Anytime anyone had asked him what he was searching for here in his self-imposed exile, his answer had always been the same: peace and quiet. Taking another drink of water, he pulled on a fresh linen shirt and began to pull the cart back towards the farm.

Something was coming, and Henry prayed it was only the wind. Inside the farmhouse, Henry hung his hat on the peg by the back door and lathered his hands with soap at the entryway washbasin. Fingers gentle against sunburned skin, he washed the dirt and perspiration from his face, feeling the long, raised white scar running from cheek to collarbone. There were other scars, less visible, but this one was his favorite. It let him play the role of disgruntled hermit nicely.

His stomach rumbling at the welcome smell of roasting fish, Henry crossed the stone courtyard to join his family at the outdoor table for dinner. His cousins were there already. Gerald was telling everyone about a pretty girl he'd met in town, gesturing wildly and his eyes twinkling. Maurice was setting a huge platter of grilled fish on a table already laden with crusty bread and heaping plates of vegetables. The crisp rosé wine was flowing freely. The harvest was over now, the wine-making season in full swing. Uncle Martin bustled out of the house with a crock full of fresh butter for the bread, his white apron still bearing the grape-juice splatters from today's pressing.

"*Bonsoir*, Henry!" His uncle said jovially, greeting his nephew in French. "The sky is as a blushing maiden tonight, is it not? It cannot be that they have such beautiful skies in England!"

Henry only spoke French with his family as was his preference. They had welcomed him with a warmth he had not expected when the war was over. He'd shown up unannounced, covered in battle scars both literal and figurative, and they'd taken him in. His relatives here loved to tease him about his home country, but he knew he was as much at home here in Provence as he could ask for.

"*Non, Oncle*," he answered as always. "Nothing like this. This —" he waved his arm around to gesture to the farm, the fields, and the sky, "—is heaven, of course."

"*Non, mon petit chou.*" Henry's grandmother padded out of the kitchen with the help of her cane, a bottle of rosé tucked under her other arm. "Heaven is where the Good Lord lives. But Provence is our little preview, no?" She patted him gently on the cheek.

Henry gave her a roguish smile and kissed her cheek.

"Well, madame, it may not quite be heaven, but you are certainly an angel. You and this place have certainly helped me find solace."

His cousins were lighting the oil lamps hung around the patio, and a fire crackled merrily in the outdoor hearth. The atmosphere was one of contentment and plenty—not the austere, gilded wealth of his childhood, but a contentment born of having everything one needed, and nothing one didn't. Despite his restlessness of late, he was eternally grateful for all his family and this place had given him. He was little more than a boy when he came here; now he was a man, not quite without regrets, but more at peace with himself and the world.

"Your journey is not quite done yet, my love." She interrupted his thoughts as she looked into the last vestiges of the sunset lingering on the horizon. "You have one more battle left to fight."

Surprised, Henry looked at his grandmere. Despite her some eighty-odd years, she wasn't usually prone to these slips in memory. It was one of the inevitabilities of aging, he supposed.

"*Non, Grandmere,*" he answered gently, "the war was over nearly ten years ago. I am done with the army now."

His grandmere smacked him, hard, on the arm.

"I am not yet so old I have lost my wits." She winked, pulling a letter out of the pocket of her apron.

"*Voila. Ta lettre.* This came for you today, from England."

Henry took it and glanced at the handwriting. Not his mother's, neither was it his sister's hand. Neither elder brother nor father ever wrote to him, but he would have still recognized their haughty scrawls. Then who? Panic gripped him. Was his mother ill, or worse?

"Read it before you worry yourself to death."

He looked up and raised an eyebrow, but his grandmere held up a hand.

"I know you, Henri." She used the French pronunciation of his name. She only called him "HEN-ry" when she was cross.

"I see panic written all across your face, even though you keep your emotions like this,"—she patted her chest, her fingers under her shawl—"as you say, close to the vest."

"I have not read your mail, but there I think you will find your next adventure. I have a feeling, too."

She gave him a kiss on the cheek and shuffled off towards the table and their evening meal. Bewildered, Henry opened the letter and began to read.

Staring into the embers of a dying fire as if they held answers, Henry sat in semi-darkness in the cottage library. His family had all retired for the night, and the mistral was picking up. The windows rattled in their frames, the fire flaring as the occasional gust snuck in under the door. Henry looked at the empty glass in his hand and considered pouring something a bit stronger than the wine he'd been drinking with dinner.

Rachel Gates

A quiet shuffling sound indicated his grandmother was coming to join him. He'd been waiting for her. They always stayed up late together in the library when there was something important to discuss. When he'd received word his younger brother died at sea, his grandmother had sat with him, smoking a pipe and silently praying down her rosary, until dawn began to dance over the edge of the hills.

She sat and waited. She was as patient and stubborn as a stone, and he knew he could not leave here until he told her all—or, in this case, at least most of it. Henry grimaced, took his spectacles back out of his waistcoat pocket and glanced back over the letter one more time.

"I've received a letter from my former commander, Colonel Phillips. He wants my help with something."

His grandmere nodded her head ever so slightly and waited again. He wouldn't tell her Phillips now worked for the War Office and was actively engaged in espionage against England's enemies. That most likely included the French, and the thought of his birth country spying on his adopted country…well, Henry knew it happened, but dwelling on it made him uncomfortable.

He cleared his throat, mentally sifting through the information in Phillips' letter.

"There is a stretch of coastline in England, it's near where Charles' ship…" Henry's voice wavered, and he pinched the bridge of his nose and started again, slipping into what his fellow soldiers had called "battle mode" to keep the emotions at bay. He'd deal with those later, in his own way.

"It is close to where Charles' ship ran aground. It's always been a particularly dangerous spot, where merchant ships dodge sharp rocks to follow the coastline up to the Thames estuary. It takes skill in the best of weather. In storms or fog it can be next to impossible."

Facts. Stick to the facts.

"In recent years, there has been an increase in casualties. More

A Brilliant Convergence

ships are being caught on the rocks, and there seems to be a...sharp decrease in the number of survivors."

"*Quel dommage*," murmured the elderly woman beside him.

"*Oui, Grandmere.*"

Henry leaned forward and stirred the dying embers in the fireplace.

"There is a man here in France. Monsieur Fresnel. You may have read of him in the newspapers. He has invented a lighthouse lens apparatus that is magnitudes brighter than anything we have now, and that makes it possible to see the lighthouse from miles out to sea! Colonel Phillips wants me to go visit Fresnel in Paris, see if one of these lenses might be helpful for this town in England, and then go there and persuade the local landowner to install one."

"*Oui, mon Cherie.* And what is the catch."

His grandmother was a sharp one.

"Phillips thinks there may be more than bad weather at play here. He suspects smugglers of assisting ships towards their untimely demise, but how no one knows. He wants me to pose as an investor eager to install the new lens, which of course if it is anything like they say, I would certainly be. Any device which has the ability to keep more sailors safe I am certainly all for. But more than that, he wants me to quietly investigate around the area, and figure out what might be happening there."

Henry did not add the reason he was chosen for this somewhat grim investigation was a band of French smugglers was believed to be operating in the area, and Phillips wanted someone who could also easily blend in with the coarse sailors. Henry didn't know whether to be flattered or appalled.

"It sounds *tres dangereux*." His grandmother's eyes sparkled. She knew he wasn't telling her the whole story, but thankfully didn't press him for details. "Like just what you need to get the blood flowing."

"Perhaps." Henry swirled the last few drops of wine in his glass like a miniature tempest. "But grandmere, going back to England again…" Henry struggled to put his hesitations to words.

"I'm not a soldier anymore. I'm not sure I'm even entirely English anymore. I did my duty, obeyed my father, and served my country honorably, but I planned never to go back there. I certainly don't want to ever have to pick a side again. And I'm certainly not a bloody spy." His vehemence surprised even him. He thought in French, dreamed in French even, but apparently he still cursed in English.

"God has no nationality, *mon Cherie*, you know this. England is not right. France is not right. We are all only human, no? Doing the best we can with where we find ourselves. You will do what is right, Henri, not because of who is around you, but because what is *inside* of you."

Reaching over, the old woman patted his chest.

"This I know."

Swallowing, Henry fought against the lump in his throat.

"You think I should go then? Can I go back to England—back home—after all this time?

"You will always have a home here, my love," she reassured him. "It is my dearest wish you will marry a nice French girl, and have many children that will run wild in the fields of Provence and sneak me my favorite sweets when no one is looking. But you will never truly be at home here, until you make peace with a few things you've left behind."

Henry could think of a few things he'd left behind he had no desire to make peace with, particularly his father. The Viscount had pressed Henry into the army and Charles into the navy, to continue the "glorious line" of Rockcliff men that had made his family proud. Henry had wanted a different, more scholarly path in the law or the church, and he'd never quite understood why such a noble calling had been denied him. He was strong, was a good soldier, and had that uncanny sixth sense. In his two short years in the army, he had quickly advanced up the ranks and earned the respect of his men. But as soon as the war was over, he'd cashed in his commission, had saddled up his horse, and was headed towards Provence less than two days after the last shot was fired.

He hadn't set foot in England since.

Maybe it was time to go back, if only for some closure. And Monsieur Fresnel's new lens sounded like a miracle of science and genius. If it could indeed save other sailors, he owed it to Charles' memory to try.

He turned towards his grandmother, raising a brow, and allowed the ghost of a smile to flit across his face.

"But how will you survive the winemaking season without me?"

His grandmother's shoulders started to shake. A full-throated chuckle escaped, quickly turning into deep, rich laughter. She laughed until tears streamed out of her eyes.

"Henri, our family has worked this land for two-hundred years, and we've managed perfectly fine without you until now," gasped his grandmere when she could breathe again. Getting up out of her seat, she began to shuffle out of the library. She paused at the door. "Besides, my love, you are good at many things. The vines thrive under your care, my garden has never been more productive, and you keep me entertained with such stimulating conversation, no? But you are an Englishman through and through—you have no finesse for wine."

Henry heard her cackling all the way to her bedroom.

CHAPTER 2

COLLINGTON
KENT, ENGLAND

April 1825

There were no mistrals on the coast of England, but it was a breeze of a very different sort that stopped Henry in his tracks today. He and his valet, Rogers, were riding down a quiet country lane when a straw bonnet edged in yellow ribbon blew right across the road and was nearly crushed by the horses' hooves. It was a fetching bonnet, made of high quality materials but simply trimmed. It boasted only a few yellow and white daisies for embellishment, none of the horrid stuffed birds or enormous plumes of feathers Henry had seen ladies wearing of late in Paris.

"Ho ho! It looks like the ocean breeze has done some poor woman a disservice." Henry reined in his horse and scooped up the wayward topper before it could blow any further. "I wonder where the lady in question has run off to."

Shielding his eyes from the bright afternoon sun, he looked around. The sea was sparkling and the road down to the village quaint and scenic, but he saw no one else in sight.

"That's rather odd. Ladies don't normally let themselves wander very far from their bonnets while out in public. While the breeze is brisk, I doubt it could have carried this all the way from the village."

As he scanned the horizon again, two tiny figures appeared

off to his right, gaining in size as they appeared to be running straight towards him.

"What in the world?"

The two young people came closer as they raced over the hill. One, a young man, was dressed in his shirtsleeves and waistcoat but missing a coat and hat. The other, a young lady, was properly attired in a golden walking dress but lacking a bonnet and—judging from the number of curls flowing free behind her—also a number of hairpins.

"Must be a local farmer's children, me Lord," Rogers offered.

"Perhaps they know when the Baron might return. They seem to be his nearest neighbors."

Henry had been in town less than twenty-four hours, and already his mission was stalled. He'd just come from the estate of the local Baron, a Lord Warwick, who was supposed to give him permission to install a Fresnel lens in the town's lighthouse, which sat on his land. Lacking his blessing, there was only so much snooping around the lighthouse Henry could do without getting arrested. It turned out that the Baron, however, hadn't been home in nearly a decade. The manor's dour-faced butler had looked down his nose at Henry—an impressive feat considering he was at least a head shorter—and told him his master was due to return any day now, and Henry could take the matter up with him then. Hopefully the man was right and not just trying to rid himself of a troublesome interloper.

Looking down at the girl's bonnet in his hands, Henry smiled and considered the two young people making their way towards him. His siblings would have never been caught gallivanting across a field thus attired. His younger sister Angelica, now married and mother of two children—at least so he was told—never left the house without a hat, for she feared the sun would brown her skin. He chuckled and looked down at his own tanned hands. If she could only see him now.

At least he looked a bit less like a farm-hand at present.

Handing his reins to Rogers, Henry dismounted and patted the horse's neck. The horse had been purchased by Colonel Phillips and left for Henry at Dover when he arrived in England. He could have just borrowed a horse, as was his plan, but Phillips wanted him to arrive in style. The chestnut was one of the finest horses Henry had ever seen. He suspected the Colonel had called in a few favors to find him such a magnificent creature, and he hadn't let Henry pay him.

"Give him to me when you go back to France, if you must," the man had written, "or take the fellow with you."

The horse wasn't the only effort that had gone into making Henry presentable. While he'd been meeting with Monsieur Fresnel and his associates in Paris, he'd visited a fine tailoring house and ordered a new wardrobe. If he wished to mingle in society, his grandmere had admonished him, he could hardly show up dressed as a field hand. As Henry had given himself one last cursory glance in the mirror this morning on the way out of the inn, he'd barely recognized the man looking back at him. Gone were the loose linen trousers and open shirts of a French laborer. In their place he sported a pale yellow linen waistcoat, smartly tied cravat, and a coat of blue superfine that clung like a second skin to his broad shoulders. A pair of lightweight fawn-colored trousers and gleaming hessians completed the look.

Henry approached the fence separating him from the youths as the runners slowed their pace and walked towards him.

"Excuse me, miss! I believe this bonnet may belong to you."

The girl had stopped to catch her breath, bending at the waist, while the young man at her side was rather flushed with thick, dark hair standing on end like a lion's mane. Henry grinned, still holding the bonnet, and couldn't help but tease them.

"Unless of course, good sir, this is your topper. While it is quite lovely I believe it would be a rather unorthodox choice."

The girl straightened as she laughed heartily, and Henry felt his stomach drop to his toes. *Well that was curious.* He quickly glanced around them, wondering if they were in imminent danger. No, nothing but rolling fields and gentle sea breezes. His gut had never failed him before, but this was new. There was no danger about, nor was it restlessness as he'd felt back in France. Henry looked back at the girl's face.

She was older than he'd first believed, not quite a schoolroom miss, but a young woman with sparkling brown eyes and an attractive spray of freckles across her face. Her skin had a healthy glow, which suggested this wasn't the first time she'd been caught outside without her bonnet. Her dress was tidy and well-made, but, like her bonnet, it lacked any unnecessary adornments. Henry suspected she could wear a flour sack and still be breathtaking.

"Thank you, sir, for saving my bonnet, and do please forgive us our lack of propriety."

She smiled at him, blushing, whether at the *faux pas* of being caught without her hat, or the fact that Henry was now unashamedly staring at her, he wasn't sure. She gently took the proffered bonnet and set to work tying the ribbons under her chin. It did little to tame the riot of curls still poking out from all directions.

"You see, I told my brother here he'd grown too old and fusty and could no longer beat me to that tower and back." She pointed to a crumbling ruin about a kilometer in the distance. "And obviously, I could not run fast enough in my bonnet."

"Obviously," repeated Henry dumbly, still captivated. "I'm honestly impressed that you managed to do so in a dress." He stared at her a moment longer, and the girl, far from being embarrassed, simply raised an eyebrow.

Henry cringed, and the girl's brother chuckled.

"Forgive me, both of you, where are my manners," he added quickly, "I am Mr. Henry Rockcliff, in town on business."

The young man smiled at Henry and offered his hand.

"I am Mr. Pierce Seaton, and this is my sister, Miss Emelia Seaton," he said, putting his other arm around his sister affectionately.

"Sorry you had to witness our little display of indecorum," he added grinning. "Hardly anyone ever comes down this road, with the manor being uninhabited for so long; we've become used to treating it like an extension of our property. Just come from Seaton House, you see, and we're about to walk to the village. Care to join us, old chap?"

Mr. Seaton shot a quick glance at his sister as he made his invitation, as if daring her to contradict him.

"I was just heading to the village myself," answered Henry. "I'm staying at the inn for a couple of weeks while I work on a project. Shall we walk that way?"

"Oh no, we can't do that," protested Miss Seaton.

Henry glanced at her and tilted his head, waiting.

"I mean," she added hurriedly, "not until our friends join us."

Sure enough, two more young people were walking towards them through the field. Henry had been so entranced by the lovely Miss Seaton, he hadn't even noticed the others approaching. An exquisitely-dressed young dandy carried an extra coat draped over his arm and a hat in his hand. Joining the siblings, he handed them to Mr. Seaton with a nod. At his side was a girl, perhaps a few years younger than Miss Seaton. She was shorter and curvier, with golden blonde ringlets peeking out from her straw bonnet, and her cheeks dimpled as she smiled at Henry. She was objectively quite pretty, he thought, but curiously his stomach gave no response.

After Mr. Seaton had shrugged his shoulders into the well-fitted coat and donned his hat, he turned to introduce his friends.

"This is Arbuckle, a good friend of mine on holiday from London, and Miss Clara Appleton, our nearest neighbor and dearest friend." Mr. Seaton winked roguishly at Miss Appleton, and she hiccuped a giggle. Definitely younger than Miss Seaton, then, thought Henry. He looked back and saw her watching him curiously.

"I've just been to the Manor to see Lord Warwick, but I'm told he's been away for quite some time," he explained, sensing the young woman's curiosity, and waved an arm towards the property now far behind them.

"Ah, good old Eddie!" exclaimed Mr. Seaton. "Hasn't even made it home yet and already he's bringing new and interesting visitors to town. How lucky for us," he added in an low voice, gazing pointedly at his sister, who smiled sweetly at Henry. He pretended not to notice that she'd also stepped swiftly on her brother's foot.

"Dash it all, Emmie, I—" Mr. Seaton began,

"Now that our friends have joined us, won't you walk with us, Mr. Rockcliff," interrupted Miss Seaton. "We'd love to show you around town. Since you're heading that way, of course."

He looked at her kind smile and sparkling eyes, a riot of curls still proclaiming their independence around the edges of that oh-so-very-fetching bonnet, and glanced back at Rogers with a look of bemusement.

"Rogers, my good man, there's nothing for it. You take my horse, and I'll meet you back at the inn."

Chapter 3

Seaton House
Collington, Kent

"'Pon my word, Emelia, you're a bit haggard this morning," Emelia Seaton's brother, Pierce, declared as he spooned kippers onto his plate at the breakfast table.

Rolling her eyes, Emelia stifled a yawn as she shuffled to her spot in the morning room, adjusting the stray pins her unruly curls threatened to send scattering about the room. The sun was well into the sky, and the French doors open to the patio let in an invigorating sea breeze and warm spring sunshine. The unseasonably warm weather had the whole family sunning like cats at every available opportunity.

"If I'm looking haggard—a situation which I vehemently deny—then it is entirely your fault." Emelia grimaced, knowing her dimpled cheek added unwanted levity to the situation. With her wildly curly hair, spattering of freckles, and that stubbornly optimistic dimple, Emelia often struggled to school her countenance into something serious enough to accompany her scholarly thoughts.

Ignoring the unruly dimple, she began again.

"If you and Mr. Arbuckle hadn't woken the entire house while you were thrashing about the stairs in your cups last night, I wouldn't have had to study Thomas Young's *Experiments and Calculations Relative to Physical Optics* until the wee hours."

Pierce had the grace to blush but quickly recovered.

"Dash it all, Emmie, ought not to read such things." He deftly redirected the conversation away from his perceived transgressions. "Not the thing for a young girl! No ordinary man wants a blue stocking of a wife."

Emelia snorted, attempted to pass it off as a cough, then raised a demure eyebrow as she scooted her seat farther towards the table.

"Well it's a good thing I'm not in the market for a husband, at least not an *ordinary* one. I'll not have one of these marriages of convenience to a man I hardly know."

In fact, marriage of any kind wasn't high on Emelia's priority list. Perhaps she could be persuaded to consider marriage built on deep friendship like her mother and father's had been. But the marriages of her peers, most often little more than business arrangements, hadn't inspired in her a great confidence in the institution. And when one had received the kind of education and freedom usually only afforded to sons, well, marriage was decidedly a step down in life.

"Likely I shall be an old maid and spend all my time doting upon your ten children."

The thought of spending her days as a doting aunt rather than a proper, boring housewife cheered her, and she happily snagged a piece of buttered toast off the rack.

At his sister's revelation, Pierce's eye became as wide as the saucers their coffee cups sat upon.

"Ten children! Good Lord, Emmie, you know I ain't in the petticoat line, and I have zero interest in becoming leg shackled anytime in the near future."

"I beg your pardon?" inquired Emelia, knowing full well what her brother meant but not able to resist giving him grief anyway.

Likely perceiving the previous line of conversation to be safer for his happy bachelorhood, Pierce tried a defensive tactic.

"I'll have you know, I was *not* in my cups last night, well, maybe we'd drunk a brandy or two by the fire, but that don't signify. We were designing a most exciting curricle race, it's going to be a bang-up course! As for thrashing about, well if we didn't have that damned suit of armor in the entrance hall, there would have been nothing to it. Why father insisted on retaining that relic when the rest of the house is quite the thing, I'll never know."

Her brother seemed satisfied with this shifting of blame to ease his somewhat limited conscience. He helped himself to another piece of toast and attacked his kippers with gusto, and the family balance was restored.

Emelia slid her chair slightly to the left to take full advantage of an inviting beam of sunlight coming in through the open doors, and poured herself a cup of coffee. While the house was not what most in London would consider up-to-the-moment in fashion, it *was* a lovely modern estate, full of light and large windows oriented toward rolling green hills sloped gently towards the sea. The house had been built in the Georgian style, with stately columns, and light and airy rooms decorated tastefully in shades which reminded one of the outdoor setting in which the estate was located. Large French doors in the breakfast room opened onto a generous balcony for enjoying the sea breezes.

Thanking Davis, the family's elderly butler, for the plate of toast and eggs he set in front of her, Emelia allowed herself several full minutes of comfortable silence to sip her coffee. Her brother cleared the last of his breakfast with an enthusiasm that suggested he was honest about his lack of indulgence the night before.

"Come to think of it, where *is* the delightful Mr. Arbuckle?" Emelia and Pierce's mother asked, finally poking her head out from behind her newspaper and peering at them owl-like over her spectacles. "I confess, having him as a houseguest has been the most amusement I've had in ages. One just gets used to his finely-honed air of nonchalance, and then someone mentions parents or bills, and the poor lad suddenly looks like a startled horse and bolts out of the room."

Emelia chortled and choked on a mouthful of coffee, her brother glaring at her even as he pounded her back to help her catch her breath.

"Arbuckle's a most exquisite tulip of the *ton*, Mama," defended Pierce as Emelia coughed into her napkin, "one of the leading names in fashion at the moment, and from one of the best families in town."

He took an enormous bite of toast. "Can't hep if sound eff un asket."

"I'm sorry, darling. What did you say?" Mrs. Seaton abandoned her newspaper altogether and looked pointedly at her son. Emelia knew that while her mother might overlook the cant that slipped into her son's vocabulary, talking with a full mouth at the table was never acceptable.

Unabashed, Pierce washed his toast down with some coffee.

"I said, he can't help it if he finds himself in the basket. Fellow barely gets an allowance from his father, and he had to purchase a whole new wardrobe for the season of course. His father won't return from India in time to ensure Weston can do the thing justice."

"How dreadful it would be to be seen sporting last season's fashions," agreed Mrs. Seaton, with what Emelia thought was an admirable attempt at a straight face.

"Yes, dreadful," said her seemingly oblivious son. "Besides that, Arbuckle has had a dashed run of bad luck at the tables as of late. Safer for him to rusticate with me for a spell, at least till his father comes home to settle matters. He'd do the same for me, of course."

"How fortunate of him to have a kind friend such as you." Mrs. Seaton's eyes twinkled. "But let us hope you never have need of such a service, as you are the head of the household now, and if you ever find yourself, as you said—in the basket—well, that would hardly bode well for the rest of us."

Emelia knew there was little chance of that happening, as her brother had been content to let his mother handle the bulk of their affairs since their father died three years ago. Pierce had inherited the estate while most young men his age were still cutting a lark about town, and, at least in Emelia's opinion, had not yet grown into his role as the head of the household.

Wiping the last of her eggs off the plate with a bit of toast,

Emelia glanced at her brother again across the table. Five years her senior at twenty-five, he did cut a rather dashing figure with his wavy brown hair cut short in the Brutus style, and simple but impeccable taste in clothes. The only member of the family who traveled regularly to London, Pierce loved nothing more than an exciting curricle race, a boxing session at Gentleman Jackson's, or long evenings of cards with his cronies. He was not a bad sort, however, and she would be the first to defend him. His manners were all that was proper, and he was kind towards Lord and tenant alike. Overall she was very fond of her brother.

"To answer your question, Mother." Pierce interrupted Emelia's thoughts. "Arbuckle never rises before noon. He keeps town hours, and we shouldn't expect to see him before luncheon, at least."

Emelia thought that sounded lovely, as she was prone to while away the nighttime hours tucked in bed with an interesting book. It took a few cups of coffee before her tired brain was ready to face the day. And last night had been extra late because of the crashing armor—oh! Armor! She set down her cup with a clatter. "Armor! Pierce, last night I had the greatest notion!"

Her brother, used to her outbursts, merely turned toward her with polite interest.

"You're right of course, that old suit of armor is certainly in the way." Emelia smiled sweetly, as she'd done since she was about three and discovered her adoring glances would earn her just about anything from her brother.

"Let's move it out to the garden! I've been wanting to test the strength and durability of several materials I'm experimenting with for my arrowheads, but I've lacked a sufficient target."

"For some reason, Davis has yet to agree to hold one for her." Mrs. Seaton winked at the man at his post in the corner, and he bowed in acknowledgment.

"The armor would be a perfect target: even my strongest arrows would be unlikely to damage it." Emelia chewed her lip as she made the calculations in her head. "Well, perhaps not much."

"Splendid notion, Emmie!" Her brother lifted his coffee cup in a toast. "Much better use for it than cluttering up the hall, if Mother's alright with it of course."

"Emmie, darling." Her mother peered at her again through her spectacles. "You *do* realize that armor is an antique, and could possibly be very valuable?"

Her breakfast abandoned, Emelia was already bouncing up from the table. She turned back with a smile.

"What better value than science, Mother! You always say the acquisition of knowledge is our most valuable pursuit."

"I do, don't I?" Mrs. Seaton shrugged and reclaimed her newspaper. "Very well, dear. Don't forget to take notes. A scientist is nothing without proper documentation!"

A collection of round wooden targets tucked under her arm, Emelia made her way through the back garden. A knot of red ribbons hung from one elbow. Davis, two footmen, and the gardener had carried the ancient—and very heavy—armor to a lovely open space between the hedges, and she was ready to hang the appropriate targets and begin her daily archery practice. Glancing around the magnificent gardens, tucked in between stately castle ruins, she breathed in the salty air blowing in from the ocean just over the hill to her east.

The family had lived at Seaton House for a mere quarter of a century. Emelia's father, though robust and hearty in both appearance and manner, lived in fear of his family taking a chill in London. As his more-than-adequate fortune allowed, he quickly whisked his wife away to the coastal hamlet of Collington as soon as she was found to be increasing in the early months of their marriage. Mr. Seaton had spared no expense, and the estate and grounds were built upon the site of an ancient castle ruin overlooking the sea in the south east of the country. The castle had been mostly reduced to a very atmospheric but useless pile of rubble, but there remained one perfect tower at the northwest of the grounds. Over the years it had served as a storage shed for the gardener, a fantastical play house for Pierce and Emelia, and most recently, Emelia's workshop. It lent an air of gravitas to the whole estate.

The family had lived quite happily at Seaton House until Mr. Seaton had surprised everyone by taking the sudden chill he lived in dread of and passing away three years prior. Emelia still missed him terribly, and knew her mother and brother did, too. For a while, she thought she would never be able to walk these grounds or enter a room without his presence; it just seemed so wrong to be at Seaton House without him. She was grateful for their life together, however, and for the peaceful home her father had created for his family. He'd poured his heart and soul into the place, and so long as she was here, she would always have a part of him.

After tying the targets to several locations on the suit of armor, Emelia stepped back to her makeshift target line behind a row of flowerpots overflowing with forget-me-nots, took a few deep breaths to release the tension from her shoulders, and took aim. This daily target practice was as necessary to her well-being as breathing the sea air.

While archery wasn't that unusual of a pastime for young women her age, Emelia was not content to simply send arrows flying across a field. That was far too tame. She was fascinated by the physics of the sport, and was continually working on improving her aim and adjusting her materials. In any number of weather conditions, she could be found in the back garden, testing her arrows against wind speed and rain, on a cloudless moonlit night, and on one unfortunate occasion, attempting to accurately hit a target lit only by lightning flashes in a raging storm. After lightning split the nearest tree from top to bottom, leaving Emelia unharmed but a bit shaken, her mother made her promise to cease practice at the first rumble of thunder.

After a few shots, she adjusted the targets and retreated back behind her firing line, her mind wandering to the man they'd met on their walk to the village yesterday. Mr. Rockcliff was intriguing, to say the least. He was clearly a gentleman of some import, with perfect manners and pleasing speech, yet he had a casual, relaxed way about him. It wasn't as if Emelia hadn't met other gentlemen, but as her family had been in mourning for her father the year Emelia would have made her come-out in London, she'd had relatively little interaction with society.

In the years since, she'd kept postponing her London debut as they settled into their new roles and routines, attempting to adjust without her father. Thus, while quite not an old maid at nearly twenty years of age, Emelia was not yet married like most girls of her age and station. This wasn't quite the black mark upon her out here in the country as it would have been if they mixed in town society. She couldn't say, however, she had any particular desire to mix in society anyway. Her friends in the village accepted her quirks and odd hobbies, but Emelia's limited interactions amongst the *ton* told her the rest of the world might not be so forgiving. The inevitable result—for most, the goal—of coming out in society was to be married, anyway. There could be nothing more stifling than being married to a man who couldn't love her as she was, or worse, who would try to change her. If necessary, she would happily live out her days in a cottage by the sea with an extensive library for company. But that didn't stop her curiosity about Mr. Rockcliff, with his suntanned skin and calloused fingertips. There was something about him that didn't quite fit, and Emelia liked things to fit.

"Halloo!" A familiar friendly voice broke through her thoughts and Emelia quickly lowered her bow. "Emmie, dearest, I'm coming around the hedge, please hold your arrows!"

The smiling, apple-cheeked face of her best friend Clara popped out from around the bushes.

"As much as I adore you and your strange hobbies, I'd hate to end up skewered like that lovely goose you brought us the other day. Charlie and Ashley were quite impressed and spent the entire afternoon fashioning bows for themselves out of branches and Cook's kitchen twine."

Two years younger than Emelia, Clara Appleton and her five rambunctious younger brothers lived with their family on a sprawling farm just down the lane from Seaton House. Emelia and Clara had been best friends since Clara could walk, and her friendship was one of the main reasons Emelia was content with a quiet life in the country.

"How did you know I was practicing archery?"

"I would hardly expect you to remain indoors on such a lovely day as this, and it's still a bit early for you to be calling on friends in the village. Can I join you today when you deliver baskets?"

"It would be my pleasure! I've got some fresh vegetables to bring over to Mr. Barlow. You know he would live on sweets and ale if left on his own too long. Plus we've got a nice salted ham and some embroidery thread Pierce brought back from London for Mrs. Oaks."

Clara was rewinding a bit of golden hair into a tidy braid wrapped around her head, her bonnet dangling loosely over one arm from its mint green ribbons. She smiled widely, displaying a row of perfectly even white teeth. As often as Emelia attempted to appear poised and elegant, Clara just came by it naturally. It was one of the many things Emelia appreciated about her friend.

"Oh, Mrs. Oaks! I haven't seen her in ages." Clara clapped her hands in delight. "She always has the best stories of dashing adventures in London in her younger years, gallivanting around with the *beau monde*."

Once her friend was safely behind the flowerpots, Emelia reshouldered her bow, adjusted her aim, and let a few arrows fly toward her next target.

"Perhaps we'll even run into Lord Warwick! Pierce said he's due home any day now. Oh! How droll! You have a new helper." Clara giggled at the suit of armor, still holding Emelia's targets but none the worse for wear as of yet. "We shall have to name him."

"Rusty, Lord of Seaton," Emelia offered cheekily.

"Sir Rustalot!"

"Lord Clank, Duke of Arrowton."

"Mr. Ironpants!"

They continued in this fashion as Emelia shot a few more arrows, managing to hit most of her targets despite the stitch in her side from trying to laugh with minimal movement. A sudden and loud clearing of the throat turned Clara's laughter into a fit of the hiccups as Emelia's last arrow went wide and buried itself into the hedge.

"Pierce!" Emelia frowned at her brother. "You shouldn't startle me so! I could have shot you."

"Been calling you since I left the house, Emmie. If you two hadn't been giggling like schoolgirls, you would have heard me."

"You're just sore because you didn't get to name Sir Ironsides."

"Oh that's a—" Clara hiccuped loudly.

"*Gazheundit*," offered Pierce.

Emelia laid down her bow and extended her hand in a peace offering. "What can I do for you, Pierce? Does Mr. Arbuckle need anything?"

"Matter of fact, was going to ask if we could accompany you to town. Arbuckle needs to post a letter to his father, and I need to check in on one of the tenant farmers near the village."

Emelia blinked at him. "I've never known you to take an interest in the tenants, Pierce. Do you not have curricles to race or new neckcloth knots to learn?"

"You, my sister, have a talent for seeing only what you want to see. Don't you wish for me to join you?"

Emelia felt slightly abashed.

"Of course! I'd like nothing better. It's just that, well, you're always busy going to town or playing cards or staking out your next horse. You never want to make social calls with us."

Waving his hat toward the blue, cloudless sky, Pierce executed a credible bow.

"It's a glorious day! What could I have to do that's better than accompanying two beautiful ladies on a trip to the village?"

He offered each lady an arm.

"Get those delivery baskets I know you always have, and maybe we'll even have time for a walk along the beach."

Chapter 4

Collington Village
Kent, England

Emelia and Clara strolled down the sidewalk, a fine picture of rural English charm with their cheeks rosy from exercise and a basket tucked under each of their arms. Pierce and a slightly hungover Mr. Arbuckle trailed along behind.

That young man, whom Pierce reported to be an aspiring dandy of exquisite taste, was perfectly dressed for the occasion. He sported a mint green and pale yellow striped waistcoat and matching striped cane, effulgent hessians, numerous dangling fobs which made a slight tinkling noise as he walked, and—as appropriate to his trip to the sea side—a straw topper. To achieve the air of decided nonchalance necessary to his role as dandy, as well as to keep the sun off his still-woozy head, Mr. Arbuckle kept the brim of this hat pulled low over his eyes as he gazed casually out at the sparkling sea, stopping only to tip his hat politely to any lady that crossed their path, showing off a perfectly-parted Bedford crop as he did so. Emelia found the whole effect rather ridiculous, but Mr. Arbuckle was a kind young man, and she couldn't help but like him.

"Miss Seaton! Miss Appleton!" A bubbly and effusive voice rang out over the cobblestones, drowning out the sound of crashing waves and screeching gulls. Mr. Arbuckle winced slightly.

"Ah, and you've brought visitors today! What a gorgeous day for a stroll!"

The young people turned and saw Mrs. Oaks hanging out of an upper window, waving a lace handkerchief in their direction. Tall and well-figured, Mrs. Oaks had been a beauty in her day. While her hair was more gray than brown these days and her movements slow, she remained a handsome woman.

As she knocked on the front door, Emelia turned to Mr. Arbuckle and explained in a low voice, "Mrs. Oaks was the toast of the town during her come out years ago. She always likes to tell a story or two from her salad days, so do try to be patient with her. She is the kindest soul and is quite lonely, I fear, as she lives here with only her servants for company."

Always respectful of a lady's request, Mr. Arbuckle nodded enthusiastically, grimaced, and then nodded again ever so slightly.

"Yes! She was wealthy and beautiful and could have married anyone she pleased," added Clara, misty-eyed, "but she fell in love with a farmer and didn't give a fig for what anyone else would say! Isn't it romantic!?" She lowered her voice conspiratorially. "Her husband died years ago in a terrible farm accident, and she moved into this house in the village. She could go back to London to live with her grown son and his family, but she says she could never leave the sea, because that's where her beloved was laid to rest, and all of her happiest memories are here. Isn't it tragically beautiful?!"

At this Clara sighed contentedly and turned back towards the door. Mr. Arbuckle's eyes widened slightly, Emelia shrugged, and Pierce grinned. Clara loved nothing so much as a Gothic romance.

After being admitted by a maid who curtsied and took their hats, they entered the small parlor. Mrs. Oaks was sitting on a settee near the window, shutters thrown open to let in the sunlight and a cool breeze.

"Welcome! Welcome my dears! Isn't it an invigorating morning?! Such warm weather we're having for early spring!"

She lay down her embroidery and rose to greet them as Emelia smiled and handed her a basket.

"Pierce has brought you the embroidery thread you requested, the latest colors from London, and some silk ribbon he thought you would enjoy."

"Oh! How beautiful! Thank you so much, Mr. Seaton, you are too kind!" Mrs. Oaks beamed at Pierce. "Having all of the notions shops at my disposal is the thing I miss most about London! And for you to come deliver them in person, well it's such a treat."

"My pleasure, ma'am," answered Pierce with a bow. "Your embroidery skills are renowned throughout the village, and it's been far too long since I've stopped by to say hello. Why, my mother still talks about that reticule you embroidered for her last Christmas. May I present to you my friend Arbuckle? He is visiting us from town for a few weeks."

Despite his aching head, Mr. Arbuckle executed a perfect bow and placed a delicate kiss on Mrs. Oaks hand.

"The pleasure is mine, ma'am, I assure you."

"Oh my! What a delightful young man! Please, please sit down and I will ring for tea!"

Emelia and Clara settled themselves on a small sofa near the fireplace, leaving Pierce and Mr. Arbuckle to the adjacent arm chairs.

"Now, how do you come to be in the country, Mr. Arbuckle, do tell me," Mrs. Oaks coaxed as she leaned forward to look at Mr. Arbuckle. "I sense a story here, since you are obviously a London man, and the season is nearly upon us, I would imagine there must be a good reason for you to join us here in the wilds by the sea."

Mr. Arbuckle looked wistfully at the door, but manfully collected himself and nodded politely.

"Well, ma'am, needed to leave town for a spell. A rum friend, Pierce is, and invited me to rusticate with him until my father returns from India."

"Ah, I can see it all," exclaimed Mrs Oaks. "In trouble with some over-enthusiastic creditors, I dare say."

Mr. Arbuckle had the grace to blush, but nodded genially in her direction.

"Yes ma'am. In my eagerness to ready my wardrobe for the season, I may have outrun the constable a bit, and well—it seemed safer to wait here for a while."

"Come, let us allow Mr. Arbuckle some remaining dignity," said Emelia with an attempt at primness, but her dimple gave her away as always. She turned to her hostess, knowing the older lady couldn't resist a bit of gossip. "Mrs. Oaks, have you heard that Lord Warwick is soon to return to Ernside Manor?"

"Oh! Is the new Baron the handsome stranger that is said to be staying at the inn? All of the young maids were quite aflutter at Susie Hinkleton's description of him, you know."

Pierce chuckled.

"No, I believe that was Mr. Rockcliff, a man we met yesterday who apparently is in town on some sort of business in shipping or trade or something like that. You remember Eddie Warwick, I dare say, as we were children together. Eddie and Emmie and I used to play knights and invaders for hours and hours. Our property just touches his on the northwest corner. He's Lord Warwick now, since he inherited his father's estate. Wrote to me just last week and said he'd be home soon."

Emelia had many fond memories of her childhood friend. The same age as Pierce, Edwin Warwick had grown up at the stately manor bordering the Seaton's property. They had run like wild animals around the hills between their properties, spending warm summer days swimming in the sea, and cold winters huddled up in the Seaton's library, reading and acting out plays that Edwin wrote and directed. While Pierce despised school and chose to be educated at home by his father's old tutor, at age thirteen Edwin went off to Eton and hadn't returned home since.

Only eight at the time, Emelia had been heartbroken when he left. Edwin had often boasted that as soon as he was old enough to leave, he was never coming back. His mother had died in childbirth, and his father was a miserly old fellow who kept to himself and spared no love even for his son. Years later, Emelia learned from a servant of the manor that Edwin had gone on to Cambridge, and from there he left to tour the Continent. His father had died several years ago and still the wayward son had not returned, so until last week's letter, Emelia had assumed he'd kept his promise and was never coming back.

Mrs. Oaks poured her another cup of tea just as Pierce was clearing the last of the crumbs from his plate, and with an indulgent smile she gave him a second plate of sandwiches. He accepted it without hesitation, and set to work on the food as though he hadn't just finished breakfast. Emelia wondered as always how in the world he managed to eat so much and still retain his lanky figure.

"I've heard Lord Warwick has been touring the Continent ever since he finished at Cambridge." Clara was always the expert on young gentlemen. "I'll bet he's seen some amazing places—and to come back here to boring old Collington after all of that, can you imagine!"

Emelia buried a quick stab of jealousy. She loved her home, she truly did. But it was really quite unfair that young men were so often afforded the opportunity to travel while the young women were expected to stay at home and stitch samplers, or learn some other skill to make them good wives.

"Some of us don't think it's boring, love." Pierce teased Clara. "Guess Eddie does have a home here to put to rights, even if he don't intend to stay. Will be good to see the old boy!"

Mrs. Oaks leaned forward conspiratorially.

"I've *heard* that he's terribly handsome, and ever so charming, *and* that he's coming home because he's decided it's time to settle down and find a wife."

At that, Emelia started out of her reverie with a giggle.

"How funny it is that every titled gentleman is always assumed to be looking for a wife. I'm sure there is no reason he would come here for one after bearing witness to all the beauties of the Continent!"

"Well, dear," Mrs. Oaks said matter-of-factly, "foreign beauties are all right for having a bit of fun, but when a man looks for a wife, he usually looks a bit closer to home."

Pierce grinned and elbowed Emelia in the side.

"Might not need to snare a husband after all, Emmie! Maybe a rich and handsome Lord will come looking for you!"

She returned his grin and discretely stepped on his foot.

"Gadzooks, Em, I—"

"Pierce, do tell us about your recent trip to London," Clara, always the peacemaker, asked smoothly. "Did you go see that new play I've been hearing all about?"

The conversation then turned to the upcoming London season, and this was Emelia's cue to smile politely while Pierce and Mr. Arbuckle filled Mrs. Oaks and Clara in on the newest plays and promising young actors, who gave the best pre-season dinner party, and which families were planning on hosting come-out balls for their daughters. Clara listened with rapt attention, and Mrs. Oaks interjected here and there with questions about her friends and acquaintances, but Emelia found it all rather boring. It wasn't that she disliked London. They'd traveled there often enough when her father was alive, but she found society's obsession with always being at the height of fashion a waste of time and intelligence.

Emelia had never cared much for the theater, and she'd been too young to attend the grand balls. When it came to clothing, she preferred simply and elegantly cut dresses, in her favorite flattering shades of blue, red, and gold; none of these pastel confections which, in her opinion, turned girls her age into walking tea cakes. Today, for example, she wore her favorite rust-colored walking dress—which admirably hid the dirt from archery sessions and walks along the beach—and a matching bonnet trimmed in rust and cream floral ribbon. Simple and serviceable, she thought, with none of the frippery that she didn't need. Her hair was pulled into a simple braided knot at the nape of her neck, her unruly curls escaping a bit due to the strong sea breeze, but she knew any efforts to tame it further would be in vain, since they just had to walk back home in that same breeze shortly. But all in all, there were far more important things to spend time and effort on than building a new wardrobe every season—even if Mr. Arbuckle did look very dashing in his.

"Emmie, dear, what do you think about that," asked Clara, turning to face her on the settee.

"I am so sorry, I was woolgathering, I'm afraid," Emelia answered, attempting to bring her attention back to the present. "What do I think about what?"

"Mr. Arbuckle was just telling us of his need to return to London to have his hair cut, and Mrs. Oaks suggested he visit the village barber instead. You know Mr. Lampitt don't you? Do you think he'd do a good job?"

Emelia considered the matter for a moment.

"Well, Mr. Arbuckle, I can't say I've ever had my hair trimmed by him, as he is primarily a men's barber and my maid is more than adequate with the scissors. But he is well-regarded around town, and I know he studied in London under an excellent barber."

"He did a bang-up job last Autumn for a friend who was in a pinch," offered Pierce. "He said it was just as good as his usual man in London."

So they said their goodbyes with Mrs. Oaks and parted ways, Emelia and Clara off to deliver the remaining basket to Mr. Barlow, and Pierce and Mr. Arbuckle off to the barber. While Mr. Arbuckle still expressed some doubt about the trustworthiness of a fellow so far removed from the metropolis, the discomfort of trying out a new and unproven barber was still less than the discomfort waiting for him in London, so he calmly accepted his fate, and they strolled off down the street.

Emelia and Clara found the worthy Mr. Barlow not in his house, but sitting on a bench overlooking the ocean, perfectly upright but sound asleep. Clara scrunched up her cute button nose, regarding him curiously.

"How can he sleep like that, with the noise of the street right behind us, and the gulls screeching overhead?"

"I suspect it has something to do with the sound of the ocean." Emelia closed her eyes and smiled, listening to the waves and smelling the comforting aromas of salt, fish, and fresh-baked bread from the bakery down the street. "Papa used to say it put him fast asleep whenever he left the windows open at night. He also said that's why we could never go sailing, because he'd just fall asleep right on the boat, but I suspect anxiety played a greater role than the sound of the waves."

At this Mr. Barlow let out a huge snore, tilted his head down onto one shoulder, and continued with his nap. Looking at the basket on her arm, Emelia wondered if they should just set it on the bench and leave the old man to rest.

"Yer wasting yer time, love," said a gravelly Yorkshire drawl behind her. "'E's sleeping more and more these days, and if you wake 'im, it'll lief as not confuse 'im."

"Mr. Aveyard!" Emelia turned towards the weathered old fisherman walking up the path behind her, voice low as to not wake their slumbering friend. "How lovely to see you. We were just bringing Mr. Barlow his weekly basket of vegetables from our garden."

"Aye miss, and 'tis good of you. We know that ye've taken good care of 'im since 'is old lady passed."

A grunt and gruff nod emanated from the man at Mr. Aveyard's side. Mr. Cofferey, another elderly villager whose fishing days were long past, was still tall and well-built, never hunched over despite his age, and carried himself with the dignity of an old family retainer. He always had a ready smile for Emelia, but she'd never heard him speak a word in her presence, or anyone else's for that matter. She'd always assumed him mute somehow, though she didn't know that for certain.

The three men were some of her favorite companions in the village, always ready to regale her with exciting tales from the sea, and send her home with one of their younger son's freshest catches of the day. For Emelia, who'd never been out further than she could swim, life at sea sounded like about the most exciting and daring thing imaginable. Most of her daydreams involved sailing to distant lands. So many merchant vessels had come to their splintered end on the rocks just up the coast, however, that she also had a great deal of respect for the water. The difference between a short fishing trip within sight of shore and a long voyage out to sea was what had allowed her elderly fishermen friends to live long enough to complain of rheumatism and poor eyesight. Many young sailors had been denied that privilege.

It was an odd life, living near the sea. You were at once spellbound by its beauty, invigorated by its breezes, and reminded of its brutal power during a storm or after a shipwreck. It was a curious mingling of love and grief, and allowed her to feel a gratitude and passion for life and a respect for nature she wasn't sure she would have if she had grown up strictly in London.

Handing her basket to Mr. Aveyard, she requested he pass it along to Mr. Barlow after he woke from his morning slumber.

On the walk back to Seaton House, Clara and the newly-shorn Mr. Arbuckle strolled ahead, deep in discussion on whether the new machine-made netting could ever be as elegant as hand-knotted lace. Emelia and Pierce walked behind, watching the younger man in front of them finger his well-cut curls and fiddle with a fob on his waistcoat as he thought about an apparently tricky answer regarding old lace.

"He's not a particularly deep-thinker, is he." Emelia whispered to her brother *sotto voce*. "Will he be okay, do you think? When his father gets back."

Pierce might be indolent at times, but he was not a fool. She had never doubted his ability to land on his own two feet when he needed to. As proper as his manners were, Mr. Arbuckle seemed a floundering sort, with no parents or guardians around to guide him.

"Oh, he'll rub along fine, I think." Pierce slowed to let the others get a little further ahead. "He's a bit green, and his father knows it. Keeps a hold of the purse strings rather tightly so he doesn't return from India to find himself in over his head. Arbuckle's mother died when he was very young, I believe, and his father was often abroad. He's got no head for the bills, and he can be a bit bird-witted at times, but he's a good lad."

"A good lad!" Despite her genuine concern for Mr. Arbuckle, Emelia could not hold off her laughter for long. "Listen to you, Pierce, talking as though you were quite the old man. One would think you were a responsible land-owning gentleman! Oh wait, perhaps you are."

Her eyes sparkled with mirth, and she jabbed her brother with an elbow. He grinned good-naturedly, then stopped in his tracks.

"You know. Been thinking about that, Emmie. Perhaps it's time—I mean, I have some ideas about the estate, only I've been hesitant to approach Mother. She does seem to enjoy looking after things so."

Emelia stopped too, surprised, and looked up at her brother.

"Pierce, I think she's a woman of sense, and has cared for things only until you felt yourself able. I'm sure she would be overjoyed to hand the reins over, so to speak. What has brought this about? You're not thinking of establishing your own family, are you? You know you have merely to ask, and Mother and I can find a nice cottage by the sea somewhere, and you may start working on those ten children I mentioned earlier."

Emelia grinned at him, jesting of course, but at the same time knowing that there would come a day when their happy little family would have to expand.

"No, no, not what I meant." Pierce blushed and glanced up to make sure his friends were still ahead and in deep conversation. "I'm in no hurry to be caught in the parson's mousetrap. I met a man last time I went to Newmarket, and he was telling me how he'd built a steam-powered mill on his farm. Now the fellow grinds the entire town's grain in an afternoon! Wouldn't that be something for the tenant farms? I'd love to take one apart and see how it works, wouldn't you? Maybe you could help me."

Before Emelia could reply that she would be delighted, if only they could find someone willing to let them dismantle what was obviously a valuable piece of equipment, Clara was waving her arm to get their attention.

"Emmie, Pierce, look!"

She pointed to a gentleman on the road ahead, riding towards them. He was exquisitely dressed, attired for riding, but the cut and fabric of his waistcoat and riding coat and the polished leather of his boots proclaimed him a member of the upper echelon of the social strata. Not a local, then. Emelia and Pierce caught up with their friends and watched the newcomer.

As he drew closer, Emelia saw that he was exceedingly handsome, with dark hair perfectly curled around his face, sparkling brown eyes, and a charming smile, which he flashed at the ladies as he drew up beside them on the road.

"Can it be," the young man inquired with a wide smile. "Do my eyes deceive me, or is it possible my old playmates have grown up into the prettiest girls in England?"

"Edwin!" cried Emelia, at the same as Pierce exclaimed, "Warwick! Welcome home, old chap!"

Edwin Warwick deftly dismounted his horse and came up to Emelia, taking one of her hands in his as he extended the other to grasp Pierce's in an enthusiastic handshake.

"Let us not stand on ceremony, old friends," he instructed them, laughing heartily. "Edwin will do! Or you may call me Eddie once again if you please, though I confess if anyone else dares to do so I will box their ears."

He smiled, a dazzling smile full of perfect white teeth. While he had always been a good-looking child, he was now the most handsome man Emelia had ever seen. He bowed low and kissed her hand, and then turned to do the same for Clara.

"Miss Appleton, I presume? You must be nearly grown now, and are quite as beautiful as ever! It is a delight to see you."

At this Clara blushed prettily and stammered, and Pierce stepped forward to clap Edwin heartily on the back.

"Eddie! You old dog, always making up to the women, I dare say. Haven't seen you since our university years! I trust all went well on your journey through the Continent."

"It was quite the adventure, and I have many astonishing stories to tell." He spread his arms out wide and grinned delightedly. "In fact, I shall tell you all the whole of it, each story more astonishing than the last, and you can determine how much of it is true, and for how much I am simply using my imagination as we did as children."

His eyes twinkled, and Emelia decided he had not changed too much in the last decade; he had always been just as ready to laugh at himself as he had at anyone else's expense.

"May I present to you my friend, Arbuckle?" Pierce gestured to the younger man standing politely beside them.

"Honored to make your acquaintance, sir." Mr. Arbuckle executed a bow that would have been right at home among the Bond Street beaus.

"The pleasure is mine, young man." Edwin returned Mr. Arbuckle's bow with a flourish. "But! I have interrupted your little party. Where are you all off to?"

"We've been calling in the village," answered Emelia, "but are on our way home now for tea. Do say you'll come join us!"

"Nothing would give me more pleasure than to spend more time in your company, but alas, I've just arrived home this morning, and I must see to some business in the village. Another time soon, I hope? I don't have my household set up credibly yet, or I would invite you all over for dinner."

"In that case, you most certainly should come dine with us," Pierce offered. "Tomorrow night, then?"

"You always were the best of fellows! You can depend on it!

I'm eager to see your mother again. I heard of your father's passing." Edwin's eyes grew misty and his voice thick. "I extend my utmost condolences to you all. He was the best man I ever met."

Pierce coughed into a stylish handkerchief and patted Edwin on the back once more.

"Thank you, Edwin," offered Emelia. "Mother will be very pleased to see you, I am sure."

"Then it is settled." Edwin clasped each of their hands again briefly. "Enjoy your walk back home my friends, and I will count the minutes until I am back with you on the morrow."

At this last pronouncement, his gaze lingered decidedly on Emelia, a warmth there that she had not expected. For a full second she stood there, mouth open and stray hairs blowing in the wind, all witty retorts banished from her mind. She might have stood like that indefinitely, but, fortunately for her composure, he quickly looked away and climbed back on his horse.

The friends all called their goodbyes, and the foursome continued walking back towards Seaton house. Her thoughts muddled, Emelia could not help feeling a few butterflies in her stomach on the way home. It had been quite some time since anything—much less anyone—had rendered her speechless.

Chapter 5

Ernside Manor
Collington, Kent

Henry stared up at the imposing estate in front of him, hat in one hand, his other hand combing through sun-streaked hair in a nervous gesture. It was time to approach Lord Warwick about Monsieur Fresnel's lens, and Henry wondered if he could remember how to behave in society after all this time. Tucking loose strands of hair back into his ribbon, Henry smiled wryly at the thought that his hair was the only thing about himself that he recognized. He'd left it much longer than was fashionable, just brushing the tops of his shoulders. His tanned skin had faded a bit over the winter, as it had been cold and wet in Paris, but there was no denying he was a man used to the outdoors. He only hoped centuries of breeding and two decades of living as a Viscount's son would enable him to persuade this young Baron to take up the cause of a new Fresnel lens and allow Henry access to his lighthouse. And Colonel Phillips was counting on Henry's ability to fade into the background of country life to enable him to investigate these shipwrecks around town without arousing suspicion.

It was a fine line to walk, thought Henry, but perhaps his experiences made him uniquely suited to the task. He'd been a quiet child, more inclined to his books and philosophical discussions than sporting or gaming like his older brother and father. This subjected him to endless teasing from the former, and abject disdain from the latter. At age nineteen, sick of the tension and ready to make his own way in the world, he caved to his father's endless badgering to let the army "make a man out of him," purchased his commission, and was shipped off to France to fight Napoleon within a fortnight. His younger brother, Charles, had done the same two years later, only it was the Navy that had captured his interest. He'd been begging to sail since he could walk, and with a boyish naivety Henry had foolishly thought him safe since the war with France had by then ended.

Now, beginning this mad investigation, was the first time in his life Henry felt that perhaps there was a purpose to everything he'd been through. He'd always felt like Fate had made a mistake, allowing Henry's life to be ruled by the whims of a cruel father and a horrible war. But now, a decade later, having experienced so much joy and healing with his family in Provence, he could see the hard years for how they had shaped him and turned him into who he was today. Perhaps now was his chance to use his experiences to accomplish something good.

"I'll be beggin' your pardon, my Lord, but shouldn't we be banging on the cove's door or whatnot?"

Startled, Henry turned to Rogers, his old batman turned valet and personal assistant.

"I apologize, Rogers, I confess I was lost in thought. Do I look passable?"

"A rum thing to quiz your valet, sir. Yer quite up to snuff, as if I'd let you go runnin' about in anything less, my Lord. My repyeeetation's at stake, it is, sir."

"Well, don't work yourself up, my good man." Henry attempted to fight the smile threatening to spread across his face. "Pardon the slight, I wasn't questioning your abilities. It's just been so long since I've needed to fill the role of gentleman. In my defense, you have only been a valet for two weeks now, so I believe this is all a bit new for both of us."

Henry had run into Rogers while he'd been in Paris, and the two had repaired to a local watering hole to share a drink and remembrances of their wartime cronies. Rogers had always been a loyal companion, and he certainly didn't lack pluck, and Henry had come upon the unorthodox idea of asking him to act as valet for the journey to England. A *gentleman's gentleman* Rogers was not, but if the going got tough, he'd rather have a man that was handy in a scuffle than one proficient in tying the latest cravats. Between jobs, Rogers had eagerly accepted his offer, and the two set about turning him into a passable valet in what little time was available to them.

He hadn't expected it to be April by the time he reached English soil, but here they were. All together, Henry had been in Paris for two months. He'd written to Monsieur Fresnel as soon as he'd received Colonel Phillips' letter, but the inventor had been unable to meet with him until after Christmas. So Henry had stayed in Provence, helping his family through winemaking season after all, all the time wondering how many more ships were being lost. For someone who'd spent the better part of a decade more or less in hiding, Henry was restless once he'd received a mission. It felt like the longest winemaking season he'd ever experienced.

Eventually, he'd spent a cold and wet winter in Paris, meeting with Monsieur Fresnel and other scientists. When the cold weather became too much for Monsieur Fresnel's sickly constitution, Henry had accepted the man's invitation to visit Bordeaux for a few weeks. He found the young scientist truly brilliant, and his lens—well, Henry was confident it had the power to change the world. Hopefully starting with this little corner of England.

Taking a deep breath and squaring his shoulders, Henry knocked on the door, which was opened by the haughty butler. Henry smiled his most winning smile and handed the man his card.

"Hello! You'll remember me from the other day. I'm here to see Lord Warwick."

The butler gave him a long, disapproving look from head to toe. For a full five seconds, he made no move to announce Henry or invite him in. Just when Henry wondered if perhaps the man was senile and he should try introducing himself again, the butler lowered his glare to the card in his palm, then back up at Henry, and then slowly stepped inside and motioned for him to follow.

"If you'd follow me, sir."

Walking through the main hall, Henry's main impression was one of cold antiquity. The stone walls were ancient and drafty, but the furnishings were heavy and gilded, and every stick of silver so highly polished you could see your face in it. It was obvious this family had been ruling here since feudal times.

The sitting room Henry was ushered into was surprisingly more welcoming than the rest of the house. Some effort had been made to lighten the atmosphere—the shutters were open to let in light and fresh air, there was a cracking fire in the fireplace, and the furnishings here were lighter and more modern.

A polished wood desk stood on one side of the room, and a handsome young man with thick, dark curls was sitting at it. The elderly butler did not soften when he saw his master, but said in a gravelly voice, "The Honorable Henry Dufort Rockcliff, my Lord." His brows raised on the honorific, as if doubting the truth of such a title.

"Ah, Mr. Rockcliff," Lord Warwick said, rising from his seat and coming around the desk to greet Henry. "I apologize for missing you the other day. It is an honor to meet you."

"Likewise," answered Henry. "It is quite a magnificent place you've got here."

Warwick chuckled and gestured to a pair of comfortable armchairs by the fire.

"Steeped in history, true," answered his host as they were seated, "but I'm afraid it's a bit cold and impersonal for my taste. My father, God rest his soul, was so taken with the family lineage, that he refused to change one stick of furniture or a single tapestry. It's all well and good for a museum, but not much fun to live in."

"I can definitely understand that. My father is also a stickler for preserving the family history. When I was growing up, I tended to stick to my mother's sitting rooms; she always liked things to be bright and comfortable."

"Ah yes, a woman's touch makes all the difference. I'm afraid that's been lacking around here for decades. It is the way of these old homes, isn't it, to cling to one's history? I had the staff freshen this room before I arrived, but I firmly intend to bring the whole house up to date once I've settled in a bit. I've been touring the Continent since I graduated Oxford, and I'm afraid I haven't been home in many years. I hadn't realized it had fallen into such disrepair. Tell me, Mr. Rockcliff, are you also from Kent?"

"No, my family is from Gloucestershire, however I've been living in Provence for the last ten years."

"France! How fascinating. I very much enjoyed my travels through that country. I'm afraid we didn't spend much time in Provence, but what I saw of the countryside was very beautiful."

"It's a little piece of heaven on earth." Henry wondered how to subtly steer the conversation to the purpose of his visit. "This part of the world is also beautiful. You've a lovely little village here, and your coastline is stunning."

"Ah yes, our stunning coastline is the reason for your visit. I gathered by your letter of introduction that you have knowledge of some latest technology out of France, meant to save us all from the peril of the seas, hmm?"

"Well, something like that. This new lens could go a long way towards making voyages around the coast much safer."

Henry took a deep breath and plunged into the part he'd been dreading.

"I've learned that this is one of the most perilous stretches of coastline in England, and it is my understanding that this new lens could make navigating the area much less treacherous."

Henry focused on breathing in and out, in and out, as he had done when on the battlefield. He would not think of Charles, and how he'd met his end just a few villages up the coast. Focus on the task at hand. Henry was good at focusing on the task at hand, and that had made him particularly well-suited for battle. Hopefully, it would serve him now.

"Well, yes, the rocks along the coastline make it dangerous for all but the best of sailors, and our position along the Channel makes it a high traffic area. The two factors are sadly bound to result in more accidents." Warwick waved a dismissive hand. "How exactly does your lens rectify the situation?"

"It's certainly not *my* lens, but I was able to spend the winter with the man who invented it, and his associates. While I confess I'm not a physicist, I was most impressed. Mr. Fresnel gave several demonstrations recently in Paris. His new lens magnifies the light rather than simply reflecting it, and the resulting beam can be seen for miles out to sea."

Henry leaned forward, warming to his subject. He had never been particularly fond of physics, but he'd always loved learning about new subjects, loved the way a good narrative caused a thing to get up off the page and become alive in one's head.

"It's the difference between using lighthouses along the coast as land-bound stars along the shore, to guide you to where to make your next turn, and using a lighthouse to illuminate your way. It's the moon, if you will. At Cordouan, the first lighthouse in France where this lens has been installed, you can see its light a full nine miles out to sea on the deck, and up to 30 miles if you're up in the rigging."

"Nine miles?! Good heavens."

"Shipwrecks there have decreased by nearly forty percent just in the last few months."

"And you have seen this lens in operation?"

Henry thought for a minute, remembering the stunning flash of light that had nearly floored him with its brilliance, even though he was nearly a mile away up the Champs d'Elysee.

"Yes," he said simply. "It is all that they say and more."

"Surely a light that bright will keep all of the villagers awake as if in the noonday sun?"

"No, no, there are still special reflectors behind the lens, to ensure the light only shines out to sea."

"Well, I suppose the next question is, then, what do I have to do with any of this?"

"Well, Lord Warwick, the town's only lighthouse is on your property."

Now it was time for Henry to bend the truth a bit.

"I am willing to pay for the shipment and installation of Monsieur Fresnel's lens at no cost to you, as a goodwill gesture between our countries. I have invested heavily in Fresnel's enterprise, you see, and it's my hope that other lighthouse owners around England will see it in action and decide to purchase one for their villages as well. If it were to decrease the number of goods and lives lost by even a fraction, I can imagine it will be much sought-after by many towns with an interest in trade. You wouldn't need to do anything except grant permission and offer us access for the planning and installation."

It was a warm morning for April, but the thick manor walls left the house cold. Henry leaned closer to the warm fire in front of them, watching Warwick as he stared into the flames, and gave the man time to think. It was hard not to think of Charles and wonder if his ship could have been saved if only this apparatus had been invented a few years sooner.

Having come to some sort of a decision, Warwick finally nodded his head and stood.

"Mr. Rockcliff, you have made an interesting proposition."

Henry was mentally calculating how long it would take to measure the lighthouse and manufacture a perfectly-sized lens. He knew it was a difficult and time-consuming process, but surely they could have it here within—

"However, I confess, I am still skeptical. Having only your word to its success, how do I know that this isn't a plot by the French to undermine our country's entire shipping network? You know as well as I do that our peace is a fragile one."

"Well, yes, of course the peace is fragile, but this is a scientific advancement, hardly a military operation. It can only make both our countries safer, not to mention increase lawful trade. And increased trade always brings more incentive for peace, in fact—" Henry was just warming to his argument when Warwick held up a hand to stop him from speaking further.

"I would love, however, to continue hearing more of your work, and get the results of any further testing on *English* soil—should there be any—and I promise to review the matter thoroughly. As I've said, I've only come home, and to make any sweeping changes with such haste would be a mistake. I'm sure we can come to an arrangement within a year or two—when Mr. Fresnel's lens has been properly vetted, of course."

"But surely, Lord Warwick," tried Henry once more, "the results from the first lighthouse testing in France can indeed speak for themselves? Perhaps I can supply you with some documents verifying the outcomes from the initial year of use at Cordouan."

"And am I to take your word for it? Or that of the French government? Like I said, Mr. Rockcliff, the lens does sound like a remarkable advancement, and I'm sure we can come to an arrangement in time. I just can't agree to any sort of venture without further *reliable* information."

After a lifetime of abuse from his father and brother, Henry was not easily offended. But he had to admit to being a bit surprised that Lord Warwick did not think his word reliable, much less the research and backing of the greatest scientific minds in France. Still, he couldn't demand a peer of a realm turn over access to his property, regardless of the matter's urgency. After all, Henry was a complete stranger. Both he and Warwick had been out of the country for years, so the normal way of things—arranging an introduction by a mutual friend, being members of the same club or social set—wasn't an option in this case. He didn't blame the man for being cautious.

"Very well, Lord Warwick, I will endeavor to send you the

very latest information as soon as possible. I have one more request, however, that will enable me to better evaluate the situation, so you need not trouble yourself over details that might not apply to your village here. I would like to conduct a small, informal study of the village and surrounding cove."

Henry needed to frame his request to sound as innocuous as possible, while still leaving him the freedom to investigate around the village. He had counted on installing the prototype lens as his alibi; now he would need a new purpose.

"It's possible your lighthouse may not even be the best fit for the demonstration we have planned," he continued, "but if I may spend a couple of weeks measuring the lighthouse structure itself, and getting to know the situation of the cove and the village, I might be able to greatly reduce the amount of information you need be troubled with. Then we can determine how best to serve your village, if we decide to install the lens in the future."

Lord Warwick rose, straightening his immaculate cravat and picking an invisible speck of dust off his sleeve.

"Very well, Mr. Rockcliff." The young Baron smiled jovially at Henry. "You have my permission to study the lighthouse and anything else on my property that might be of use. There is an excellent prospect of the estuary at the far east corner of the estate that might be helpful. I only ask that you clear your visits to the lighthouse ahead of time with the Keeper. He has an important job to do, as you know, and there are certain times that you might be in the way."

"Perfectly reasonable, my Lord," Henry agreed gratefully. The morning hadn't been a complete waste. "I will endeavor to remain as inconspicuous as possible, and will of course not trouble your Keeper unless he is expecting me."

"You seem a very reasonable man, Mr. Rockcliff," Warwick said, shaking his hand as they turned to walk towards the entrance hall. "I am sure you will keep me informed of everything you learn during your studies."

"Yes," answered Henry, running a hand across his face once more as he followed Warwick to the front door. "I am sure I will."

⁓

Back in the saddle, Henry ran his fingers through his hair until he resembled nothing so much as a wind-blown mop.

"Blast it all, Rogers!" Henry groaned once they were safely out of earshot of the manor. "I nearly bungled that whole transaction," he sighed. "Viscount's son or no, I apparently have the negotiating skills of a farmer. Fitting, eh? Investor, indeed. I realize it's not as though we run in the same social circles, but being a gentleman, I would have imagined my word would carry more weight. At least he still gave me permission to do a bit of scouting, lens or no lens."

He turned in the saddle to look at Rogers, who was riding along slightly behind him as befitting a servant, and filled him in on the whole exchange with Warwick.

"If ye ask me, my boy," his old batman said a few moments later, "that cock-sure young jackanape is devilish high in the instep. Frenchies, indeed. Wonder if 'e involved in the havey-cavey business goin' on with them ships."

Colonel Phillips believed something sinister was going on in the area, but Henry didn't assume that Warwick was involved just because he was reluctant to let Henry install a Fresnel lens. The man hadn't even been around for the last few years, when most of the shipwrecks had taken place.

"I'm sure it's not as bad as that, Rogers. You do seem to see giants in every windmill. The young man just arrived home after many years away, rather like myself. It's unlikely he could have been a party to any wrongdoing while traveling abroad. It's more likely he's figuring out his place in the world and doesn't want to upset the established order too quickly."

"Well, just keep yer eyes peeled, havey-cavey business or no, there's no telling what a young buck like that may do if ye cut up 'is peace."

"I promise I'll be careful, Rogers. After all, what could he do, with you to guard my back? Between the two of us, we could more than take one man." He grinned, joking, but his smile faded at the older man's grim expression.

"Ay, that's the problem with folks like 'im, Henry my boy. There's always more than one, there is."

Chapter 6

Aldington, Kent

Donovan Mallory sat with his back to the fireplace. It wasn't that he wouldn't have welcomed the warmth on his face, but that would require turning his back on the rest of the crowded room, something he most certainly wasn't willing to do. The taproom was packed this time of night, full of regulars, and while he knew nearly all of them, he trusted less than half. He was sure they felt the same about him, so there were no hard feelings.

That's the way life was in Aldington. Half the town had turned to smuggling after the war was over. After taking the King's Shilling, those men fortunate enough to return home found jobs scarce. So they turned to what they knew how to do, and took to the seas to transport illegal goods. Only, with a lighter tax load, and less restrictions on French imports, it wasn't as profitable as it had been in its heyday. Back then, Donovan recollected warmly, smugglers were seen as heroes, bringing the people what they needed at a fraction of the cost, and able to feed their families well off of the proceeds. Now, a fellow was lucky if he could make ends meet and avoid getting hanged in the meantime.

But Donovan was good at solving problems. He and his men hauled goods from France, just like the rest of them. One stormy night, when he was perched high on the cliffs waiting for his crew to come in, he saw it. A trading vessel caught in the storm, being dashed upon the sharp rocks not two hundred yards from the shore. It was as if it had steered right to Donovan, begging him to claim its goods.

And so he did. He and the few of his men who weren't already out to sea, rowed a small dingy out to the ship, nearly capsizing in the waves. There were no survivors amongst the wreckage, so they helped themselves to as much as the dingy could hold, and came back for the rest. Six trips they made, through those choppy waters, each time risking a grisly death on the rocks. But Donovan knew it was fate. He felt that he could not possibly fail, for he had seen the future.

He knew what they had to do.

A rail-thin man in a dark overcoat stepped in the pub and shook rain off his boots. Donovan took three long, slow drags from his cigar in a signal. It was safe. The man ordered a beer from the bartender, then came and took the empty chair beside him in front of the fire.

"Mind if I join you?"

Donovan nodded in assent. The two sat in silence while the stranger sipped his beer.

"It's a frightful night out there! I ain't seen an April storm this bad since I was in the war, eleven years ago. My wife now, we have eight children you see, she says I'm just dying to get out of the house if I'm willing to go in this weather. I tell her, you'd drink too if you had to work with these three men of mine!"

Donovan gave a grunt and a nod, and continued puffing his cigar. The two sat in companionable silence while the thin man finished his beer. Then he stood and tipped his hat to Donovan.

"I best be going now. Don't like to keep the Missus waiting for too long. Enjoy your night, and thanks for sharing the fireplace."

And he was off again into the night.

Donovan took another drag off his cigar, walked to the bar, and ordered another beer.

Eleven. Eight. Three.

Message received.

Contained within this cipher was the time and location of a smuggler's vessel due to pass the coast of Collington. Someone on his team had gotten it wrong the week before and had foolishly allowed some local fishermen to see their light on the shore. It was the last mistake that unfortunate fellow would ever make. Donovan would have to have his men spread more rumors among the villagers. He couldn't afford for anyone to find out what was really happening, or to somehow spot their reflector hidden deep within a recess in the cliffs. It was better for everyone if the locals avoided the coast at night. He couldn't afford any more collateral damage.

Someone was bound to get suspicious.

Chapter 7

Seaton House, Kent

"It's so exciting, miss!" The Seaton's maid, Marietta, drawled in her thick Northern accent, standing behind Emelia at her dressing table as she attempted to tame her unruly locks. "To have your young friend back after all this time! An' I've heard in the village that he's exceedingly handsome."

The girl ran a broad-toothed comb through Emelia's curls and attempted to coax them up on top of her head, and Emelia smiled at her while attempting to stay as still as possible. It was better not to hamper any progress the young woman might be making, as styling Emelia's hair wasn't for the faint of heart.

Marietta had come to work for them as a young girl from the village, determined to make her way up in the world, and had been practicing her hairdressing skills on anyone in the household who was patient enough to sit still. Even Pierce had once returned from Eaton with his hair nearly past his shoulders and, much to his mother's dismay, had patiently allowed Marietta to curl, arrange, and then cut his hair, before he removed himself to his hairdresser in London to clean it up.

All that practice was paying off, and Marietta was becoming quite skilled. Tonight, she was piling Emelia's dark hair neatly on top of her head, leaving a few carefully-placed curls allowed to swing free around her face and down the back of her neck.

While she knew nothing about hairstyles, Emelia thought this was probably a wise idea, as more curls would most certainly escape by the end of the evening. At least this method made it look somewhat purposeful. The reunion of the Seatons and Lord Warwick was shaping up to be the most lavish dinner party of the season. Mrs. Seaton had instructed the cook to prepare an excellent joint of lamb, remembering it to be Edwin's favorite when he was young. This was to be accompanied by numerous pies, delicate poached fish, fresh local vegetables, and four different sponges for dessert. Emelia's stomach growled just thinking about all the good food waiting for them downstairs.

Emelia had spent the afternoon remembering various childhood escapades to recollect fondly with their guest and mentally cataloging questions she wished to ask him about his travels. When she'd heard Edwin was off on a grand adventure around the Continent several years ago, she'd been more than a little envious. If only she'd been born a man, she could be off gallivanting around Europe this very moment! But for a young, unmarried woman—well, it just wasn't done. To one so interested in science and other cultures, travel seemed to her as one big, fantastic experiment just waiting to be conducted. She was always wondering about the true state of Roman ruins after two thousand years exposed to the elements, or if the climate in the Alps really could leave one stranded in a sudden June snowstorm.

As had most of his contemporaries, her father had done the Grand Tour of the Continent when he was young. When Emelia was a child, they spent many cold winter evenings snuggled in his big leather chair by the fire. Her father would pull out an artifact from this country or that, pointing to a spot on the weathered map that hung above the fireplace, and they whiled away the hours with tales from far away Egypt, or Spain, or some remote island in the middle of the Mediterranean. Her father was an excellent storyteller, and Emelia would sit and listen until the last embers of the fire were dying out and it was long past time for her to be in bed.

This morning, Emelia had walked into the library for a moment after breakfast, just to look at that yellowing map and trace with her finger all of the little lines her father had carefully sketched upon it to mark his journeys. She'd closed her eyes, and for a moment she could smell the mingling of tobacco and woodsmoke, and hear his low timbre, rising into a crescendo as he got to an exciting point in the story.

Emelia's father had been much older than her mother, but to the astonishment of everyone they'd fallen in love, drawn together by their mutual love of science and the natural world. No one had believed that her father would ever marry again after his first wife, his childhood sweetheart, had died suddenly when they'd only been married a few short months. And he hadn't, for thirty long years. Emelia's mother had been just shy of thirty—most certainly off the shelf and practically an aging spinster—with a healthy fortune and lust for life; her father nearly fifty when the two met during a lecture on Egyptology and the Science of Decay. If it was not love at first sight, it was most certainly love at first conversation, and the two had been inseparable from then until his death twenty-three years later.

It was her father Emelia had been thinking about tonight as she dressed for dinner, choosing her favorite evening dress of amber-colored satin with a cream-colored sheer silk overskirt, a simple, well-fitted bodice, and tiny puffed sleeves. The amber color had always been her father's favorite, and she always felt elegant in this dress.

After she secured Emelia's hair with what felt like a whole box full of pins, Marietta tucked a few delicate pearl combs into the mess of curls on top of her head. Although Emelia usually preferred to wear no adornments, she had to admit the effect was very pretty and complemented the cream lace of her skirt very nicely.

"That's right lovely, miss." The young maid sighed. "You'll be turnin' the heads of every gentleman in Kent—well at least any of those that happen to be comin' over for dinner."

She winked at Emelia.

"Oh, I'm sure I will." Emelia smiled mischievously. "But if

the gossip below stairs has me married off by summer, I will have to think you're just wanting to get rid of me and my troublesome wardrobe."

"Oh no, miss! Well, that's not to say you aren't hard on the clothes, what with the burn marks from that fire you were usin' on the arrows, and last week when you tore your best morning dress climbing down out of that tree, or all the times you decided to wade in the surf with all your petticoats a'draggin' behind you."

Both girls shared a conspiratorial grin.

"Yes, well, I do confess I never think of the state of my garments until after a thing is done. I will try to be more careful, for your sake."

"Nay, miss, as Davis says, we'd rather you have your adventures, and us have a bit to clean up after now and then, than you be stuck at home doing embroidery or some such. Why, you'd be bored to tears, miss. I know I certainly would be. And we've no desire to be rid of you." She patted Emelia on the shoulder. "We've all tried to take good care of you and your mum and Mr. Pierce since your father died. We just want you to be happy."

Emelia felt the pricking of tears behind her eyes, and she was truly touched. Not only had she the good fortune to have a loving family and friends whose company she could always depend on, but even the family's household staff cared graciously for her—in ways she seldom noticed but from which she always benefited.

"Thank you, Marietta. And that cements it. I could never get married and leave you all, for you're a part of my family."

Marietta nodded knowingly.

"Perhaps, or maybe you've just yet to meet the right gentlemen. I myself thought I'd never settle on just one man, until I met my Jeremy." The young maid gave her a saucy wink. "But what a man he is! In fact, lately we've been talking of getting married."

"Marietta, that's wonderful!" Emelia waited as Marietta secured the last of the pearl combs and then rose to hug the girl. "I wish you a lifetime of happiness, truly."

Dinner was a splendid affair. Cook had outdone herself. Edwin proclaimed the leg of lamb the best he'd ever eaten, and Pierce devoured three helpings of sponge cake before he finally began to look a bit green about the gills and had to stop himself from accepting a fourth. Clara and her parents, Mr. and Mrs. Appleton, had been invited to join them for the evening. The five younger Appletons had declined the invitation, as Mrs. Appleton had put it, "for the sake of everyone's comfort and sanity."

The Appletons and Mrs. Seaton carried the weight of the conversation at the dinner table, inquiring upon what Edwin planned to do with the estate now that he'd returned home. Emelia listened impatiently, eager to hear about his travels abroad. She'd managed to sneak in a question regarding Roman aqueducts, another about post-revolution Paris, but when she asked him what female mountaineers wore when attempting to summit a mountain in the alps, her mother interjected with an upraised hand.

"Now Emelia, surely Lord Warwick wishes to speak of something else. Just because he was climbing in the alps, doesn't mean he was paying attention to what the mountaineer—mountaineer-esses? Goodness, is that a word?" she questioned no one in particular. "I shall have to retrieve my dictionary after supper."

At this, Edwin threw back his head and laughed heartily.

"It is good to see that things haven't changed much here. And I welcome any question Emelia can throw at me; I think she's taking a greater interest in my travels than I did myself."

He grinned cheekily at Emelia and winked, and she felt her cheeks growing warm. He then turned to Mr. Arbuckle and changed the topic of conversation, and Emelia was relieved the party's attention turned elsewhere.

Mr. Arbuckle, in immaculate evening dress and shirt points so high he could barely turn his head to converse with Clara, his dinner partner, had maintained his air of polite disinterest throughout the meal, until Edwin mentioned he'd met a man by the name of Arbuckle off the Portuguese coast.

"An older Arbuckle, maybe twenty or thirty years your senior. He said he was traveling to India, and seemed a dashing sort of fellow. Could he be any relation of yours, my good man?"

Mr. Arbuckle dipped his head forward slightly—the only movement he could make given the height of his shirt points—and dabbed a napkin at the last bit of lemon ice on his mouth.

"I believe, sir, that you've had the fortune of meeting my father," answered Arbuckle. "He was on his way to India about a year ago. I've just received a letter from him yesterday, and he should be returning to England within the month."

"Jolly good!" Pierce slapped his knee enthusiastically. "Bound to set you to rights soon enough; won't have to rusticate with us forever, I dare say."

"Pierce!" Emelia coughed, looking pointedly at Edwin and the Appletons as she kicked her brother's shin under the table. It was never polite to speak of financial affairs in front of a guest, particularly when those affairs weren't even your own to reveal.

"Ah, how exciting." Edwin deftly ignored Pierce's blunder. "Your father was a kind man, and he seemed to me a skilled diplomat. I could tell he loved both his duties and his family back home."

Glancing across the table to Emelia, he added in a soft voice, "And do not worry yourself over your brother, my dear, for I am an old friend, remember? We needn't stand on ceremony."

"Besides, Mr. Arbuckle," he continued, turning toward the younger man, "there isn't a man alive who hasn't found himself short on blunt a time or two in his life. Why, a couple of years ago I was in an establishment in Tuscany that turned out to be infamous for rigged gaming. Well, I didn't know that at the time, and my pal Gillingham and I found ourselves on the rocks quite quickly. Our secretaries could have bailed us out, of course, but we had no way of sending word back to our traveling companions, and the thugs that ran the place wouldn't let us leave without settling payment. So, well, naturally, we had to get creative."

Emelia watched Edwin's face shining with excitement as he recounted his tale. Like her father had been, he was a talented storyteller, and soon he had the entire company in stitches. When he finally concluded with a hilarious finale that involved Edwin and Mr. Gillingham dressing up as elderly gypsy women and riding back to their hotel on the back of an old farm cart filled with manure, Mrs. Seaton was taking off her spectacles to dab at the tears of laughter running down her face.

The party had been enjoying themselves so thoroughly that the ladies had forgotten to withdraw to the sitting room, and Mr. Appleton was waving off an offer of brandy from Davis in favor of coffee.

"Oh goodness," yawned Mrs. Appleton, "it is getting late. We should get back to the boys, Horace, before they lock Mrs. Drollop in her room and come up with a scheme to launch a hot air balloon off the roof, or other such nonsense."

Edwin chuckled. "I take it your boys are a lively crew then?"

"Oh yes, but they're not bad sorts at all," Clara defended her brothers. "They're very kind and respectful, only they are just curious, and Charlie is so very clever when it comes to building things, and although Tommy is little, he is so brave and will try anything the bigger boys are attempting to do."

"I seem to remember the same of you when we were younger," Edwin recollected. "You were quite a courageous little thing, even if Emmie and Pierce and I were scaling a rocky cliff, you were right behind."

"And I've been following Emelia ever since. We've been so fortunate to grow up just down the lane from each other."

"There's nothing more special than a lifelong friend, is there?" Edwin leaned towards Emelia and continued so softly only Emelia could hear him. "What a privilege to have a friend such as you."

He gazed at her intently, and Emelia felt a flutter in her

stomach as her cheeks warmed yet again. Goodness, she was going to have to get better at controlling that. The ladies began rising and moving towards the hall, and Edwin stood quickly to help Mrs. Seaton with her chair.

"Madame, that was the finest meal I've had in ages. The company was delightful, and it is so very good to be back among friends."

Emelia stifled a yawn as the whole party shuffled towards the front door, full and sleepy. Mrs. Seaton and Pierce exchanged warm goodbyes with their guests, and as Edwin came to Emelia, he bent over her hand in an old-fashioned bow and kissed her fingers gently.

"Farewell, my lady fair."

Clara giggled, and Emelia smiled, this time managing to keep her blushes in check as she saw the glint of humor in his eyes.

"Goodnight, old friend. It was truly a delightful evening."

Tipping his hat, he strode out into the darkness.

After the guests had left, her mother retired to the library to read, and Pierce and Mr. Arbuckle headed to the parlor for a few rounds of cards. Emelia climbed the stairs to her cozy bedchamber intent on reading a few chapters of her book, but found it hard to concentrate on Young's account of physical optics tonight. Instead she found herself dreaming of a pair of warm brown eyes and adventures in exotic locales.

Despite the chilly night air, Emelia threw open her shutters, wrapped herself in a warm woolen blanket, and sat on her window seat, listening to the waves crashing in the distance. It was much, much later when she finally fell asleep under a great pile of blankets, lulled by the sound of the sea through her still-open windows.

Chapter 8

Collington Village

Henry sat at a dark table in the corner of The Leaky Pint, Collington's local watering hole, but his thoughts kept straying to Miss Seaton's charming smile and spray of freckles. Rubbing a hand across the back of his neck, he took a sip of the surprisingly good ale in front of him. Devilish luck he had. He'd spent ten years working in the fields with nothing more important than grape vines to tend to, and had barely batted an eye at all the lovely French girls his family had tried to introduce him to. He'd always thought that after his parents' disastrous go of it, marriage and romance just weren't for him.

And it had nothing to do with Alathea Westinghouse, he'd often told himself, his first moon calf love when he was barely eighteen. He'd been so head over heels in love with that girl, and she'd professed her undying love in return—right up until a Duke twice her age and as rich as Croesus swept her off her feet at her come-out ball. Henry was left nursing a badly broken heart, another factor that pushed him into finally caving to his father's pressure to join the army.

This was no time to be thinking about women, past or present, Henry reminded himself. At least he'd been able to track down some reliable information over the past few days. After a charming introduction to the village by the Seatons and their friends, Henry had set to work. He was here at the tavern chatting with locals each night, consulting with the local magistrate or landowners during the day, and even conducting a highly-escorted tour of Lord Warwick's lighthouse.

What he'd learned was intriguing, but not particularly helpful.

The lighthouse visit had earned him no information, of course, except for a confirmation that he was not quite welcome there. On the surface, the Keeper was all smiles and polite small talk as he led Henry through the old stone lighthouse, up the spiral staircase, and to the old oil lantern and its soot-stained reflector. In fact, he was *more* than polite, going out of his way to point out how well-run and highly functioning the lighthouse was.

"Well, yessir, it's an old reflector to be sure," the weathered old man had told him, "but I keep it under the strictest maintenance. I always make sure the light is burning properly. I reckon there's not a more reliable lighthouse 'round these parts."

Local pride notwithstanding, Henry thought the man was laying it on rather thick. He wondered what negligence he was trying to hide. Could it be he was just wary of the poorly-visible light being blamed for the cove's many shipwrecks, and losing his job? Or was there something more nefarious at play?

The local magistrate had also proved little help, though Henry had sensed no deception there. When he'd asked the magistrate if he'd been aware of the increase of shipwrecks in the area, the older man had scratched his thick side-whiskers, thought for a moment, and declared, "Well, by Jove, there have been more haven't there. The last what, year or two? I'd say it's that damned tropical wind coming out of the south, so unpredictable-like. It leaves sailors hardly knowing which way is which."

"The wind you say?" Henry admirably managed to keep a straight face. "You think it's been extra...windy?"

"Aye, on account of all those sailors doing trade down in the tropics. They mess up the currents and bring that devilish wind back up with 'em!"

Heavens, if this was the magistrate, Henry would hate to be accused of a crime here. The man was an idiot. Henry asked a few more questions, none of which were any more productive, then shook the magistrate's hand and thanked him for his time.

As he was turning to leave, a thought struck him, and he added, "One more thing, sir: have you noticed anything else odd happening in town over the last couple of years, even if it's not related to the shipwrecks?"

The man thought in silence for a few long moments. "Well, I guess there's the matter of so many of the ships being empty."

Henry, who hadn't been expecting anything of value, felt his heart skip a beat.

"Excuse me, empty ships? What do you mean?"

"Well," the magistrate answered, scratching his whiskers again, "whenever there are survivors from a wreck, the law says we have to hold any goods that wash up from the ship for a year for them to claim, otherwise the cargo becomes property of the Crown. Usually, the goods are brought to me, and we store them at old Jessup's farm, he havin' the extra old barn and all."

Henry nodded as if that meant something to him, eager for the magistrate to continue.

"Only lately, there have been no goods. Usually the townfolks'll help themselves to a trinket or two, nothin' much, you know, just a couple bottles of brandy to pay themselves for having to deal with cleanin' up all the wreckage, that sort of thing. It don't signify; there's always plenty left to store for its rightful owner."

The magistrate looked at Henry, as if daring him to condemn this somewhat questionable practice, but as Henry only smiled and nodded politely, he continued.

"But not only have I barely received any goods to store over the last couple of years, I haven't heard nary a whisper of an extra bottle of brandy, or a little imported finery, or nothin'. I do like a strong French drink myself now and then," he added apologetically, "but no one's seemed to have any for some time."

"I thought as maybe there were fewer survivors, the goods didn't need any storin' and went directly to London as Crown

A BRILLIANT CONVERGENCE

property. But when I was up there last month, talkin' to my friend Remus, he being an agent of the Crown an' all, he said they haven't seen any sign of any goods, either. So I'm guessing it's like the old days, and folks that are smuggling illegal goods are droppin' them out in the sea to come back and find them again, as soon as they see they are about to be dashed on the rocks. That or they really are empty ships—ghost ships the local fishermen call them."

"Ghost ships?"

"Yessir. For only an invisible crew would risk sailing these waters, to carry a load of invisible goods."

Henry thanked the man for his time, mounted his horse, and rode away shaking his head. *Oh boy. There's your answer, Colonel Phillips. Ghost ships.* But for so many wrecks to have no cargo wash ashore—either they really were dropping goods off at sea, or something else was taking them before they could reach land.

The back of his neck had been tingling for the past few days, but since he didn't believe in ghosts, Henry had no idea what he was supposed to be wary of.

Back in the tavern tonight, Henry had been testing the magistrate's *ghost ship* theory with some of the local fishermen. One weathered old sailor, a Mr. Aveyard, told Henry about his life on the sea over a couple of pints. After a while, Henry felt comfortable enough to broach the subject.

"Mr. Aveyard, I was chatting with your town magistrate this morning, and he mentioned something about the locals warning of ghost ships. What do you make of it?"

Mr. Aveyard wiped the ale off of his mustache and leaned forward conspiratorially.

"Aye lad, this 'ere's always been a ragged coast, but nothing like it's been since the curse," he whispered in his strong Yorkshire brogue.

Henry choked on a sip of ale, coughing and sputtering. After a few moments, he managed to speak again, his eyes watering. "Excuse me, what curse?"

He supposed he shouldn't be surprised, after all, it wasn't a huge leap to go from ghost ships to curses, but still he was a bit taken aback.

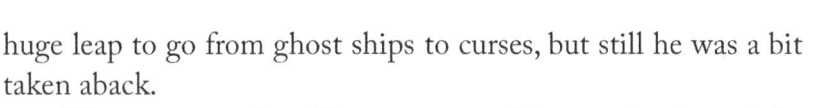

"The curse, my boy. There was an old smuggler 'anged for murder bout two, maybe three years ago. 'Twas about that time the shipwrecks became more frequent. Ships 'ave met their grisly end, not just in stormy or foggy weather, but on a clear, moonlit night. The old timers say the 'anged smuggler put a curse on these waters, dooming all the goods 'e can't 'ave into a watery grave."

The old sailor took a healthy swig of his beer, and thought for a moment. Henry regarded his own beer warily, content to listen for now.

"I don't suppose the ships are crewed by actual ghosts, mind ye, but the lack of cargo is what's really scared folks. Whether or not there really is a curse, me boy, it's changed our lives just the same. Not just the lives of them that die in the wrecks, though I know that is a terrible way to go, it is." He took his cap off and held it over his heart for a few seconds, a solemn look on his face for the lost sailors, then returned it to his head and continued. "But most of the villagers earn a little extra on the side, ye know, helping smugglers load and unload their goods. It's been that way for centuries. But as of late, there be no goods passin' through, not through this town anyways, and no extra jobs neither."

"An' 'at's another thing!" Mr Aveyard's words began to slur. "You always 'ear of some goods from a wreck coming up into town and being stored, for the rightful owners to come and claim 'em later. And as usual, a few bottles of French wine, or a bolt of silk and the like gets passed around town. Nothing 'armful like. But I ain't heard hide nor hair of—*hiccup*—anythin'."

At this point, the gentleman was starting to bob and weave slightly in his seat, and Henry knew his time was limited. The man had been dipping rather heavily this evening. Henry had been drinking as slowly as possible, but he'd still gone through three beers while waiting for Mr. Aveyard to become comfortable enough to tell his tale. He could only imagine how the older man was feeling after his five pints. Any information he could glean from here on out was unreliable at best.

"One more question, my good man, and then I believe I must call it a night. If it were your ship, what could possibly cause you to crash into the rocks here on a clear, moonless night?"

"Well—*hiccup*—disregarding the supernatural, ye mean." The old man stared into his glass for answers. "Suppose an inexperienced sailor could run aground if he couldn't judge the depth of the water, or the distance to the rocks."

"What about an experienced sailor? What could cause him to steer into the rocks?"

"Nothin' short of sabotage."

∽

The next morning Henry awoke slightly worse for wear. His tongue felt as if it was made of carpet, and a pressure that had nothing to do with danger throbbing at the base of his head. Rolling out of the bed, he padded to the washbasin in his bare feet and plunged his head into the cold water. A few seconds later he emerged, dripping and sputtering, but a bit more clear-headed.

It was a trick he'd perfected while in the army after too many late nights playing cards and drinking the local moonshine. A cup of coffee, a bite to eat, and he would soon be set to rights and able to go about his business. Hopefully. These late nights at the pub were a younger man's occupation.

Now, where were we? Henry tried to clear his head as he pulled on a fresh shirt and trousers and rang the bell for Rogers. He'd let the man practice his cravat skills, and he could use a hand getting into his coat of moss-green superfine. Henry had thought it a bit of an outlandish choice when a French tailor had first pulled out the bolt of cloth, but now that he was by the sea again, it seemed to fit in nicely with the churning swells and spraying seafoam just beyond the harbor.

Ghost ships, missing cargo—either he'd had more to drink last night than he thought, or nothing in this town was making sense. Perhaps he needed to write Colonel Phillips one more time. How was he supposed to go about his business when he wasn't even sure what that business was anymore? All he had was superstitious townspeople, a suspicious old lighthouse Keeper, and a vague inclination that all was not as it should be. That was hardly enough on which to conduct an investigation. After all, Henry was hardly a Bow Street Runner. Maybe it was time to return home to his grapevines and his library. Go home and forget England, forget his father, forget these damnable shipwrecks.

Shipwrecks. Henry rubbed the back of his throbbing head. Crazy, adventurous Charles would never get a chance to go home again. He'd been claimed in this very sea, attempting to save sailors who could not swim when their ship started taking on water. He'd always been a strong swimmer, but the storm had been too much even for him. Three sailors owed their lives to him, though. Because of Charles they'd been able to hold onto the wreckage long enough to be rescued by some passing fishermen. Charles had gone after one last sailor and had never come back.

So many sailors just like his brother had lost their lives on this rocky coast. If there was a chance he could uncover information that would save even one ship, smuggler or otherwise, he owed it to Charles to try. Henry had not even come back to England for the funeral. He regretted it deeply now, but he'd been so filled with anger at his father, and even at his older brother, Randolph, for pushing Charles to enlist. Staying away from the funeral seemed like a way to punish them, but in the end his anger had only punished himself.

He knew it was foolish now. Charles had always felt called to the sea, and he would have joined the Navy no matter the situation at home. Henry's battles were his own to fight, just as Charles' had been his own. He could not blame anyone for them, not even his father.

Rogers knocked a bit too loudly, then bustled in with a breakfast tray.

"G'day, m'Lord." He set the tray down on the breakfast table and bowed stiffly to Henry.

The sight brought a ghost of a smile to Henry's face.

"Rogers, how many times do I have to tell you that I'm not a Lord?"

"But yer pap's a Viscount, and that's a lot more mighty than some of these other young swells as think they're above your touch."

"That may be true, but I'm a mere second son. Moreover, I'm your friend, Rogers! You can just call me Henry."

"But 'twouldn't be proper, bein' yer valet an all," retorted Rogers, his nose in the air. He was doing quite a good impression of Lord Warwick's lofty butler from a few days ago, and Henry laughed.

"Leave it to you to lighten my mood, Rogers. I'm afraid I've been a bit blue-deviled this morning."

"Well, I 'ave something 'at'll cheer you right up, it will. You have an appointment with a Mr. Pierce Seaton at 11 o clock, and if i'm not mistaken, 'at'll be the young fellow with the lovely sister."

Good Lord! Today was the day he was supposed to visit Mr. Seaton, and with a devilish head, too! Henry groaned.

"Rogers, don't let it ever be said that the Fates don't have a sense of humor," he muttered, resignedly. "Let's see what can be done to make me presentable."

∽

Emelia bounced down the stairs, remembering halfway down to lift her navy striped morning dress so she didn't rend the hem. She was trying to be more careful with her garments, not that it mattered too much with this particular dress. It was one of her oldest and starting to show wear. She'd dressed for comfort and utility today. Not bothering to ring the bell for Marietta, Emelia had just braided her hair quickly down her back and secured it with a strip of linen.

The last week had been full of excitement, with Edwin stopping by or inviting them on an outing nearly every day. On Monday, they'd taken a walk down to the seaside. On Tuesday, they visited Ernside Manor so Clara and Emelia could see how the gardens had fared over the years. Clara, a talented artist, sketched some suggestions for improvements. On Thursday, Edwin had assembled a magnificent picnic on the beach and invited the entire Seaton and Appleton families. Even Clara's five younger brothers had come, their mother telling them to run off their energy in the sand. The group spent many enjoyable hours together until the sun began to set and they finally had to call it a day, salty hair, sandy hems and all.

Emelia couldn't remember when she'd had such fun, but she was starting to wish for a rainy day alone at home to catch up on some reading and thinking. She thoroughly enjoyed a good adventure, but too many packed days in a row had left her feeling a bit ragged. There were no merriments planned for today, and some ominous clouds were promising a good, solid rainy afternoon. She was hurrying out to the garden for a bit of archery practice before the skies opened up and she could enjoy the rest of her day of solitude in the library.

Heading to the back door, Emelia tied on the heavy linen pinafore she used for metalworking and went out into the garden. The air was heavy and charged for a spring thunderstorm. She needed to work quickly, and headed over to the tower-turned-workshop.

The workshop was actually the last remaining tower from the old castle ruin Seaton House was built upon. The walls connecting it to the rest of the castle had long since crumbled away, but the tower was solid, and her father had it shored up to be used as a gardening shed. "It lends us some antiquity," he used to say, a twinkle in his eye.

When she'd shown an interest in archery around the age of ten, her father had built her a special workstation in the shed, with a lathe for turning arrows out of different types of wood, and a stove, hammer, and anvil for fashioning arrowtips. The wide wooden workbench gave her plenty of room for stringing bows.

He'd also taught her how to calculate the weight of the arrow, the materials used, and to factor in the conditions around her. She'd been a quick study, and was accurately hitting targets at forty-five meters when other girls her age were still learning how to hold the bow.

Emelia glanced out the tower's small window at the darkening sky. By the time she'd fitted the arrowheads onto the arrows and made a few minor adjustments to her bow, the sky was growing darker. There was no time to drag Sir Ironsides from his home in the corner back out into the field for practice, so she'd have to settle for a few quick shots at the wild geese roaming in the field in front of the house. Tossing her quiver over one shoulder, she dashed out of the shed.

Strong breezes pulled at her dress and whisked hairs away from her braid, but the rumbling thunder was still quite a ways off in the distance. The geese were restless in the tall, spring-green grass. She'd have another goose to send to the Appletons within minutes.

Her first few shots fell close to their mark, but she heard no telltale honking or flapping, so Emelia took a deep breath, closed her eyes, and listened for rustling in the grass. There. Right on top of that little hill.

Opening her eyes, she let an arrow fly towards the noise—just as a tall, gray beaver hat came into view over the grassy knoll.

Emelia's stomach dropped.

"Look out! Get down!"

But of course, it was too late. Any arrow had long since met its mark. Dropping her bow and quiver, she ran through the long grass towards the unfortunate visitor, praying he was still alive.

Chapter 9

Seaton House

She reached the knoll at a dead run, but what Emelia saw brought her to a quick halt. There stood Mr. Rockcliff, their new acquaintance from last week, very much alive, but staring at her with a look of utter astonishment. Fresh blood was dripping down his cheek from a sizable gash that could only have been made by her arrow.

"What just…who—*you* shot me?" The confounded gentleman stood, mouth agape, heedless of the blood trickling down towards his cravat.

"I am terribly sorry, sir, but you had the misfortune of walking up right behind my goose." Emelia picked up the hat that now lay several feet away from him in the grass.

"*Your* goose?"

"Well, the one I was aiming for. I do believe I would have had him, too, if you hadn't walked up behind him and scared him off. What in the world were you doing walking through this field?"

"My apologies, miss. I could have hardly known you would use me for target practice."

"Yes, well, I thought the field was quite deserted. There's never anyone here but these wretched geese. They've quite taken over, you know."

Emelia glanced at the blood now flowing freely down Mr. Rockcliff's face and neck, and pulled out a rumpled handkerchief from her stained and dusty pinafore. She cringed. At least the handkerchief was clean.

"Here, you're spoiling your cravat." She pressed the handkerchief gently to his cheek.

"A few inches lower and it might have severed an artery," Emelia muttered, examining the wound as the mounting wind tugged at her skirts and threatened to overwhelm the ribbon holding her hair in place.

"Well, I knew it was coming so I ducked! Apparently not far enough, though."

"You heard it coming? That's impossible. You can't hear an arrow, especially not over this wind. And I shouted as soon as I saw you, but by then it was too late."

Thunder cracked, closer now, and Emelia felt a drop of rain hit her forehead.

"I didn't say that I heard it coming, I just *knew* it was coming." Mr. Rockcliff, still standing there calmly on the knoll, held his beaver hat in his hand as if they were discussing the weather—which they were going to need to do very soon or they would both be struck by lightning.

"And if I hadn't ducked I would have been shot through the throat like that goose you were trying to hit. I am sorry I scared it away; hopefully you weren't planning on roast goose for dinner."

"Dinner? What? Oh no. Just target practice. Well, it would have been someone's dinner, I suppose."

Poor man must be in shock. Emelia thought he had seemed unusually calm for this odd predicament. *Knew it was coming!* But she had not been raised to be impolite to strange gentlemen, so she just smiled at Mr. Rockcliff and hoped she didn't spook him further.

"Come on, it doesn't appear to be a deep wound. We can clean it up at the house. I'm sure mother has a tincture that would aid in its healing."

"A...tincture?" Mr. Rockcliff looked fascinated, as if she'd just told him she had a rare artifact on display. What an odd man.

He nodded his assent, then stopped and stared at her.

"What is that black substance all over your hands?"

"What? Oh that. It's just dust from my arrowheads. I make all my own, you see. Are you sure you're okay? You didn't fall and hit your head when the arrow grazed you?"

Emelia glanced at his pupils. He didn't seem to have a concussion.

"Oh no, I'm quite alright. Quite."

Mr. Rockcliff still stared at her with a queer expression on his face.

Heavens! Perhaps he wasn't addled in the head, but was just trying to figure out how to politely excuse himself and get as far away from her as possible! The last time they met she was running through the fields like a hoyden, and here she was as filthy as a blacksmith, her braid running down her back like a schoolgirl, shooting geese before a thunderstorm. And she'd shot *him!*

"I truly am sorry." Emelia apologized again as fat raindrops began to fall in earnest around them. Oh well, in for a penny, in for a pound. It was either come with her or catch his death of a cold, at least for now. "Come, let's go into the house and get you cleaned up."

Since he was still standing there looking slightly bewildered and the rain was coming down in hard sheets now, Emelia grabbed Mr. Rockcliff's hand and began to run towards the house. She didn't want to hurt him if he had a head injury, but she also didn't want to leave him out in this field to get struck by lightning. The air was heavy and charged with electricity.

The pair ran until they reached the portico over the front door, and Emelia stopped to catch her breath. Her arm tingled where her hand touched Mr. Rockcliff's, but surely the imminent lightning was to blame for that. She looked down and realized with some surprise she was still holding on to his hand. Dropping it quickly, she looked up into his face. The handkerchief had been forgotten on their mad dash to the house, not that it mattered as they were entirely soaked from the rain. Her bow and quiver were still out there in the grass somewhere too, but she would come back to retrieve them when the rain stopped. She had to get Mr. Rockcliff inside and tend to his wound.

"Are you okay?"

She looked up into his eyes, checking his pupils again. He was a full head taller than she, and the fine cut of his coat could not disguise his broad shoulders beneath. She was immensely grateful she had not injured him more severely. It would have been impossible for her to carry him back to the house.

"Yes, I believe everything is going to be just fine." He absently smeared the blood on his cheek. His eyes searched her face for a moment, but just when she thought he was about to say something profound, he added, "Would it be possible for us to go indoors now?"

"Oh! Oh yes of course. Come, let's get you patched up."

She turned to go into the house, making a conscious effort not to take his hand again. She didn't wait for Davis to open the door, but strode in as if she weren't dripping all over the floor, and led Mr. Rockcliff to the sitting room. Her mother always kept a warm fire going in here, especially on wet days like this one.

"You can wait here in front of the fire while I fetch some first aid supplies. I believe mother is in the library, I will see if she can assist us. I know Pierce was expecting a business call this morning. He is in his study, but I am sure he will want to see you as well."

"*Erm*, that was me, you see." Mr. Rockcliff looked rather bashful.

"What was you?"

"Your brother's business call. I was coming to meet him when my horse lost a shoe, so I told Rogers to take him back to the inn, and I would continue on foot. I had the, um, bright idea of cutting across your field. Thus my inopportune interruption of your hunting expedition.'"

"Oh! I see. Well, that does make more sense. I don't usually have strange men walking across the field in front of my house, you see."

"You think I'm strange?"

Well, yes, obviously! "No, no, I meant—it's just—let me go get those bandages."

Her cheeks burning, Emelia turned and ran from the room.

She returned a few moments later, slightly more collected and carrying a fresh pitcher of water, a clean towel, and a bar of soap. She'd been unable to locate Davis or her mother, so she'd settled for grabbing the first supplies she could find. She found Mr. Rockcliff still standing in front of the fire, holding a freshly torn piece of his cravat to the wound. He shrugged.

"It was ruined anyway, and it has slowed the bleeding. The wound is starting to clot, so it's nothing much to worry about. I've had many worse."

He smiled, and then the smile turned into a chuckle, and the chuckle turned into a hearty laugh. Soon he was laughing so hard his shoulders were shaking and tears were streaming out of his eyes. At least Emelia thought they were tears. It was hard to tell since there was so much blood and water still all over his face.

"Now I *know* I have done you a head injury," she sighed, pulling a wooden stool over in front of the fire and motioning for him to sit down. Retrieving the washbasin in the corner, she laid out her supplies on the table next to the fire.

Emelia watched Mr. Rockcliff carefully as he dried his tears of laughter, then lowered his hand and gingerly touched his cheek. He grimaced, then grinned at her, which was quite disarming. This man had more than enough cause to hate her, but here he was grinning as though they were lads causing mischief at boarding school! Surely he needed a doctor, but she'd best get him cleaned up first. It was the least she could do for him.

"I do beg your pardon," began Mr Rockcliff, still drying his face. "I confess I was a bit hungover this morning, and the absurdity of this whole situation just struck me. I have just realized that I made it through the war and its many injuries, lived a peaceful life in France among my once-enemies for years, and here I finally come back to England and am nearly skewered by a mere slip of a girl out hunting for dinner!"

He laughed again, and she couldn't help but smile a bit when he put it that way.

"Well, I truly am sorry. I'm really grateful you weren't injured worse. You hardly seem old enough to have fought in the war, though, you can't be all that much older than I am."

Mr. Rockcliff chuckled again.

"I'm twenty-nine years old, so I'm sure I have at least a decade on you. I was barely more than a boy when I left to fight Napoleon."

Emelia began lathering her filthy hands with soap and washing them in the basin.

"I'm not neglecting your wounds, Mr. Rockcliff, I just felt like it would be a good idea to clean up a bit first." She then wet the clean towel with water from the pitcher and began to gently clean the blood off of Mr. Rockcliff's face.

"You're not at all squeamish for a gently-bred young lady, are you?"

"Is that an insult, sir, or a compliment?" asked Emelia wryly.

"Oh a compliment, I assure you. You've kept a very level head, too. You would put some of the men in my old regiment to shame."

"I take it you're no longer in the military, then."

"Oh no, I left right after the war ended, nearly ten years ago now. Or I should say, I never came back. I've been living in Provence with my grandmother for a decade. I only set foot on English soil again a week ago."

Emelia set the bloodied towel down and studied the wound. It tracked from his left cheek nearly to his hairline, but it wasn't as deep as she would have thought by the amount of blood. She studied his face, noticing a small scar above his left eyebrow, and another long, white line running down the right side of his jaw and disappearing into his shirt collar. He certainly had been a soldier, and had seen quite a bit of action by the looks of it. She quickly looked back up into his eyes, not wanting for him to see her gawking. His cool blue eyes looked clear and alert. No head injury, then.

"I don't think you'll need stitches, Mr. Rockcliff. The wound may bleed a bit more but it's shallow, and we should be able to bandage it acceptably."

"Oh! Good afternoon," said a voice from the doorway. "Emelia, you didn't tell me we have visitors."

Emelia glanced at her mother, who seemed entirely unperturbed at the stranger bleeding on her carpet. She gestured towards Mr. Rockcliff with the bloodied towel.

"Mother, meet Mr. Rockcliff. Mr. Rockcliff, my mother, Mrs. Seaton."

Mr. Rockcliff stepped forward to extend a hand, noticed it was covered in blood, and quickly withdrew it, wiping it on the ruined cravat.

"Please, excuse me, ma'am. It is a pleasure to meet you."

"Thank you Mr. Rockcliff." She whisked into the room and took a seat on the settee. "Let me ring for some tea and sustenance, and then I'll get some salve for that gash on your face and you can tell me the whole story."

"That's what I was afraid of," muttered Emelia.

After Emelia had thoroughly cleaned the wound, she'd applied some of her mother's salve and bandaged it gently. Mr. Rockcliff had brightened at the sight of the salve, sniffed it, and politely requested a full catalog of its ingredients from her mother, who insisted he take the remainder of the tin home with him to apply over the next few days.

They'd then drunk a bracing cup of tea brought by Joseph, the footman, Mr. Rockcliff from his wooden stool by the fire and Emelia from where she stood. Mrs. Seaton sipped her tea from the settee, looking every bit the genteel hostess enjoying a normal social call. After a few moments, she looked the pair of still-wet young people up and down.

"Now, Emelia, your teeth are beginning to chatter. Please go upstairs and change out of your wet things. I've already instructed Marietta to draw you a bath."

Emelia opened her mouth to protest, but her mother held up a finger and turned to Mr. Rockcliff.

"Mr. Rockcliff, it won't do for you to remain in those clothes either, seeing as you're soaked to the bone. I would send you home in the carriage but I let Davis, our butler, take it to visit his mother for the afternoon since it looked like rain. We can't have you venturing out on horseback, because if that wound gets wet right now it'll likely start bleeding all over again. There's nothing for it but to get you into some dry things and wait out the storm."

Glancing outside, Emelia saw the thunderstorm was still raging. She hadn't even noticed in all the commotion. Mrs. Seaton reached behind the settee and rang the bell.

"I'm going to have James, my son's valet, take you upstairs and find you something to wear," she instructed matter-of-factly. "You and Pierce appear to be about the same height, though you're considerably broader in the shoulders, but surely he can find you something to wear while your things dry."

Emelia waited for Mr. Rockcliff to make his excuses and flee this crazy family as fast as possible, but he just smiled demurely and nodded.

"Thank you, ma'am. That is most kind."

"Emelia, upstairs you go." Her mother looked at her sternly. "Don't come back until you're dry and warm. I'll have a light luncheon brought in when you return."

Emelia climbed the stairs to her room, knees shaking. She was properly chilled now that the excitement was wearing off, and perhaps in a bit of shock herself. Dispassionately, she assessed her pulse and temperature, and once in her room allowed Marietta to divest her of her ruined garments. Her maid would have fussed over her more, but Emelia climbed into the bath, insisting she needed a few minutes of alone time to decompress, so she was left to marinate in the steaming water. Scrubbing quickly, Emelia removed Mr. Rockcliff's blood from her hands, spending an extra few moments on the stubborn stains under her fingernails. As macabre as it was, it was also oddly intimate. She'd never so much as touched a man's bare hand before, let alone his face, nor felt the pulse at his neck with her fingertips.

She still had no idea what Mr. Rockcliff was doing here, both here in the village and here to visit Pierce. He had mentioned being here on business, but the only people that ever came through Collington were sailors and traders. Mr. Rockcliff had been a soldier, so he was likely not a firstborn son, but he was definitely a gentleman. He wouldn't have been here to make his fortune in trade. Emelia had lived in Collington for twenty years, and could count on one hand the number of gentlemen that had stayed in town longer than to change horses or catch a boat to France. And when they'd walked with Mr. Rockcliff to the village the other day, he'd mentioned needing to pay a call on Edwin, who had only just arrived in town himself. It was really all quite a puzzle. Emelia enjoyed puzzles.

Once her temperature had returned to normal, Emelia climbed out of the bath and quickly dressed in a clean blue morning dress. After twisting her still-damp curls into a knot on top of her head, Emelia put on her warmest wool stockings in an attempt to prevent becoming chilled again. She gave a hurried glance in the mirror on the way back down the stairs—still a bit pale and perhaps not her most put-together, but it was certainly better than the disheveled mess she'd been before.

Walking back into the sitting room, she was stopped in her tracks at the sight of Mr. Rockcliff sitting in an oversized leather armchair by the fire. She threw a hand over her mouth to suppress an unladylike giggle. The man was reading a book and looking as perfectly at home as he would in his own salon. He wore a pair of dark pantaloons and a white shirt that had obviously come from Pierce's wardrobe, but in lieu of a waistcoat or coat, he was wearing one of her father's old dressing gowns over his clothes.

Her father had had a habit of collecting dressing gowns from his travels, the more ostentatious the better. This one was made of a patchwork of colorful silks from India. She felt sure her mother had chosen one of the more outlandish dressing gowns on purpose. This, combined with the long hair now flowing freely around his shoulders and the fresh wound on his cheek, lent him the air of a rather dashing pirate. This effect was only slightly spoiled by the pair of spectacles perched on the end of his nose.

Having finally noticed she'd entered the room, Mr. Rockcliff stood, removed his spectacles, and bowed slightly in her direction. Her mother was nowhere to be seen.

"I'm afraid I've made myself at home." He held up the book with a grin. "I saw this copy of *The Flora of the West Indies* on the side table and had to take a look. I've always been rather interested in botany."

"Really?" Emelia managed to keep a straight face and took a seat on the settee across from him. "I had no idea pirates were such plant lovers."

"Pirates? Oh! The outfit." He grinned again, a habit that seemed to come easily to him. "I suppose I do look a bit roguish. Unfortunately your brother is a bit more narrow in the shoulders than I, so your mother and the valet had to improvise."

"Father did love his outrageous dressing gowns. He collected them on his travels. How's your face feeling?"

"Oh fine," he said dismissively, as though he were grazed by an arrow every day. "I dare say I won't even feel it tomorrow. And I'm sure your mother's salve will heal it up nicely. There might not even be a scar." He waved his hand to indicate his other scars, and Emelia found herself wondering how far down the scar on his collar went, then blushed at the impropriety of such a thought and quickly redirected the conversation.

"So you're interested in botany?"

"Yes! Botany particularly, but also zoology...any of the natural sciences really. I also went through quite a philosophy phase in my youth. I spent many hours hiding in the woods behind our house with a great stack of books. My reading habits irked my father, but my mother supplied me with whatever subject was my fancy that week."

Emelia smiled at the image of a young boy with a pilfered library taking refuge in the woods. She'd had no need to hide her love of reading, but the great stacks of books had been an integral part of her childhood as well.

"I confess I tend to stick more to physics and mathematics myself, but botany does seem to be all the rage right now. My mother is well-read on the subject, and is particularly interested in plants with medicinal values."

"Ah, thus the salve," he murmured, absently touching his cheek. "I'd just been reading about the efficacy of arnica in preventing swelling and scarring. You all seem to be quite the well-read family. Is your brother as bookish as you and your mother?"

Emelia was grateful he'd asked without a hint of judgment in his voice. Most gentlemen weren't as accepting of her and her mother's reading habits.

"Afraid Pierce doesn't share in our proclivities. I suppose he's always been a bit of the black sheep of the family," she added with a fond smile. "He's much more modish and fashionable than the rest of us. Don't let him fool you though, he's highly intelligent. He's always fascinated with the mechanics of things, though these days his tastes run more to the races at Newmarket and running up to London for the latest boxing match or gaming tournament."

"Ah, well, he's very young yet, I'm sure he'll find gainful employment soon enough. And what about you? You seem to have your own sort of restlessness about you, though not in a negative way," Mr. Rockcliff quickly added. He gave her a look which Emelia swore she could feel directly to her bones. "You strike me as contained energy, just waiting for a purpose."

Emelia's jaw dropped slightly. Who was this man? She'd been in his company for less than an hour in total, and here he was presuming to look into her very soul! And even more eerily, he was oddly perceptive. What a strange man, indeed.

Rather than answering, she jumped off the settee and clapped her hands together.

"Goodness, listen to me blabbering on as if we have all the time in the world, without any further thought to your welfare! Where is mother? I believe we need to get you something to eat as soon as possible. No doubt all of that loss of blood has left you quite famished."

She was just turning to leave the room again, when her mother bustled in carrying a small tray of scones, Cook behind her with a much larger tray laden with sandwiches, cold meats, cheeses, and fruit.

"I thought we needed a bit more luncheon than usual after this morning's excitement," Mrs. Seaton explained, and began piling a plate high with food.

"Here we go Mr. Rockcliff. So sorry to have kept you waiting. You should know that your things have been hung in front of the kitchen fire, so they shall be dry in no time. In the meantime, I want to hear all about what you're doing in Collington—besides serving as target practice for my daughter."

Handing Mr. Rockcliff a plate that could have easily fed three, she began nibbling on a sandwich. Emelia was left to fend for herself.

After polishing off several sandwiches and a scone, Mr. Rockcliff handed his cup to Mrs. Seaton for another cup of tea, crossed an ankle over one knee, and leaned forward to tell his tale.

"I first had the pleasure of meeting your son and daughter earlier this week as I was leaving your neighbor Lord Warwick's estate," he began.

"Ah! You're the mysterious stranger Pierce mentioned," interrupted Mrs. Seaton. "He kept going on about coats and bonnets and running into Adonis, who I now see clearly was you."

Emelia nearly choked on her sandwich. Pierce's Adonis was

certainly well-built and golden-haired, but she wasn't sure she would count him among the most handsome men of her acquaintance. In addition to the scars, his nose looked as if it had been broken at some point and set poorly, and while he'd been impeccably dressed and well-groomed, his overly long hair was certainly not in keeping with the current fashions. No, he was not as classically handsome as some—say particularly Edwin—but there was something quite intriguing about him. His shoulders and his jaw gave him a look that was entirely tough and unyielding, but his eyes held a sparkle of mischief, and there was something fascinating about his mouth…

Emelia was forced to abandon the study of her subject when he looked straight into her eyes and said with a look of utter sincerity, "I am sorry about that, by the way."

She blinked.

"Sorry? About what?"

"Emelia," chided her mother, "you must try to pay more attention when we have guests. She is always off in a world of her own, you see, completing mathematical equations or designing a new longbow," she explained airily to Mr. Rockcliff, with a look at Emelia that plainly said "*mind your manners.*"

Emelia's cheeks burned. If only her mother knew exactly what she'd been contemplating.

"I said," repeated Mr. Rockcliff patiently, "I was sorry for being a dull bore on our walk to town the other day. I confess I was trying to make some important business plans right before I met your party, and I was a bit distracted. I did enjoy hearing your brother's introduction to Collington, however, it was most amusing."

"Yes, Pierce has always been the entertaining one of the family," Mrs. Seaton said indulgently. "Speaking of, I attempted to tell him that you were in here with us and would have to reschedule your business meeting, but he seems to be nowhere to be found. He likely went off on some errand with Mr. Arbuckle and was detained, but perhaps it was all for the best today."

Emelia couldn't contain her curiosity any longer.

"And what exactly is your business with my brother, Mr. Rockcliff?"

"Please, call me Henry, both of you. I believe our acquaintanceship justifies first names after today." The corner of his mouth twitched up in a half smile.

"Very well, Henry, since we are such good friends, I'd love to hear more about how you interrupted a decade-long sojourn in France to come to our little town on a somewhat vague errand of business."

"Emelia!"

"No, no, she is quite right. It is very odd. I am here because of the shipwrecks."

That made Emelia pause for a moment.

"Oh! Well, there are very many shipwrecks in this area, that is true, but what can you possibly do about them?"

"I am here on behalf of a French inventor named Augustin Fresnel. Perhaps you've heard of him?"

Emelia chewed the inside of her cheek in thought. That did sound familiar.

"I believe I read something about him inventing a brighter light for a lighthouse off the coast of France?"

"Yes, but...well, that's like saying the sun is brighter than a candle. The difference is revolutionary. Shipwrecks off the coast of France have been cut nearly in half in the last six months. The new lens enables a ship to see the light up to nine miles out to sea."

"Nine miles!" exclaimed Mrs. Seaton, "that would be incredible."

"It is," he said simply. "Mr. Fresnel's associates want to install a copy of that new lens right here in Collington, in Lord Warwick's lighthouse. As you know, it's one of the most dangerous stretches of coastline in England. They're hoping that if England can be shown its efficacy, orders for the new lens will start coming in as quickly as they can make them."

Mr. Rockcliff—Henry—leaned forward excitedly, warming to his subject.

"I was in Paris for several weeks before I sailed to England, watching and working with Mr. Fresnel and his associates, and the process was astonishing. It is at once a triumph of science and a work of art."

"How does it work?" Emelia was intrigued.

"I'm afraid it would take a physicist to explain it to you properly. I certainly am not, but my understanding is that Fresnel has designed a new shape of lens that magnifies the light rather than simply reflecting it."

He pulled a folded sheet of paper out of the dressing gown's pocket. It was slightly damp, but otherwise looked none the worse for wear.

"I brought this sketch to show your brother," he said, offering her the paper. "I laid it near the fireplace to dry while I was dressing. You can probably understand the lens's function better than I."

Emelia carefully unfolded the paper, and was looking at a drawing of a beehive shaped lens, with concentric circles around each of its six sides resembling ripples in a still pond when a stone is dropped. Even given her somewhat limited knowledge of optics, she could see how it was miles more sophisticated than anything currently in use.

"This is exciting. Imagine if even a few ships were saved each year, how many lives would be spared! When does installation begin?"

"Ah, that, I'm afraid, is the question of the day. You see, I visited Lord Warwick earlier this week, and he will not give his permission for me to install the lens."

"Is there a catch then?" Mrs. Seaton looked thoughtful. "Is the lens much more expensive to operate, or somehow unreliable or dangerous?"

"It is my understanding that the Fresnel lens takes less fuel to operate, and is just as safe and reliable as any other lens. Lord Warwick, well—"

Henry looked down, as if unsure how to proceed.

"Lord Warwick is being extremely cautious. He expressed

concern about trusting a French innovation, and I believe he was hesitant to make changes too quickly after just arriving home."

"That seems very unlike Edwin." Emelia spoke mostly to herself. "He was always one to rush headlong into a project and then ask questions later. Perhaps coming home and taking over the estate has left him more overwhelmed than he lets on."

"That would make sense, dear," agreed her mother. "His father was such a recluse after Edwin's mother died, it would not be surprising if he inherited a great deal of work to do."

"Although," she nodded to Henry, "the rate these shipwrecks have been occurring the last couple years, if this lens has any chance of helping then the sooner, the better. Being friends, perhaps we can speak with him and help him see the wisdom in allowing your Frenchman to install this lens. If it's anything less than you've claimed it to be, he can always go back to the old lens with nothing lost."

"I would most appreciate it if you would encourage him in that direction. My time here is limited. I am planning to stay for only a few more weeks, and I am afraid the offer might leave with me."

Emelia looked up at him, surprised.

"But you said you've only just returned to England! Surely you're not heading back to France already?"

Henry laughed, but it was with amusement, not condescension.

"Well, there's a lot more to England than Collington. I am planning to visit my mother in London, and my sister in Sussex, and I do need to be back in France by harvest. My grandmother and uncle run a winery in Provence, and the work requires all of us come September."

"How lovely!" exclaimed Mrs. Seaton. "I understand Provence to be a beautiful part of the world. My husband often said he longed to go back there."

"Yes, ma'am, it is quite remarkable. I have been very happy there."

Emelia wanted to ask so many questions. Why he'd left England all those years ago. Why he'd never come back to visit, especially if his mother was still living in London. Why he left a genteel occupation in the military to become a farmer, of all things! She had no judgment for his choices, only curiosity. But, despite the forced intimacy of the day, she reminded herself she barely knew this man. Such questions would be an impertinence. So she racked her brain for an easy, impersonal question.

"What kind of wine do you make in Provence, Henry?"

"Mostly the light pink wine locals call Rosé. It is quite refreshing in the arid climate. Tell me, Miss Seaton, do you—"

Emelia never heard what he was going to ask her, as at that moment Pierce burst into the room, wearing a sodden greatcoat and wide-brimmed hat.

"By Jove, Rockcliff, there you are! Sorry I'm late. Devilish weather we're having."

He removed his coat and hat and hung them on the back of a wooden chair near the fire.

"Got any more tea, Mother? Chilled to the bone. I'd ring for Davis but the fellow was nowhere to be found, that's why I was dripping all over your rug with that deuced coat."

"No wonder I couldn't find you in your office, Pierce," his mother said. "I didn't know you were out. I thought you'd be here awaiting Henry, but it's all for the best as he met with a bit of an accident."

"Sorry about that, old chap," apologized Pierce, stuffing a sandwich in his mouth in one bite, and washing it down with half a cup of tea. "I—*erm*—was a bit held up."

"Yes, so we had gathered," said his mother dryly.

Pierce colored slightly, and looked at his plate of sandwiches, but offered no further information.

"Henry was just telling us of his vineyards in Provence," offered Emelia, sensing her brother's discomfort. Likely he was off playing cards or betting on a horse race, but he was a grown man, and he had no need to give an account of himself to his mother and sister in front of a guest.

"That so? You're a winemaker, then?" Pierce looked up at Henry in surprise. "Quite different from an inventor, or an investor, or whatever it is you're here doing."

"Yes, yes it is," admitted Henry. "And it's even worse than that! My uncle does the winemaking, I simply tend the vines. My skills run more towards botany than chemistry."

"A farmer? By Jove! And Arbuckle was just explaining to me how your father is a Viscount. Suppose you can do whatever you want, then."

He seemed to be about to discuss this surprising fact further, when he looked fully at Henry for the first time.

"'Pon rep! You're dressed rather queerly, old chap. That one of my father's old dressing gowns? And what happened to your face? You weren't in a brawl were you? Fancy that! I missed all the fun! Who was the other fellow?"

"No Pierce," Emelia said quickly, blushing, "Mr. Rockcliff—I mean, Henry—was not in a fight, we just had a bit of an accident. He, well…"

"Your sister shot me with an arrow," Henry supplied, still maddeningly calm about the whole thing.

"That so!" Pierce exclaimed politely, as if he hadn't just been told his sister had nearly killed his morning caller. "She's a devilish good shot, so since you're alive I'd say she was aiming for something else, and you got in the way."

Emelia felt a rush of affection for her brother.

"Pierce! I think that's the nicest thing you've ever said about me!"

"Well it's true, ain't it? But you weren't out shooting geese in this mess, were you?"

"No! Well yes, but rather, just before. Henry came over the little knoll just as I was aiming for one of those pesky geese."

"As I understand, the sky opened up on them while they were tending to the wound," added Mrs. Seaton, "and we couldn't have Henry catching a cold from his wet clothes, so he's borrowing your clothes and one of your father's old dressing gowns until we can get his things dried."

"Thought I recognized those trousers! Not one of my newer pairs, but Weston does make 'em to last! Devilishly fine tailoring if I do say so myself."

Pierce waved a sandwich at the trousers in question.

"Thank you sir, for your raiment," Henry offered with a grin. "I would have walked home, my horse having been taken back to the village on account of a thrown horseshoe, you see, but your mother and sister would hear none of it."

"Right smart of them, too! Hardly do for you to catch your death before you can help us with this newfangled lens of yours! Why, I just heard another ship ran aground last night! Has got to stop, Rockcliff!"

"Oh dear," exclaimed Emelia, unaware of the news. "*Another* ship, really?"

"Just a small fishing vessel and no one was injured. Poor devils swam to shore, thank God. They said they got confused about where the shore was in the fog!"

"I've heard most of the local fishermen won't go out at night anymore." Henry looked thoughtful.

"Older ones won't. The young bloods are more reckless. But even then I hear they stay within easy sight of shore, just to be safe."

Pierce set down his plate at last and drummed his fingers on his knee, studying the fire.

"Wouldn't say this to just anyone, Rockcliff, but you seem a dependable fellow. Think there's something devilish queer going on out there on the water. Folks who've been sailing all their lives are suddenly losing their way. Makes sense for the larger shipping vessels to have trouble, these waters are rocky and dangerous and always have been. But I hear the talk around the village. Superstitious, they all are. But I figure, wherever there's a superstition, there's an underlying cause somewhere."

Emelia was taken aback. She'd never heard her brother speak of current affairs or known him to listen to talk in the village. In fact, she felt a little ashamed of herself, as she prided herself on being informed on all the local news. But she knew little about the danger beyond her father's fear of going out on the water and a vague inclination that their area was more treacherous than average. She'd assumed most of the wrecks were shipping or smuggling vessels from France, as none of the local villagers ever seemed to be directly affected. She'd chalked the tragedies up to the sad realities of a dangerous profession and a highly-trafficked, difficult to navigate waterway. She'd never been aware of being consciously sheltered, but perhaps Emelia was more wrapped up in her own little world than she realized.

Henry looked to be on the verge of commenting on Pierce's suspicions, but seemed to think better of it. He simply nodded, and added, "I can't think of a better time to introduce the new lens, then."

Just then, there was a knock at the door, and Davis entered. The butler was neat as a pin as always, and despite the still-pouring rain sported neither a damp collar nor muddy shoes, a testament to the Seaton's fine traveling carriage having been put to good use.

"Ah Davis!" Mrs. Seaton greeted the butler warmly. "Do come in! I trust your mother was well today."

"Yes ma'am. She gets along quite nicely, despite being nearly to her ninetieth birthday. She sends special thanks for the goose Miss Emelia provided her last week, ma'am."

"Ah, so you really do hunt the geese." Henry turned to Emelia, looking delighted. "They're not just for target practice."

Davis responded with a bow before Emelia could think of a clever retort.

"Yes, sir, we have quite the over-population on the hill. If Miss Emelia were not so skilled in hunting them, we would be quite overrun. Between that and Cook's excellent vegetable garden, Miss Emelia feeds half the town," he added proudly, loyally pretending not to notice Henry's strange ensemble or the now-crusting gash on his cheek.

Emelia blushed, suddenly self-conscious. She realized that hunting geese was not a gentlewoman's occupation.

"Thank you, Davis, I am quite glad your mother enjoyed the goose."

"Yes, Miss Emelia. But I am remiss. I came in not to convey my mother's gratitude, but to announce a visitor who arrived right on my heels. Lord Warwick has come to call, ma'am."

"Good heavens!" exclaimed Mrs. Seaton, "Do send the poor boy in, Davis, thank you. And now that you're here, would you send up a fresh pot of tea?"

"Certainly, madam," he glanced at Pierce's still damp collar and cravat, spared a brief look for Henry's strange raiment, and took in the downpour outside. "Shall I bring some tea cakes as well?"

"Yes, yes of course, a little extra treat would be welcome today. Thank you, Davis. Show in Lord Warwick if you please."

Davis bowed and left the room, and was replaced in the doorway by an enthusiastic Edwin, impeccably dressed in a coat of bottle-green superfine and matching striped waistcoat. Despite the conditions outside, not a hair or thread was out of place.

"Ah, what a cozy party! The perfect solution for an afternoon such as this one. Mrs. Seaton, you look resplendent, as always. Emelia, Pierce, how fortunate to find you both at home." He winked at Emelia and nodded to her brother.

"And Mr. Rockcliff! How nice to see you again. I had no idea you were acquainted with the Seatons." He glanced at Henry in the armchair with his borrowed clothes, looking quite at home, and raised an eyebrow. "Quite well acquainted from the looks of it."

Edwin smiled charmingly at their guest.

"Yes, we were but little acquainted," Henry answered, unflappably, "but they were kind enough to take me in today when I had a bit of an accident. Horse threw a shoe." Gratefully, Henry omitted all the pertinent facts of the mishap and allowed Warwick to draw his own conclusions.

"Ah, 'tis a pity, but I'm glad to see you sustained no serious injuries. How comes your work in Collington?"

"Slow." Henry returned the raised eyebrow, still smiling politely, and Emelia wondered if he was alluding to Edwin's reluctance to install the lens.

"Yes, well, these things take time, do they not? And all the better!" Edwin clapped his hands together excitingly. "You'll be in town long enough to join us for a real treat! I was just coming to invite the Seatons, and you should come along too!"

"Lovely, dear. You can tell us all about it, but please sit down and have some tea," commanded Mrs. Seaton.

"You'll never guess my treat!" Edwin sat next to Emelia on the settee and was supplied with tea and cake by her mother. "What is something you've always longed to do?"

Emelia couldn't help but smile at his infectious enthusiasm.

"Well, travel the world, but I hardly think we can manage that in an afternoon outing."

Her friend grinned.

"Okay, a little closer to home than that, but no less exciting!"

"Oh! You do not mean sailing?"

She glanced anxiously at her mother, who looked at Edwin for further clarification.

"Yes! My yacht is being delivered next week, and as soon as she has docked in Collington, I want you all to spend an afternoon sailing with me!"

He turned to Mrs. Seaton to make his case.

"Just in the cove, mind you, ma'am. We will never go out of sight of the shore, and shall only sail on a beautiful, clear day, with every safety precaution."

"Well! How can I say no to that?" Emelia's mother pursed her lips, attempting to look stern but failing miserably. "Anyway, I have no real objection to sailing, if done in the daytime. As you know, Mr. Seaton lived in fear of his children going out on the water, but he was so very protective in his old age. Why, he himself had to sail across the channel on his Grand Tour. He told me later that he was miserably sick in his cabin the whole time, and I'm sure that contributed to his dislike of the sea. But I think as long as it is daylight and you know what you're doing, Edwin, the whole scheme is a delightful idea."

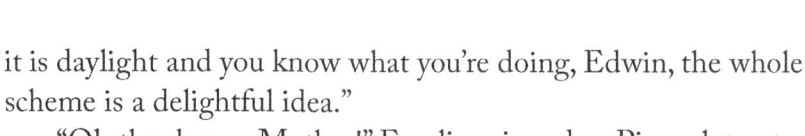

"Oh thank you, Mother!" Emelia grinned as Pierce let out a whoop and a "Capital!"

"And you must join us of course, Mr. Rockcliff," entreated Warwick, "though I'm sure you're no novice to sailing, it is such an invigorating thing to be zipping along on a yacht on a beautiful day, is it not?"

Henry hesitated for a moment, then dipped his head in acknowledgment. "I would be pleased to accompany you, thank you."

"And of course we will invite Clara and her parents too if they wish to come! We shall have a merry little party! I don't know when I've anticipated an outing more. Especially if it means fulfilling a life-long dream of some very special friends."

Edwin turned and winked at Emelia again. She suddenly felt self-conscious and very aware of their guest. She quickly moved to pour herself another cup of tea. As the storm died down to a drizzle, the conversation turned to friends and happenings in the village for a few moments.

After another tea cake, Edwin bounced back up on his feet and excused himself, practically vibrating with anticipation. Emelia shook her head, but couldn't help but smile at his excitement. He'd always been a bundle of energy, tearing from one adventure to the next. She'd always been game for these adventures, her logic and practicality keeping the boys out of any serious trouble. It was part of the reason they'd gotten along so well together as children.

When she looked up, she saw Henry watching her carefully.

"I'm afraid I must be going, too. My man Rogers will start worrying about me if I've not returned soon, he is like a mother hen."

He smiled at Mrs. Seaton.

"If you'll just show me the way to the kitchen, I'll fetch my garments and trespass upon your hospitality no longer."

Mrs. Seaton stood, reaching for the bell.

"I'll ring for James. You're welcome anytime you like, Henry, and I promise no more, *erm*, accidents."

Smiling at Mrs. Seaton, likely to show her he didn't hold a grudge, he bowed, dressing gown floating regally behind him like a train.

"I shall never stray from the road again, ma'am."

Chapter 10

The English Channel

Emelia stood on the deck of the Opportunity, Edwin's gleaming sailboat, and gazed out at the sparkling water. She never tired of looking at the sea, and now, out in the middle of it, she was entranced by it all over again.

The boat was new and elegant, all polished wood and gorgeous silk sails, and the cabins below deck offered all the comforts of home. It wasn't a huge boat—at least not compared to the big shipping vessels that sailed through the channel regularly—but it was large enough to hold a dozen passengers and crew comfortably. The four crew members scurried about, deftly maneuvering large sails. After watching excitingly from the rails as they sailed out to sea, the rest of their party was comfortably lounging on a beautifully carved wooden bench behind her, enjoying the magnificent views and talking animatedly.

Emelia pulled her chilly hands up into the sleeves of her heavy woolen coat. She was glad that Marietta had insisted she wear her warmest coat, a beautiful bottle-green with shiny gold buttons down the front. The morning had dawned clear and cold for April, and it was even chillier out here over the water. Still, the chill couldn't dampen her spirits, and she was delighted to be sailing at last.

She glanced back over her shoulder and saw Clara give a full-throated laugh to something Mr. Arbuckle had said. *Maybe the two of them would suit?* Emelia wondered. Her friend was so lovely and kind, she deserved an excellent match. Mr. Arbuckle was charming, to be sure, but he was very young. Perhaps her friend was falling for his pretty face and stylish air? She supposed Clara could do worse.

"Penny for your thoughts?"

Emelia turned and smiled at Edwin.

"I was just contemplating what a lovely party this turned out to be! Thank you so much for including Clara and Mr. Arbuckle—and Mr. Rockcliff." She nodded towards Henry, standing slightly away from the group and cheerfully carrying on a discussion with one of the crew, which from the gestures of their arms, appeared to have something to do with the sails.

"Any friend of the Seatons is a friend of mine, of course!" Edwin grinned. "He is a rather odd fellow, though to be sure."

Emelia chuckled.

"Yes, he is! But he seems kind enough, and Pierce has declared him a 'capital fellow.' I confess I've felt a bit awkward anytime he's around lately. I'm still just so mortified that I actually shot him!"

"Now, you mustn't blame yourself for that, Emmie. It could have happened to anyone. How were you to know a stranger would be stalking through your fields? But, you should really take more care of yourself." Edwin's tone suddenly turned serious, and he took her cold hand in his, rubbing it for warmth. "Out in the fields in a thunderstorm! You could have been injured."

He looked genuinely worried, and Emelia was touched, until he continued.

"Perhaps you should take up a safer hobby, like painting."

"I was fully aware of the conditions," she defended, bristling, "and I would have been inside long before even a drop of rain fell if I hadn't been aiding Mr. Rockcliff."

"Besides, I'm terrible at painting! You know Clara has always been the gifted one when it comes to art."

Emelia had no desire to quarrel with him, so she quickly changed the subject.

"Your boat is just lovely! Thank you so much for taking me out today. It's been one of the few things I've always desired to do but have never been able to!"

He took the hand still held in his and kissed it, leaving her cheeks a pink that had nothing to do with the cold.

"It's truly my pleasure. Just to see you so happy has been a delight. In fact, you have a slight dimple in your left cheek when you smile that big. The one in your right cheek, of course, is legendary."

Emelia laughed, all annoyance at her friend forgotten in his sudden show of affection, her aforementioned right dimple on full display.

"Yes, it did often give me away when we were children. No matter how I've tried, I can't seem to look serious with this blasted dimple."

"Well," Edwin continued, delight on his face "I've never noticed the left one before today. I simply must do something else to bring it back. Tell me, is there anything else you've always longed to do that you haven't been able to yet? You always wanted a dog. Did you ever get one?"

"I never did, no! Father was allergic, and I couldn't bear to leave a poor puppy out in the barn all the time, so we never got one. I might have to get one someday, now that Father is gone—though I can't say anything will ever be able to beat this experience!"

She looked back out at the sparkling sea, grateful to have her old friend back in her life once more.

"You know, I've lived next to the water all my life, but it looks completely different when you're out here. The sky and the sea are nearly the same color. It's like gliding on a mirror."

Emelia squinted into the distance, a tiny imperfection appearing on her "mirror."

"Wait, I think I see land! Is that France? How long does it take to get there?"

Edwin followed her gaze across the water.

"It is. If the wind and tides are right, we could be there in a couple of hours. But it can take a whole day if the wind isn't in your favor. I once had to wait at Dover for three days for the winds to turn, but as soon as everything was blowing in the right direction, we left after luncheon and arrived before tea. And speaking of tea," he added with a flourish, "I have a grand repast prepared for us today. My cook has packed us a delightful hamper of pastries and sandwiches. You wouldn't know it from the looks of them, but my crew is actually quite skillful at brewing up a strong pot of tea, though I don't think I shall ask them to pour."

Emelia's stomach rumbled and she laughed again.

"That sounds delightful. I think all this brisk sea air has given me quite an appetite."

"It's always a bit colder out on the water. As I was just telling the rest of our little party, I have quite a stash of cozy quilts belowstairs if anyone gets chilled. May I fetch you one? It would never do to have you catching cold. Your mother would never let you go out with me again, and that would put quite a damper on my future plans."

He winked at her.

Before Emelia could ponder what he meant by *his future plans*, Pierce joined them at the railing.

"What do you think, Emmie? Live up to your expectations, this sailing?"

"Oh yes, Pierce isn't it delightful?"

"Let's go tell these salty sailors it's about time for tea, my boy." Edwin pounded Pierce heartily on the back. "On our way I'll show you how this mast works, it's really quite amazing! I know you've always liked to see the workings behind things…"

Edwin trailed on as they sauntered off to discuss masts and rigging, Edwin's eyes shining and Pierce laughing as though they were still schoolboys.

Clara and Henry had also walked up to the rails to enjoy the view, Henry pointing out something across the water, and Clara smiling prettily. Clara looked over at her and waved, and Emelia grinned and waved back, thinking that she'd better not attempt to play matchmaker for her friend. She thought no one suitable! Glancing at Henry's chiseled face, she noticed his wound from the arrow was healing over nicely. He still resembled a pirate, but perhaps it was the way his eyes sparkled or his quiet confidence that made him feel...safe. A safe pirate. Emelia laughed out loud. It was an odd thought, to be sure. She barely knew the man, but she thought that if she had to, she could trust him with her life. Why then did the thought of Clara marrying Henry make her slightly queasy?

While Edwin was showing Pierce how to shift the sails, Mr. Arbuckle joined Clara at the rail and was apparently reenacting a famous French dual, complete with a terrible French accent that Emelia caught snippets of on the breeze. Clara was laughing heartily, her cheeks rosy and her eyes sparkling. Henry had moved aft to watch the waves churning behind them. Emelia was delighted that everyone seemed to enjoy the outing as much as she. Closing her eyes, she breathed in the salty sea air. Sailing may have been her dream, but sharing the experience with people she cared about made it so much more rewarding. She might never get to see the Continent, or sail away to far off lands like she'd daydreamed about as a girl, but today Emelia was content. There was beauty around her every day, she reminded herself. Her little corner of the world was no less inspiring than the rest, just more familiar.

Heart full of gratitude and stomach rumbling, Emelia turned to join her friends and ask about that tea. She was just aware of a fluttering of white in her peripheral vision, before all the air left her lungs with a woosh and Emelia felt herself falling, falling into cold darkness.

∽

A sudden headache struck without warning, and Henry knew immediately that it was Emelia who was in danger. She'd barely hit the water before he'd tossed off his coat and shoes, and he dove off the side of the boat before the others even knew what happened. He'd never been more grateful to Charles for insisting he learn to swim than he was in this moment.

The water was so icy it took his breath away, and Henry took in a great gulp of air and looked around. Panic rose within him. He couldn't see Emelia anywhere. She took a hard hit with that piece of rigging and could be unconscious. Even if she wasn't, her heavy woolen cloak would be like a dead weight pulling her down. He fought off a wave of nausea, picturing Charles fighting the waves so close to here. Diving underneath the water again, the icy sea water stung his eyes, his lungs burning from lack of oxygen.

Three feet to his left he saw ripples beneath the murky water. In two powerful strokes he was there and dove under, his fingers just brushing wet wool. Brushing and missing. Coming up for air, Henry was just about to go under again when Emelia's head shot up out of the water a few feet in front of him. She was coughing and gasping, but very much alive.

"Emelia!" Henry heard the half call, half sob escaping from his own lips. He quickly swam the distance between them and treaded water, supporting Emelia's head and shoulders while she coughed out mouthfuls of cold sea water.

"Had...*gurgle...cough*...to unbutton...my coat." She gave him a weak smile. "Hard."

Oh, poor girl. If she hadn't been such a strong swimmer, she wouldn't have been able to stay up long enough to get the coat off. He didn't think he could have reached her in time, and his stomach churned at the thought.

By now everyone on the boat had been alerted to the near-tragedy. The boat had slowed and was attempting to turn around. They were too far away for Henry to hear, but Lord Warwick seemed to be shouting at the helmsman and gesturing in their direction. Arbuckle was staring in shock, a handkerchief clutched over his mouth. A distraught-looking Pierce was holding Clara, who was sobbing onto his shoulder. Henry had the sudden realization that if he hadn't been here, Emelia's plight would have been discovered too late. Still treading water, he looked over to find her pale, her arms starting to slow. Linking one of his arms gently under hers, he began to swim the two of them towards the boat.

There was a great clamoring of people aboard waiting to help them back up onto the deck. Still treading water and holding Emelia up with one arm, Henry pointed to the sturdiest looking deckhand and barked, "You!" His choice was a good one, as the burly man gently lifted Emelia over the edge as if she were a ragdoll. In fact, she'd gone limp as a rag doll, and that worried Henry. Shock or hypothermia were very real possibilities now.

He grabbed Pierce's offered arm and hauled himself up over the edge of the boat. Everyone was talking at once, Clara was still crying, and Lord Warwick was trying to pick a shivering Emelia up off the deck. His military training kicking in, Henry started giving orders.

"Pierce, gather up all those quilts I saw below deck. Hurry. Warwick, that stove you mentioned—have the men get a fire going and boil us some water. Tea if you have it. Clara, stop crying at once. Emelia needs you to pull yourself together. I'm going to carry her downstairs and you're going to take her clothes off."

Henry didn't even allow himself the time to blush.

"Anything that's wet needs to be off of her as soon as possible. Then, wrap her up in those quilts Pierce is going to bring you."

He scooped Emelia, now shivering convulsively, and ran down the stairs to the cabin. He set her on a small wooden bench as gently as possible, and lifted her chattering chin so he could look into her eyes.

"I'm going to leave you now. Try to help Clara get you out of your wet things as quickly as possible. With any luck, Warwick will have you a nice cup of tea waiting when you're done, all right?"

She managed a weak smile that nearly destroyed him.

Henry ran back up the stars two at a time, trying to get some blood flowing into his now-shivering body. He didn't want to take any of the quilts away from Emelia, but he was going to have to figure out a way to get himself warm too.

Luckily, one of the weathered old sailors was a quick thinker, and had an old woolen blanket, a thick fisherman's sweater, and someone's extra pair of work pants ready for him. The girls safely below deck, he stripped as quickly as he could with cold, fumbling fingers, and pulled the sweater over his head. It smelled faintly of fish, but it was soft and warm, lovingly stitched by someone's wife or mother. Another deckhand, with enormous ears and a gap-toothed smile, shyly brought him a pair of thick woolen socks, and Henry thanked the man graciously. His teeth had nearly ceased chattering by the time the sailor returned with a steaming cup of tea.

"Bless you, man."

Henry clutched the teacup and ran back downstairs just as Pierce was offering Emelia a cup.

"Lots of sugar," Henry ordered. "For the shock."

Emelia was still shivering, but she was wrapped in quilts from head to toe and looking a bit stronger now. Clara, now in full mastery of her emotions, sat behind her on the bench and was gently drying Emelia's hair with a towel.

Even her curls had less life in them, and Henry felt a shiver that wasn't from cold steal over him. That had been entirely too close. He crouched in front of her and examined her face.

"How are you feeling?"

"Much warmer now, thank you, though I admit I feel very tired."

"You can't sleep until you've drunk all the tea, you must bring your temperature up."

"Yes, sir."

She gave a jaunty little salute with one quilted hand and Henry smiled. She was a tough one.

The sailors had turned back towards shore right after Henry and Emelia had been scooped out of the channel, and they were nearly back to the harbor. Warwick came rushing down the stairs, looking anxious and agitated. Henry could imagine the guilt the other man felt. It was an accident that could have happened to anyone, but to have it happen to a young lady who was a guest under your protection—it was enough to leave any man shaken.

"We're nearly to the dock, and my carriage should be waiting. We will be early, but they had orders to stay just in case we needed anything. We can carry Emelia to the carriage and get her back home as quickly as possible."

"I can do that. It's the least I can do," Pierce offered, looking anguished. Putting a reassuring hand on his shoulder, Henry pulled him aside.

"It was an accident, Pierce." Henry needed the younger man to understand, lest he blame himself. "That rigging could have failed even if you and Warwick hadn't touched it. Emelia was in the wrong place at the wrong time, but she's going to be okay."

"Yes, yes you're right. Thank you, so much, but—" Pierce broke off, looking puzzled. "Rockcliff, how did you know? She was barely in the water before you were diving in after her. Almost as if you knew before it happened."

Henry swallowed, suddenly feeling very old and foolish.

"I have a…sense. I can tell when danger is at hand, sometimes before it happens. It saved my life a few times, and the lives of my men."

Even to Henry's ears it sounded ridiculous, and he knew it to be the truth.

"It's not something I go around telling everyone," he added quickly. He trusted Pierce, but it wasn't exactly information he wanted public.

"Of course." Pierce looked thoughtful. The two men looked at each other for a moment, as if unsure where to go from there, when someone shouted from above deck, "We're 'ere, my Lord!"

By then Emelia had finished drinking her tea, so Pierce gently picked her up and started above deck. She looked tiny bundled in her quilts, but the color was returning to her face, and she had the strength to jest with her brother. "Now Pierce, I've put on a few pounds lately, maybe you should let one of the other gentlemen lend you a hand."

She winked at her brother, and Henry knew she didn't hold him responsible for her near-drowning. It took quite a woman not to faint away with a fit of the vapors after such an experience, but then again Henry didn't think she was the type of woman to succumb to such things.

Once she was settled inside, Henry poked his head into the carriage to make sure Emelia was safely tucked in next to Clara. She gave him a little wave and a half smile.

"Thank you again! Perhaps now, we're even?"

In spite of himself, Henry laughed.

"I'm not sure that's how it works."

He clasped her cold hand in his, and briefly brought it to his lips.

"I'm just grateful I was there."

He bid Clara and Pierce goodbye, and then watched the carriage pull away as he turned to say his farewell to Warwick. Henry was bone-tired and ready for a hot bath and a stiff drink—likely both at the same time.

"I can't thank you enough, old chap." Warwick clapped Henry on the back. "You've the quickest reflexes I've ever seen. You were in the water after her before we even heard a sound."

Warwick ran a hand over his face, looking as tired as Henry felt and older than his years.

Henry nodded.

"It kept me alive on the Peninsula."

Unlike with Pierce, he didn't feel the need to elaborate.

"Something like that never goes away, I suppose." Warwick looked as if he needed a stiff drink as well. "I can't say—what would I have done if…if anything had happened to Emelia, I would have been most grieved. If I may speak in confidence, it is my dearest hope that she will one day soon consent to become Lady Warwick."

Henry's face remained calm, but his insides started as if he'd hit the icy water all over again. No wonder Warwick looked so wretched. He'd known the man was flirting with Emelia, but hadn't been able to tell if he was just the type of man to dally with a pretty girl to pass the time.

Henry had never liked that type of man.

Too tired to sort through his thoughts, Henry nodded his understanding.

"I expect we both need some rest now. Send word if you hear of anything the Seatons need."

Henry declined the offer of a ride to his hotel, bid Warwick goodbye, and started off at a brisk pace down the sidewalk. He was only a couple of blocks from the inn, and the exercise would help warm him and give him a chance to think.

Emelia was safe. No one drowned today.

Why then did he feel as though he'd been punched in the stomach?

CHAPTER 11

SEATON HOUSE

Glancing over her shoulder at the solemn face peering at her through the French doors, Emelia sighed.

"Will you please stop making that face? I'll let you in if you promise not to attack Mother's embroidery basket again."

She set aside the book she'd been reading, threw off the heavy woolen blanket Dr. Eldermeyer had insisted she keep tucked about her at all times, and opened the door. The shaggy mongrel staring up at her was a sight to behold. A canine of indeterminate parentage, he was quite the largest dog Emelia had ever seen, with shaggy black fur, floppy ears, and a tail that spelled death to any delicate objects that happened to sit upon a nearby table. Giving her a slobbery grin, he happily rubbed around her legs, nearly causing her to stumble with his weight, and bounded over to a comfortable spot on the rug in front of the fireplace.

"You know," she continued conversationally, "I suppose that if I'm stuck with you I may as well give you a name. It will have to be something mighty, for you're a great beast of an animal. Perhaps one of the Greek gods."

The dog cocked his head as if approving the notion.

"Apollo? No, too overdone. Chaos?"

The dog whined and laid his head down on his paws.

"Well after what you've done, you deserve it. Attacking Mother's embroidery right off her lap! I'm sure you thought it was a furry beast that needed to be vanquished, but honestly if you were a civilized dog at all you'd recognize a tangle of thread."

In addition to the sudden dispatching of embroidery, the dog had mangled one of Pierce's best riding boots (much to the dismay of his valet), stolen two Cornish hens right off the roasting spit ("It'd serve him right to have his tongue burned right off!" Cook had cried), and dispatched three of the wild geese—burying them upside down outside the kitchen door, their feet sticking right out of the ground. The kitchen maid had found them while sweeping the next morning and had gone into hysterics, believing it to be some sort of bad omen. Emelia didn't mind so much about the geese, as they *were* overpopulated and a nuisance, but they couldn't be forever tripping over fowl feet in the yard. Apparently her new dog had a thing for poultry.

Emelia coughed a few times, took a sip of her now-tepid tea, and leaned back against a pile of pillows on the sofa. She'd taken to her bed as soon as she'd returned from their sailing trip, chilled and shaken but very much grateful to be alive. Edwin was so worried about her he was nearly in tears. Touched, Emelia assured him she would be right as rain in the morning, but it was not to be. By morning she was feverish and had a headache, and Dr. Eldermeyer was sent for.

Gratefully, it had proved nothing more serious than a bad cold, but the doctor had prescribed complete bed rest, hot broth and tea, and as much marrow on toast as Emelia could get down. She'd spent the past week being clucked and fretted over by her mother, Clara, and the entire household staff. Edwin had stopped by every day to check on her progress, bringing flowers, cards, and on one occasion, chocolates, which were quickly swept away with a glare from Davis.

"Sweets, my Lord, are unfit for the ill," the butler had informed him loftily. Davis had set up a post in the hall outside Emelia's room and proved a fierce gatekeeper, allowing visitors other than Mrs. Seaton or Pierce in for only fifteen minutes at a time, strictly no sweets or heavy food, and enforced quiet on the whole floor so Emelia could rest.

Admittedly, Emelia was grateful for all the care, and for a few days she felt rather dreadful indeed. She was exhausted from coughing through the night, and too ill to protest any of her mother's tinctures and even Cook's favorite cure of restorative pork jelly.

After a week of rest, she was starting to feel much more herself. Although she still had a lingering cough, Dr. Eldermeyer had given her the okay to come down to the sitting room during the day for a change of scenery.

It was here that Edwin had come bounding into the room two days ago—two days that felt like half a lifetime to Emelia—his eyes shining, bouncing on his heels with excitement.

"Emmie! Emmie dear, I have a present for you!"

"For me? What for?"

"Well, I've been wracking my brain all this last week trying to figure out what to give you to make up for my sailboat throwing you into the sea, but all I kept coming back to was the thing you wanted most almost killed you, and I had no idea how to follow that for better or worse. Until! Then I knew just what you needed!"

Emelia had looked up at him with his empty hands, confused. Tucking the woolen blanket around her more tightly, she ventured cautiously, "And, what do I need, exactly?"

"This!" he cried delightedly, turning back towards the open door. "Davis, bring him in, would you?"

Davis struggled in, an enormous black dog lumbering in on the end of a fancy gold leash. The beast had been much cleaner than he was now, his fur handsomely groomed and smoothed. For a fleeting moment he was on his best behavior, sitting politely at Edwin's command and regarding his new mistress with an air of aloof disinterest.

Surprise must have caused Emelia to choke a bit, for she succumbed to a coughing spell, which spurred the dog into action. He must have decided then she was desperately in need of his protection, for in a flash he had pulled the leash out of Davis' grasp, crossed the room in a single leap, and was on the sofa on top of Emelia, licking her face profusely.

Edwin and Mrs. Seaton, who had entered the room behind Davis, were most alarmed and rushed to her side, believing the dog to be a mauling menace. When they saw he was only licking her face, and that she was laughing, they slowed their rush to her defense and instead began to coax the dog back onto the floor with one of Emelia's tea biscuits. Removing himself from her person, the dog accepted the biscuit and promptly curled up as close to the sofa as possible and installed himself as her protector.

"Wherever did you find this great beast?" Emelia wiped her slobbered face with her handkerchief with one hand while scratching the delighted dog behind the ears with the other.

Edwin looked sheepish.

"I asked my steward to bring me a puppy while he was in London on business this week, something small and fashionable. Apparently no puppies were to be had, but the breeder assured him this mongrel was barely grown and a rare specimen of hound. I'm afraid my steward is a rather retiring sort, and he couldn't bring himself to argue, so he came home with this mutt."

The dog harrumphed from his spot at Emelia's side.

"No, darling," she crooned, patting his giant head, "you can't be held responsible for your parentage or Edwin's steward's momentary lapse of judgment."

"Since he seems decidedly attached to me, I guess I'll have to keep him. Thank you for the gift—I think."

Edwin blushed.

"If you don't like him, I'll have him returned to London right away."

"Nonsense. I have always wanted a dog, and although I never imagined one quite this, *erm*...big, well, how much trouble can he be?"

Emelia regretted her words within the hour, when her mother

sat down to join her in the parlor. The dog, mistakenly believing her tangle of threads a small animal bent on Emelia's destruction, hopped up from his post and snatched the embroidery right out of her mother's hands. He'd begun shredding it to bits, knocking over an end table and an expensive vase in the process. Emelia had carefully extracted the ruined tangle from the dog's mouth, his tail wagging with pride as her mother and Davis set the room to rights, and then as all the excitement had brought about another fit of coughing, Emelia's mother promptly banished the animal to the back garden.

In the dog's defense, it had been while trying to get back inside to Emelia that he jumped through an open window in front of which Pierce's valet had been blacking boots. Apparently the sight of so much toothsome leather had been too much for the beleaguered animal.

The buried geese Emelia had no excuse for, except that the dog had terribly bad manners. While she liked to think that perhaps he had picked up on her dislike of geese, she knew the truth was she had been saddled with an unruly, misbehaving beast of a dog.

Who really ought to have a name.

Emelia sighed and summoned him from his place near the fire, upon which he gleefully climbed back into her lap and promptly fell asleep.

They spent the rest of the afternoon thus happily situated, until Davis came to announce a caller.

"Mr. Rockcliff to see you, miss."

Henry! Emelia started to jump up, then remembered the sleeping dog on her lap.

She hadn't seen Henry since that day on the boat. Since he'd saved her life. There was no way she could have made it safely back to the boat without him, much less known what to do once she was on it. She blushed. How do you say thank you to a man for rescuing you from drowning and hypothermia? He'd been close to tears as he left her to Clara's care in the bottom of the boat, and she remembered his watchful gaze as Pierce had carefully carried her, bundled up to the neck, to the carriage as soon as the boat had docked. Once she was tucked inside, Henry had gently grasped her chilled hand and brought it to his chapped lips, telling her he was grateful he'd been there to save her. She thought he was going to say something else, but instead he turned and bowed to Pierce and Clara, spoke a few quiet words with Edwin, and was off down the street in his borrowed fisherman's clothes, presumably in a hurry to change and warm up himself.

Emelia had thought about him often this week while confined to her sickbed. Why hadn't he stopped by to check on her? Had he also fallen ill? And honestly, she was annoyed with herself for expecting him to come. She barely knew the man, yet after first the arrow incident and then the near-drowning, she felt as if their fates were tied together somehow. Still, she had no claim on him, she reminded herself again and again this week, he was nothing more than an acquaintance. She'd told herself she was only curious about his welfare, wondering if he'd succumbed to the cold the same as she.

Emelia quickly smoothed her dress and tucked a stray curl behind her ear.

"Please bring him in, Davis."

Her new pet sat straight up, jumped off his cozy spot on her lap, and positioned himself between her and the doorway. Emelia smiled.

"At least you're good for something."

"And what exactly am I good for?" The voice came from the doorway.

"Oh, no, I was talking to the dog." She grinned. "Although you've proven yourself useful, too. I must thank you again for saving my life."

Rather than dismissing her politely, Henry strode into the room, stopped short when he saw the enormous beast, and slowly retreated to the settee across from her. After apparently deciding he was not about to be mauled, he looked earnestly into her eyes.

"And did I? Save you, that is. Are you quite alright? I heard you've been ill, and it distresses me that I couldn't come to visit you sooner."

"Oh! Were you ill as well? I'd been hoping you'd escaped the chill."

"Only a few sniffles, thank goodness. I escaped relatively unscathed. My body has too many memories of nights spent shivering in trenches to worry too much about a swim in the drink."

He smiled, and Emelia knew it was an attempt at levity, but she could see the worry in his eyes. She wanted to ask what had kept him away then, why it had taken him nearly two weeks to visit, but stopped herself just in time.

He glanced from her to the dog, and grinned.

"I see you have a new protector. What's its name?"

"Well, it's a he, but I haven't found a name that fits yet. Pierce wants to name him Midnight, after a magnificent black horse he once had, but I don't think it fits. Edwin suggested Shaggy or Urchin, as he's quite a deplorable fellow once he's allowed out into the garden to get dirty. The dog I mean, not Edwin."

She grinned, wrinkling her nose.

"I, however, am leaning towards one of the Greek gods. He needs something that fits both his size and demeanor. I ruled out Apollo and Chaos. Though the latter is tempting, I want to believe he'll grow out of some of his roguish tendencies."

She gave Henry a brief summary of the dog's recent exploits.

"Hmm..." Rockcliff looked the dog up and down, and then up at Emelia. He grinned.

"Cerus."

"I'm afraid my mythology is a little rusty," she admitted.

"Cerus was a massive wild bull who destroyed everything in his path, and no one could tame him."

Emelia started to interject but he held up his hand.

"*Until*...along came the lovely Persephone. She tamed the beast, and he became docile and patient. They would ride together every spring, sowing beautiful flowers behind them."

At that the dog left his post, crossed the distance between the two sofas in a single step, and laid his head adoringly on Henry's knees.

"Well, I guess that settles it. He adores his new name and you, apparently." She grinned impishly, and couldn't help teasing him. "And, thank you, Henry, I have to say I don't mind being compared to the goddess of spring."

Henry's cheeks colored slightly under his scars.

"I shall endeavor to keep the lovely Persephone from being carried off to the underworld," he joked with a half smile and a bow.

Since she wasn't kidding when she said her Greek myths were a bit rusty, she started to ask him to explain this, but just then the dog's hair stood on end. He abandoned his comfortable position on Henry's lap, faced the door, and growled.

"Oh dear. He's been doing this whenever we have visitors. Cerus! Come!"

Cerus retreated to her side, but still faced the door and growled softly.

"At least he seems to know his new name."

"I think it's more likely he knows his mistress means business."

"He didn't growl at me when I came in."

"You're right. Curious."

Emelia stroked the dog's head and waited for Davis to come announce their visitor. She wasn't sure what happened—a momentary spasm perhaps—but suddenly she found herself blurting out "Where were you?"

"Excuse me—where was I when?"

"Where were you the last week and a half? I kept expecting you to call, but…"

There was a glimmer of something in his eye that she couldn't quite make out.

"I'm afraid that I wasn't in Collington. The day after the boating trip, I was traveling up and down Kent and Sussex."

"To see if they want to install your new lens, too?"

"Not exactly."

Emelia wanted to ask more, and thought perhaps there was more he wanted to tell her, but Davis appeared in the doorway.

"Lord Warwick, to see you, Miss," Davis announced, with a cautious look at Cerus. He stepped aside just as Edwin entered the room. The dog, apparently, took this as his cue, and lunged for their visitor.

Henry let out a breath he hadn't realized he'd been holding as the dog stopped inches from Warwick, stood on his hind legs, and began licking the man's face affectionately.

"Cerus!" Emelia threw off her blankets and struggled to her feet, speaking to the dog in a commanding voice. "We do not *lick* our visitors! Come here, and leave Edwin alone. You'll ruin his clothes."

The dog stopped his assault of affection and retreated to his mistress' side, where she rewarded him with a bit of discarded biscuit from the tea tray on the side table.

"I am so, so sorry, Edwin. He has no manners at all." Emelia frowned at the dog, then brightened. "Though he does finally have a name. And it's Cerus, after the mythological Greek bull, you see."

"He is a bit of a bull, isn't he?" Warwick laughed, brushing dust and stray dog hairs off of his jacket and attempting to repair a rumpled cravat. "But at least he holds me in affection. I dare say he remembers that I was the one who had him rescued from London. And however appalling his manners, I take comfort in the fact that he's become attached to you, Emmie."

For some reason Henry felt a bit disgruntled that the dog was so affectionate towards Lord Warwick.

"Nice to see you, Rockcliff," said Warwick, taking the seat closest to Henry and furthest away from Cerus' adoring glances. "I expected to see more of you the last couple of weeks. I trust you haven't been laid ill as well?"

"No, I am quite well, thank you. I merely had some business along the coast."

"Ah, attempting to pawn your French invention off on other unsuspecting land owners, I see." Warwick grinned.

"Something like that, yes," answered Henry, though he knew he'd been doing nothing of the sort.

In fact, Henry had spent the last two weeks talking to villagers and excisemen up and down the coast, attempting to learn something about the general state of smuggling in this region. It appeared smuggling had been on the rise again in the last decade, as men returned from the war and were unable to find gainful employment. Most of the townsfolk in nearby villages accepted smuggling as a way of life, with its dangers not that different from most other jobs for the lower classes. Until lately. They were starting to worry about their menfolk out to sea. Henry had learned something that surprised him and made him more determined than ever to get to the bottom of this mystery—nearly all the ships that had wrecked near Collington in recent years were smuggling ships. This information had taken him a while to track down, as people seemed afraid to share. But there was definitely some outside evil at work here. Nature could never be so selective.

It made sense, Henry had thought. In a way it was the perfect crime. A merchant or trading ship could report the sabotage and work with the law to avenge their destruction, but a smuggling vessel had no such rights. And it explained why there were no goods to store or claim either—whoever was sabotaging the ships was obviously taking the stores for themselves. As no one could report smuggled goods stolen, they simply vanished into the night, likely to turn up on the black market of London for a quick sale and easy cash.

Henry returned his attention to the room, and saw Warwick already jumping up. Cerus sat up too, but didn't leave his post.

"I was simply dropping by to check on you," Warwick was saying, "I must leave. Important business, you know."

Emelia looked confused but stood, her canine protector bounding towards his hero, and bid Warwick goodbye. Henry fought the pressure in his chest as Warwick took both her hands, bent down and kissed them, and then said in a low voice that Henry could just make out, "I was hoping to have a private word with you, but I will return tomorrow." His voice raised, and he continued, "just continue to rest my dear, you need your strength. I am sure exciting things are ahead for you this spring—exciting and hopefully much less dangerous."

Warwick turned as if to nod goodbye to Henry, smiling, but Henry saw a warning flash in his eyes. Henry nodded once, but did not return the smile. He understood completely.

For all his smiles and jovial air, Warwick saw Henry as a threat and was marking his territory.

Henry understood. He had no plans to pursue a woman, however much he admired her, who was courting someone else. And despite his hesitancy to let Henry install Fresnel's lens, Henry liked Warwick. But if he was involved in the smuggler's operation in any way, Henry had to find out, before Emelia agreed to marry Warwick and was tied to his fate forever.

Not wanting to wear Emelia out so soon after her recovery, Henry too said his goodbyes, patting a now yawning and stretching Cerus on the head and bidding him to watch over his mistress. As he rode his horse back towards the village, he couldn't shake the image of Warwick, dressed as Hades, carrying a flower-crowned Emelia off to the underworld.

Chapter 12

Sparks flying, Emelia pounded furiously on the glowing arrowhead atop her anvil. She stopped to wipe at her now-dripping nose with her sleeve, handkerchief long forgotten in her agitation. The rest of her dress was already streaked with ore and grime, so it mattered little.

Dr. Eldermeyer hadn't yet cleared her to resume her normal activities, but she would go crazy if she was forced to stay cooped up in the sitting room for one more day. Despite the still-running nose, she was feeling much more herself, and her mind always struggled to process without being able to move her body.

And she certainly had a lot of processing to do. Edwin had come by again yesterday, uncharacteristically serious, professing his undying love and asking for her hand in marriage. Emelia was in shock. She knew Edwin liked her, and had attempted to strike up a bit of a flirtation since he'd returned home, but that was normal for Edwin. She never imagined he was serious enough to pursue marriage, and certainly not with her. Emelia hardly knew how to answer him. She liked Edwin, enjoyed his company, and thought they would rub along well enough. Perhaps in time they might even grow to hold each other in affection. But surely that wasn't sufficient motivation for marriage?

How did ladies make decisions like these based on a man's wealth and social connections alone? Were there any women of her class that were fortunate enough to find they loved their husbands after they were married? For so long the idea of marriage had been little more than an intellectual exercise, something to think over and laugh about with her family, but hardly earth-shattering. But now that she had a real-life decision staring her in the face, it hardly seemed a laughing matter.

Emelia had answered Edwin honestly, telling him she was honored and flattered. She would seriously consider his proposal, but needed some time to decide. He had been all smiles and gently kissed her hand.

"You can take all the time you need, my love. Only once you decide, take pity on my heart and do not hold me in suspense a moment longer than necessary."

He'd bowed and winked at her, his jovial nature intact despite her delay in answering his suit, and taken his leave.

Her mother came in then, and sat quietly while a confused Emelia poured out the whole encounter. Mrs. Seaton confessed that while she liked Edwin immensely and always had, she too felt that this proposal was a bit sudden. Surprising Emelia by pulling her up into a fierce hug, her mother had held her tight for a moment, then looked at her with too-bright eyes. "It's times like these I most miss your father. We could use his wisdom right about now."

"I'm afraid I'm not going to find answers in a book as I usually do." Emelia glanced longingly at the side table where her stack of sickbed reading still sat.

"With your father, I just felt connected to him so quickly. After a few conversations, I knew we would suit. But our compatibility was a rare gift, I know. Most of my friends were not as fortunate in their choice of partners," Emelia's mother admitted with a grimace. "Don't feel you have to make a decision quickly. The rest of your life is quite a long time."

And so Emelia found herself out in her shed, pounding and pondering, the two activities working together surprisingly well. Sweat mingled with tears as Emelia poured her heart out into her craft. She was just fitting the last arrowhead onto a slender birch arrow when her mother burst into the shed, spectacles askew on top of her head, and shouted, "I've got it!"

Emelia wiped grimy hands on her pinafore and blinked at her mother through damp eyelashes.

"What do you have?"

"An idea! I was just making some tinctures at my desk, and the most marvelous idea popped into my head. We'll go to London!"

"Go to London? For what?"

"For the season of course. The season you never had."

"And how will that help me make a decision whether to marry Edwin, exactly?"

"I don't want you to settle for the first offer of marriage you've received without at least meeting a few other men and considering what qualities you want in a future partner. Maybe it'll help you figure out your own heart in regards to Edwin. He can't object to you having a season, after all. I'm sure he'd want you to be introduced into polite society if you are to be married. We'll go to London, stay with Lady Ravenscroft, and go to all the balls and Almack's, oh and the museums! It'll be such fun."

Emelia had never seen her mother so excited, and in her bewildered state she was struggling to keep up.

"Lady Ravenscroft? My Godmother?"

"Yes. She still lives in London, and has extended us a standing offer to stay with her anytime. I haven't seen her in ages, but we correspond frequently. We'll need to pack, but of course there'll be new wardrobes to order. I'd better make an appointment right away. There'll be theater reservations, new gloves…"

Her mother wandered out of the shed and back towards the house, counting her list off on her fingers. She hadn't bothered to ask Emelia if she wanted to go, but there was no way Emelia was going to put a damper on her mother's enthusiasm. She hadn't seen her this excited about anything since her father was alive.

And she supposed it would be nice to finally have a London season, even though she would be a couple of years older than the other debutantes. If nothing else, she supposed it would give her an excuse to take plenty of time before she had to give an answer to Edwin. In fact, the more she thought about it, the more she liked the idea. There would be museums, and music recitals, and—oh!—perhaps she could even meet with some of her father's old scientific contacts and encourage them to look at Mr. Fresnel's new lens. She must tell Henry.

Henry! If they were leaving for London, they must do so very soon, as the season had already begun. She doubted she would see Henry many more times, if ever. Brushing away a distinct feeling of disappointment, Emelia looked down at her filthy hands and stained dress. Heavens! If they were leaving for London soon, she'd better get to work.

~

Standing in the enormous hallway of Lady Ravenscroft's home, Emelia tried hard not to gape. She knew her father had been quite wealthy, but he had chosen to live quietly and elegantly—and far below his means. The Ravenscroft Mansion was like another world entirely. Every corner of it screamed opulence and wealth, and Emelia wondered if the family ever got lost in its mammoth hallways. She knew that Lady Ravenscroft had been widowed a few years before Emelia's mother. Her only child, Lord Andrew, was apparently away in India or someplace doing important government work, and Lady Ravenscroft had been living alone in this enormous house for years. As the footman took their coats and hats, Emelia thought she would much prefer a quiet life in a cottage to rattling around in this pristine mansion all by herself. She hadn't seen Lady Ravenscroft for many years, and imagined her to be an ethereal, wispy woman, floating around from room to room a bit like a ghost. She swallowed a giggle. Apparently she'd read too many of Clara's Gothic mysteries while she was on bed rest.

Emelia stifled a yawn. It had been barely a week since her mother had come bursting into her workshop with her grand idea, but it felt like a month to her tired body. The journey to London had been a pleasant one, only a few hours by carriage, and the weather was sunny and clear. But Emalia was still tired from her illness and the whirlwind of packing over the last few days, and she hoped they would not be expected to mingle in society immediately. The only company she longed for tonight was that of a hot bath and a good book.

"If you will just follow me, ma'am, miss, Lady Ravenscroft will see you in the orange sitting room."

"Elizabeth, Emelia, darlings!" a voice boomed from the sitting room doorway. Lady Ravenscroft was nothing like Emelia had imagined. She was a buxom woman, her ample curves dressed smartly and colorfully in a pink and yellow satin morning dress. Her dark hair held not even a hint of gray, and her brown eyes sparkled. She was shorter than both Emelia and her mother, but her larger-than-life personality seemed to fill the whole room.

"Oh my dears, I thought you'd never come. I've been waiting on pins and needles ever since I got your letter!"

She ran forward and embraced Emelia's mother warmly.

"Alice, dear," laughed Mrs Seaton, embracing her friend, "it's only been a week. I'm amazed we got here as quickly as we did, with all those preparations to make. But you've been such a help, making appointments and the like."

"Elizabeth, I've been waiting for this visit for twenty-five years. You'd better believe I'd do everything in my power to get you here as fast as possible."

Lady Ravenscroft turned to Emelia.

"Now, child, let me look at you. I haven't seen you since you were in short dresses and braids! You're the spitting image of your mother when she was your age. I believe you will be quite overrun with gentlemen in no time."

She must have sensed Emelia's uncertainty, because she patted Emelia's cheek and said in a gentler voice, "Your mother tells me you already have some sorting through of that nature to do. Don't worry, I have a feeling a little stay in the city is just what you need."

She winked and threw an arm around Emelia's shoulders.

"Don't worry, pet. We'll sort you out. Every one of us is faced with these decisions sooner or later."

Emelia was surprised that her eyes were moist. She must be more worn out from the journey than she thought, and she forced a smile.

"I'm sure I'll be right as rain after a bit of rest. I confess I'm not quite used to traveling, and with all of the preparations this week, I haven't slept much."

"And with you still recovering from your illness. Poor duck. What an exciting few weeks you've had. Come with me." Lady Ravenscroft linked one arm in Emelia's and one in Mrs. Seaton's. "We'll have a bracing cup of tea, and a nice chat about something frivolous and inconsequential, like hat trimmings."

Emelia smiled, feeling quite at home already.

Chapter 13

Village Inn
Collington, Kent

Henry stared at the charred remnants of Colonel Phillips' letter in the fireplace grate. His old comrade had requested that Henry ride up to Aldington and stay at the village inn for a night. He was to be approached by a contact there, though as to who it was Phillips gave no details. Only that the man would find him and offer him a snifter of Black Crow brandy. Henry paced back and forth in front of the fireplace. This was all getting a bit too cloak and dagger for his liking. Phillips had even requested he burn the letter when he was through. Henry was seriously considering telling him to find another man. He'd been a soldier, yes, but he was not a deuced spy!

He supposed it was time to leave Collington anyway. There wasn't anything left to learn here. He'd stopped by to check on Emelia again a few days ago, only to find Pierce and Mr. Arbuckle home alone. Apparently Emelia and her mother had left in a hurry to London to give Emelia the come-out season she'd never had. Henry had thought this sudden need to be in the metropolis rather curious, until Pierce had also let slip that Warwick had proposed to Emelia. She wasn't sure how to answer him, so they'd used the season as a good opportunity to give Emelia some space to think it over.

Pierce had patted him on the shoulder, looking far older than his twenty-five years, and murmured, "Sorry about that, old chap. Still hope, though, eh?"

Henry couldn't imagine what he was talking about. Just because he'd pulled Emelia out of the sea—which, of course, he would have done for anyone—here Pierce and even Lord Warwick were imagining he had some sort of designs on Emelia's affections. Sure, his stomach engaged in acrobatics when she was around. Henry's senses often did strange things, but that was completely unrelated to matrimony—wasn't it? Why then did he feel a sweeping sense of relief that Emelia hadn't yet agreed to marry Warwick?

Pierce had told him he and Arbuckle were to join the family in London in another few weeks, when Arbuckle's father was expected home from India. They enthusiastically invited Henry to join them, which made him feel strangely warm inside, but he had to decline for now. He had to get to the bottom of this mystery first.

So here he was, looking at the charred remains of a cryptic letter, off to meet some mysterious contact. Henry sighed. *La vie etait plus simple en Provence.*

Barely an hour later, Henry was on the road to Aldington. He gave his horse—which he had finally named Gideon, seeing as how they were going to be together for the foreseeable future—free reign, and rode off some of his frustrations on the way. After paying the stable boy an extra guinea to rub Gideon down properly and give him some extra oats, Henry entered the dark taproom of the Sailor's Rest.

The evening rush was in full swing, and patrons ate, drank, laughed, and smoked under the dark wooden beams of the old great room. This inn had probably been here for centuries, and held centuries worth of secrets. He wished it could share a few of those and give him some idea of what he was doing here.

A buxom, blonde young woman with a suggestive smile showed him to a table tucked in a tight corner near the kitchen. It suited his purpose, so he nodded his thanks and asked for the evening's special and a pint. He might as well have dinner while he waited for Colonel Phillips' man to find him.

The ale was cold, the food piping hot, and Henry felt some

of his frustration slip away as he tucked into a surprisingly good dish of cottage pie. He watched the room as he ate. The air was convivial, but guarded. There were rumors that this town was a hub for smugglers. Since nearly every town along the coast participated in some sort of smuggling from time to time, that in and of itself wasn't terribly remarkable. What was different about this town, Phillips had written, was that the smugglers were well-organized and well-armed. And if the estimates were to be believed, they trafficked more illegal goods in a month than anywhere else in England did all year.

Henry sopped the last of his meal from the bowl with a scrap of brown bread. He wondered how long he would have to wait before this man found him. He didn't smoke, but he wished he had a pipe to light so he could blend in a little. He'd better drink his beer as slowly as possible. Perhaps he could ask the bar wench to bring him a newspaper—it would look odd if he just sat here and stared at the room. He should have thought ahead and brought something, but Henry was new to espionage, and it's not as though Colonel Phillips had given him a manual.

Coming back to take his plates, the barmaid flirted mercilessly with Henry, batting her eyelashes and giggling like a schoolgirl. He smiled politely and requested a newspaper, attempting to keep his eyes on her face and not on the vast expanse of chest spilling out over her low cut dress.

"'Ere's yer newspaper, and a little somethin' extra for ye." She returned quickly with the paper and a plate of warm biscuits for Henry. "Will ye be needin' anythin' else?"

She looked at him expectantly and winked.

"No, thank you, but if I do, I'll be sure to let you know."

Henry nodded, giving her a few extra coins. He wasn't about to encourage her advances, but it might be useful to gain her favor if he had some questions later.

After another half hour spent half-reading the newspaper and eating biscuits, Henry felt a presence to his right. He looked up, surprised, because he had watched each man that came in the building, wondering if this was his contact, but no one other than the barmaid had approached him all evening. In the dim light he saw an older man, slim and shaggy with a long beard and crooked nose. Henry knew that crooked nose well—he had broken it himself.

"Jim!" A genuine smile spread across Henry's face. "I never expected to see you here. What brings you to these parts?"

"Just seein' our mutual friend up the coast, thought I'd rest 'ere a spell before goin' on to London. I 'ear they 'ave the best Black Crow brandy, care t' join me fer a snifter?"

Ah! So Jim was his contact. It made sense that Phillips would trust one of his former soldiers for such a task. He wondered how Jim was involved in all this.

"It'd be my honor. I haven't seen you since…well, since I broke your nose." Henry grinned, and the other man cackled and showed a smile missing several teeth.

"I would've been dissepointed in ye if ye'd done any less."

The pair took a few moments to recollect the incident, in which Jim had become so drunk on Spanish moonshine, he'd begun calling himself Wellington and chasing around several terrified women in the village near which they were camping. Henry had gone to drag him back to camp. Needless to say, Jim hadn't come willingly. He was wiry, but strong, and Henry sported a cut lip and a shiner before landing Jim a solid facer, knocking him out cold. When he came to the next day, Jim had been sorely embarrassed about his behavior—and nervous about assaulting an officer—but Henry had assured him there were no hard feelings. Jim had been badly wounded in the next battle and sent home, and Henry hadn't seen him since.

They spent the next few minutes reminiscing, Henry asking about other comrades who'd survived the war. Finally, though he had an inkling, Henry asked what Jim had been doing since returning to England.

"Well, once me leg healed enough to be walkin' again, I've

been in the shipping business." Henry understood Jim meant he'd been smuggling.

"Understandable. Has business been good?"

Jim lowered his voice.

"'Twas till about two years back. Our ships coming across the channel keep running into some bad luck. On clear, moonlit nights, they're usually fine—except the usual things like inexperienced sailors hitting the rocks. But on cloudy or stormy nights, we lose them all. You know, we used to pick cloudy nights on purpose. No moon means no one sees. But now we've started to sail only on clear nights. Even with the high risk of getting seen by the excise men, it's better than losing whole crews to a watery death. So the ships that do make it are often caught, and the ships that dare sail in clouds or storm never make it."

"That does sound like a run of bad luck."

"The funny thing is, all our ships come to bad ends within a few miles of each other. Just when they see the light of the Collington lighthouse and start to turn up the shore, they hit rocks where there should be clear sailing."

"Could someone be...planting explosives, out in the water?" Henry felt it was a stupid question, but he had to ask.

Jim rubbed his beard thoughtfully.

"Not likely. We'd be able to see them on the clear nights, but there's nothing there."

"The next logical solution," Henry lowered his voice, "is that someone is turning off the lighthouse so the ships can't find their way in the dark."

"Nae. Every ship that had survivors—and there weren't many of them, mind ye—they swore they saw the light right up until they hit the rocks."

"But surely, running aground so close to the lighthouse can't be a coincidence, right?"

Jim thought for a moment, took a swig of beer, and whistled softly through his missing teeth. "I'd say you have the right of it."

Henry crumbled the remnants of a biscuit absently with one hand.

"Obviously the Keeper would have to be in on it. Who else do you think is involved?"

Jim looked around him, cautiously.

"Can't rightly say."

Henry knew there was more Jim wanted to say, so he waited.

The older man lit a cigarette, took a few long drags, and leaned back in his chair.

"Say, you remember old Donovan Mallory, from the 16th Company?"

Henry held back a grimace. The man was a nasty piece of work. They'd been in different companies, and Mallory had been dishonorably discharged within a few months of Henry's arrival in Spain, but he'd seen enough to know he was not a man to be trifled with. He'd personally prevented Mallory from crossing a line more than once, and he'd reported several incidents to his commanding officers. In fact, Henry's intel was probably a leading factor in Mallory's dishonorable discharge. The man treated farmers like scum, village women like his personal tavern wenches, and orders from his commanding officers as suggestions. Mallory wasn't the type of man Jim would associate with, so if he'd brought him up, there was a purpose. One that Jim didn't feel he could say outright here in Aldington.

"I remember Mallory," Henry replied with a lightness that he didn't feel.

"Well, I've run into our ol' pal a few times here in Kent. Seems he's living in these parts. Close associates with a burly fellow named John Colson."

Henry nodded. These were Jim's best suspects.

"Well, if you see him around again, tell him I said hello."

The two men chatted about inconsequential matters for a few more minutes, then Jim took his leave, and Henry headed up to bed in the room he'd booked for the night. He locked his door, and stuck a chair under the handle for good measure. Even if no one but Jim knew his true purpose here, at the very least he might wake up to the barmaid standing over him and batting her lashes. Henry rolled his eyes. Over-familiar women were the least of his worries right now. Chucking off his boots and shrugging out of his coat and waistcoat, Henry collapsed into bed. He longed for the cozy chair in his library at home, and a long *tete-a-tete* with Grandmere. He was bone weary, but his mind was racing.

Jim thought that Donovan Mallory and another man named John Colson were somehow causing boats to wreck using the Collington lighthouse. Sailors claimed the light never went out, yet they found themselves miles off course, sailing over rocks they never saw coming. He wasn't sure how this all fit together, but he knew one thing for sure.

He had to get back into that lighthouse.

༄

Emelia snuggled up in a large leather easy chair in a quiet corner of Lady Ravenscroft's library, pulling a thick plaid throw tighter around her shoulders. Lord Thomas Ravenscroft, Lady Ravenscroft's son, was out of town on business, and she'd been given full reign of the library since they'd arrived two weeks ago. The days were all starting to whirl together, and Emelia was glad for a few moments to rest and gather her thoughts. Most of the last fortnight had been spent at modists, dressmakers, haberdashers, with one wild visit to the notions market in Covent Garden. Mrs. Seaton and Lady R, as Emelia had taken to calling her, would settle for nothing less than a full debutante's wardrobe for Emelia's come-out.

"I never had the pleasure of having a daughter," Lady R boomed when Emelia dared to protest at the sheer number of gowns being drawn up for her at Madame Guillere's, "and your dear mother has only one chance at this, so do let us have our fun."

She'd patted a flabbergasted Emelia on the rear and shooed her back up onto the dressmaker's box.

The two older women had been thick as thieves lately, their heads bent together over fashion plates and magazines, calling for Emelia from time to time and making her turn about as if she were a living dressmaker's dummy.

"I do think, Alice, that a slight tuck at the waist here, and a bit of a flounce around the hips here would be most becoming," Mrs. Seaton would say, and Lady R would nod approvingly and pull out a roll of trim from her handbag, which seemed suspiciously to be bottomless.

"And perhaps a bit of this brocade along the bodice," she would say, unrolling the braided trim from its spool and holding it up to the light as though it were a rare artifact straight from Egypt.

Although Emelia preferred simpler cuts and minimal trimming, she let her mother and godmother have their fun. She would have little chance to wear most of these garments once she was home in Collington, so she could put up with wearing them for a few weeks in London if only to humor her mother and Lady R.

She'd never thought of her mother as having a taste for fashion. Although her clothes were always stylish and well-made, Mrs. Seaton's wardrobe was usually made up by the local village dressmaker rather than an up-to-the-moment modist in London or Paris. But apparently she'd been quietly keeping up with current fashions all these years, because she rattled off plans for her and Emelia's new wardrobes with a vocabulary that left Emelia's mouth hanging open. This was a new side to her quiet, scientific mother, but then again, Emelia was learning a lot about her mother on this trip.

Stretching in the leather armchair, Emelia chuckled and laid aside the book on optics she'd been reading. She'd always assumed that since her mother was clearly a spinster by the time she'd married her father, she must not have had many suitors. But nothing could be further from the truth, as her mother told her off-handedly while they were having tea with Lady R earlier that week.

Apparently Elizabeth Seaton, then Elizabeth Merriweather,

had made quite the splash during her own come-out season. She had, in fact, turned down *nine* offers of marriage, simply because she hadn't been in love with any of the gentlemen.

"Half the eligible gentlemen of London were dangling after her," Lady R had confided, "and a few rather *ineligible* gentlemen as well," she'd added with a snort of laughter.

It made Emelia feel a little better about her own situation, really. If her mother could turn down nine offers of marriage holding out for someone with whom she felt true companionship, then Emelia could at least take a few weeks to decide if she wanted to marry Edwin. And if she decided not to marry him, it gave her hope that—perhaps someday—she'd meet someone she *could* imagine spending the rest of her life with.

It'd been often in her thoughts the last two weeks, but she wasn't any clearer on what she should do. Lady R kept insisting that, "Sometimes wisdom is revealed as we get out into the world and *do* things, rather than just sitting around and thinking."

Emelia had just laughed, unsure how dancing at a ball or attending a musical soirée was going to give her clarity on whom to marry, but at this point she was open to suggestions.

As the season had just begun, they'd only received a few invitations to quiet dinner parties or small card parties. Most of these Lady R had politely declined, as Emelia and Mrs. Seaton were still awaiting their full wardrobes, and Emelia had the sinking feeling they were holding out for something really grand for her debut into the *ton*. She only hoped she didn't embarrass them.

As a distraction, Emelia had picked up this book on the optics of light, which reminded her of Monsieur Fresnel's new lens and her commitment to seeking out someone who might be able to help implement this new technology. She was ashamed to admit she'd barely thought of the lens since they'd arrived in London, wondering self-consciously if she really cared about the lives that could be saved or only wanted a project to occupy her time. Emelia *wanted* to be concerned with the good of her fellow men. It was one of the reasons she brought baskets of food to the needy, and sat with shut-ins who needed company. But her worst fear was that she was really just a selfish, spoiled girl, whose care for others was really a hobby, easily put off when something more pressing for her comfort came along.

Emelia sighed, looking longingly at her book, but instead she grabbed a pencil and notebook she'd seen earlier on a side table, and started to make a list.

Find father's scientific contacts.
Discover who has power in the government to influence lighthouse owners.
Tell them about the lens, tell them what a difference it could make to save sailors lives.
Trust that they'll do the right thing?

It sounded simple enough, until it wasn't. Emelia frowned. She wasn't a skilled orator, or even a person of any standing to whom these men should listen. More importantly, she wasn't a man—just a girl from the country who read too much and fancied herself an archer. What made her think she could inspire any kind of change?

She didn't know what to say or do, but she supposed no one would be any worse off if she tried and failed. At least then she would feel like she'd done something. Emelia glanced at the clock over the mantle. It was just about time for tea. Time to see how many men of influence her mother and Lady R could think of.

CHAPTER 14

Mayfair, London

Fidgeting nervously with the lace trim on the edge of her puffed sleeves, Emelia squirmed in the carriage seat and tried not to show her mother or Lady R how nervous she was. It wasn't the crowds she objected to. She rather enjoyed talking with and meeting new people. She just wasn't sure any of these elegant people would want to keep company with *her*. If they knew her favorite hobbies involved banging on an anvil or reading obscure scientific literature, she was afraid they'd write her off as a hoyden or a bluestocking. Not to mention that business of racing across the fields like a schoolgirl. She smiled slightly as she remembered Henry's bewildered expression the day they first met. At least *he* didn't seem to mind her strange hobbies. Though he likely wasn't too keen on the archery part, seeing as how it nearly killed him.

"Are you excited about tonight's ball, dear, or are you thinking of something—or someone—else?" Lady R's eyes sparkled, and Emelia had the distinct feeling she was plotting something.

"More like remembering something ridiculous that Pierce and I did a few weeks ago." Emelia answered with a partial truth. "I wish he were going to be here tonight. Did he give any indication of when he'd be joining us in London, Mother?"

Mrs. Seaton was the picture of elegance in a jade green evening gown. A matching turban just covered the tops of her curls, golden ringlets artfully spilling out the edges.

"Pierce has been uncharacteristically vague in his letters,

Emmie. I suspect he doesn't want to embarrass Mr. Arbuckle, but he assures me they'll come to town before the season's over. Any letters from Edwin? I imagine he'll be in London before too long as well."

Emelia blushed. She'd in fact had six letters from Edwin in the two and a half weeks they'd been in London. Each was filled with the most flattering, lovesick language Emelia had ever read. Edwin certainly knew how to write a love letter. The first two letters, she thought surely he was just showing off his more than adequate skill at flirting, but the last few had seemed so tender, so heartfelt—she wondered if he truly did love her.

Heat flooded her cheeks. She was too embarrassed to tell her mother the details, however.

"Yes, he writes he has another week or two of business to take care of, and plans to join us in time for the Wilkerson's ball."

"Oh, delightful," exclaimed Lady R, but Emelia noticed her mother was examining her carefully. She tried hard not to blush again. "The Wilkerson's ball promises to be a real crush, one of the biggest events of the season."

Lady R seemed to delight in every dinner, rout party, and now, ball. She appeared to know everyone in London, and got a particular gleam in her eye whenever she spoke to Emelia of eligible gentlemen. Emelia had assured her before their first dinner party that she had no need of Lady R's matchmaking services, but only needed some time to sort out her own heart. Still, it hadn't stopped Lady R from introducing her to as many young gentlemen as crossed their path.

"You don't have to *marry* them, Emelia love," Lady R had reassured her. "Just make some friends. It might help you discover the qualities that you'd enjoy in a spouse whenever you do make that decision."

Emelia had to admit she had a point. And as Lady R was also introducing her to many young ladies she thought Emelia would get along with, perhaps she could at least make a few new friends on this trip. She missed Clara terribly, and wished her friend were here to see her and her mother dressed up in such finery. She would have sighed and gotten a dreamy look in her eyes, and proceeded to tell Emelia it was *exactly* like *The Maiden and the Rake*, or some or another romantic novel she'd recently been reading.

The carriage came to a halt outside a glittering white mansion. Luminaries lined the sidewalk, and the whole house was ablaze with candlelight.

"My goodness." Emelia forced herself to breathe slowly. "For my very first ball, you sure did pick a splendid one."

"Just wait until you get inside, dear."

After queuing to greet their hosts, an older and extremely genteel Lord and Lady Southerton, a footman took their coats and the trio walked into the great hall.

"Oh my." Emelia felt a bit breathless. It was a truly impressive entry, with an enormous curved double staircase and the largest chandelier Emelia had ever seen. As they walked up the stairs to the ballroom, Emelia noticed the banister was adorned in intricate, shiny golden geese. She stifled a giggle. How very different from the geese in Collington.

The ballroom was even more magnificent. Gilded mirrors adorned the walls every few feet, and each chandelier had been polished until they sparkled like diamonds.

"Come, come, my dear, so many people to introduce you to!" Lady R was fluttering about and clucking like a mother hen on the landing above them. Emelia's mother grinned and held out a hand.

"Shall we take the town by storm, Emmie?"

Looking her daughter over from the pearl combs in her hair to her delicately slippered feet, she smiled.

"I think we'll do, don't you?"

The next hour was a flurry of activity. Emelia met so many elegant ladies and well-dressed gentlemen, she was going to be hard-pressed to remember more than a few names. Everyone over the age of forty seemed to remember her mother, and although a few women tittered their surprise that "dearest Elizabeth" had finally returned to London after all this time, most everyone seemed genuinely happy to see her. Lady R lost no time in pulling every gentleman into Emelia's path, and her dance card was soon full.

Partway through the evening, Lady R flagged down an immaculately dressed older gentleman. His shirt points were a bit higher and waistcoat sported a few more fobs than Emelia was used to seeing on men his age. Bowing low over Emelia's hand, he kissed the air above her knuckles with a flourish.

"Emelia, this is Sir Cecil Bartlett, a physicist of some renown. I believe he was acquainted with your father. Sir Cecil, this is Miss Emelia Seaton."

Pointing to Emelia's mother, who was in the middle of a glittering circle of society matrons, she added, "Her mother, Mrs. Elizabeth Seaton, is over there."

"Ah! Yes. One could never forget your charming mother. Why, I daresay, half the gentlemen were dangling after her, and the other half wished they were."

He smiled at Emelia in a way that made her wish she could excuse herself to wash her hand.

"But yes, we were talking about Mr. Frank Seaton. He was quite a brilliant man, and a good one, too. I was very sad to hear that he'd passed."

"Thank you, sir, we miss him greatly."

Emelia jumped ahead with more enthusiasm than finesse.

"Lately, I have been desiring to meet some of his contacts in the scientific world. You see, my father was a great teacher, and I enjoy studying the sciences myself, particularly physics."

Sir Cecil looked a bit taken aback, but a smile quickly smoothed over his surprise.

"Ah, yes, your father was always quite progressive," he murmured politely. "I suspect he'd taught you as if you were the son he never had, eh?"

Taking a deep breath, Emelia attempted to push down the

annoyance rising up within her. If she wanted to speak with Sir Cecil about Mr. Fresnel's lens, she needed to stay on good terms with him.

"Actually, my brother Pierce is five years my senior, and will be joining us in London shortly. He, I'm afraid, has no interest in the sciences."

"I see." Sir Cecil nodded stiffly, as if he clearly couldn't understand why a man as smart as her father would teach his daughter science, when he had a perfectly capable son at home.

"And how are you enjoying your come-out season? Hoping to snare an eligible young gentleman, are you? Shouldn't have any trouble with a pretty face like that."

"The season has been lovely so far. Lady Ravenscroft is an excellent host. I think she knows the whole of London."

Smiling at Lady R, Emelia tried not to take offense at the implication that she was only here to find a husband. Sir Cecil was obviously old-fashioned, and that was, indeed, what most young women were hoping to accomplish with a season in London.

Sir Cecil looked her up and down, lingering a bit too long on her neckline. Emelia had insisted the bodice of her ballgown be more modest than the current fashion, but it still felt rather daring to her. She felt her face heat, but whether from rage or embarrassment she wasn't sure.

"Well, best of luck in your endeavor, my dear. You've got a lovely figure to go with that pretty face. I'm sure you'll have no problem if you keep your somewhat unusual schooling under wraps. Miss Seaton, Lady Ravenscroft, your servant."

He bowed slightly, taking his leave of them and walking across the ballroom towards the card room.

Emelia tried to school the expression on her face into a polite mask, but was afraid she was failing miserably. Lady Ravenscroft didn't even attempt to.

"Well!" Disdain dripped off her godmother's features. "I'm sorry I introduced you to him! This was one of his saner days—sometimes the man rants and raves, yet somehow he's still an important figure in the scientific community. But truly, what a cad. If he leers at you again like that, I'm going to stuff one of those shirt points up his nose."

Lady R gave a bit of a harrumph and crossed her arms. "Unusual schooling, indeed. I'm sure his somewhat limited intelligence just feels threatened."

Seeing Lady R's reaction soothed Emelia's ire a bit, and she found herself chuckling at the other woman's indignation.

"Don't worry, Lady Ravenscroft. I'm sure that father had other friends in the scientific community I can speak with about Mr. Fresnel's lens."

Lady R sighed. "However much I dislike the man, Emelia, he is right about one thing. Most people here" she waved her hand to indicate the crowded ballroom, "think it's a woman's job to look beautiful, secure a brilliant match, and bear children. As much as I agree with your family's stance on women and learning, it might be best not to mention your interest in science, at least until you get to know people a little better."

With an unladylike groan, Emelia reluctantly agreed. "I'm sure you're right, though I hate the idea of editing out who I am to be accepted."

A flash of something like pain crossed Lady R's eyes, and Emelia was surprised. She'd never seen her godmother look anything less than delighted about everything.

"You've no idea, love. But the people who truly matter will accept you just as you are, not who they want you to be."

Intrigued, Emelia wanted to ask what parts of Lady R's character *she* was hiding, but the older woman just patted her hand and sighed.

"That's for another time and place, my dear. We are in a ballroom! Let's go find the next young man on your dance card."

As she whisked her charge away into the crowd, Emelia couldn't help thinking that maybe not everything in London society was as gay and glittering as it appeared. Perhaps everyone here was presenting only the parts of themselves they wanted society to see. It struck Emelia as a truly sad way to live. She might have more enthusiasm than polish, but at least she was true to herself—wasn't she? It was a question she pondered quietly through the rest of the evening, the sparkle on her first ball a bit duller than it had been before.

Leaning back in her chair in the parlor, Emelia kicked off her shoes. It felt like they'd received every gentleman in London that morning, and a few of their mothers and sisters besides. She'd danced with so many gentlemen at the Southerton's ball last night, she was forced to ask Lady R for a brief description of each when his card was presented just to remember who was who. She supposed she should feel grateful for all the attention, but in truth Emelia was mostly overwhelmed. She felt she'd met more people last night than in the whole of her life, and it was probably true. Lord Percy Drummond was an accomplished dancer, Mr. Haversham was kind and attentive, Sir Alton told the most humorous stories. Each gentleman certainly had something to recommend him, but they were all starting to blur together a bit.

Glancing around to make sure she was still alone, Emelia sighed and began to rub her aching feet. How did people attend so many balls in a season? The dancing was fun, yes, but she wished there were easier, less formal ways to get to know people. Surely it was impossible to know one's true character after a dance or a conversation over the punch bowl. While most of the people she had been introduced to over the past couple of weeks seemed kind and genuine apart from the strict rules that governed society's interactions, everyone was so stiff and formal here in London. It almost felt like trying to get to know someone from watching them act in a stage play.

Interestingly enough, Emelia found herself comparing all

of the gentlemen she met to Edwin—not surprising considering she was deciding whether to marry him—or to Henry. That she held Henry in enough esteem to compare potential suitors to him surprised her. She considered him a friend, and she did find him intriguingly handsome. He had a genuineness about him, a steadiness of character, a lack of pretense that seemed so common here among the *ton*. Perhaps it was a result of all he'd been through in life, but Henry seemed to be a man who knew who he was, and didn't apologize for it, and that in and of itself was rather refreshing. It was unlikely that she'd ever see Henry again, but she was glad their paths had crossed, however briefly.

Stomach growling, Emelia wondered if it were time for luncheon. Lady R had stepped out to arrange something with the housekeeper, and Mrs. Seaton had run to the library to fetch a new book for the afternoon. A brisk knock sounded at the parlor door, and Carter, Lady Ravenscroft's butler, entered the room. Carter was not the sort Emelia would have pegged as a butler at all. He looked more like a prizefighter, for he was solidly built and looked strong as an ox. Now that she thought of it, his nose was slightly crooked, and one of his earlobes was missing a chunk—perhaps he *had* once been a prizefighter. His manner was perfectly stately and correct, however, and Emelia knew Lady R trusted him completely.

Carter bowed and announced guests.

"Lord Percy Drummond, Lady Lilly Drummond, The Honorable Reverend Howell, Mr. Armand Cottsworth, and Mr. Hugh Cottsworth, to see you, Miss Emelia."

Good heavens! Were they to receive *every* young person in London today? Emelia's stomach growled again in protest. She dearly hoped this was the last group of the day. She needed a quiet place to sit and think for a bit, not to mention eat. But, Emelia Seaton was never one to shy from a challenge. She squared her shoulders and quickly slipped back into her discarded shoes, standing to receive her guests.

"See them in, Carter, thank you."

The five visitors entered behind Carter. Reverend Howell was dressed in stark black, and Lady Lilly, her brother Lord Percy, and the other two gentlemen in fashionable pastels. As with all of the gentlemen present, Emelia had met Lady Lilly at the ball the night before, and had taken an immediate liking to her. A petite redhead, Lady Lilly had intelligent green eyes and spoke with candor. Emelia thought they could be friends, and had been hoping to see her again. She just hadn't expected it to be so soon. Things certainly moved fast in London.

"Miss Seaton." Lady Lilly reached out to clasp Emelia's hand. "I do hope we're not calling too close to luncheon. My brother and I were just visiting Lady Fairchild down the street, and I begged him to make one more quick stop!"

Lord Percy Drummond, Lady Lilly's brother, bowed low over Emelia's other hand.

"I never could deny my sister anything, particularly not visiting the season's newest *incomparable*."

He waggled an eyebrow, and Emelia couldn't hold back a laugh.

"Incomparable! You must be joking. You should meet my brother Pierce, I believe you two would get along, he is always ribbing me." Emelia looked at her still-standing guests and blushed. "Goodness me! I'm so sorry, I'm rather new to hosting so many people at once; I am forgetting my manners. Please, let's sit down."

Lady Lilly sat on a gilded armchair adjacent to Emelia, who resumed her seat on an elaborate settee. The gentlemen eyed one another, none wanting to be the selfish curr that stole the seat next to Emelia (or perhaps not ready to single her out just yet). Reverend Howell, a freckle-faced young man with a shock of sandy hair, resorted to standing by the fireplace with an arm propped up on the mantle. Lord Percy and the Cottsworth brothers—Emelia still wasn't sure which was Armand and which was Hugh, they both had the same wavy brown hair and prominent noses—all sat in a row on the sofa across from her. Emelia's mouth quirked to the side. With their floral embroidered waistcoats, high shirt-points, and elaborate cravats, the three gentlemen looked like a row of brightly colored Faberge eggs. In contrast, the somber Reverend Howell looked like a funeral undertaker. Emelia looked over to Lady Lilly and saw her eyes glittering, and the two shared a private smile. This was just the sort of thing Clara would have found amusing, and she was glad to have found a kindred spirit in Lady Lilly.

"But I do know him," Lord Percy was saying. "Your brother that is. We met a few years ago at a curricle race. Splendid chap, your brother. Always keeping the rest of us young bucks on the straight and narrow."

"The straight and narrow?" Emelia laughed. "Are you sure we're talking about the same Pierce Seaton?"

"Oh yes, he's quite a dependable fellow. Always making sure everyone is playing by the rules, taking the proper precautions, that sort of thing. And he's pulled me out of a scrape or two." He grinned roguishly at his sister. "Won't do for me to repeat the details in mixed company, you understand."

"Yes, he's well-respected among our set," one of the Cottsworth brothers agreed. "Mother's always eager to add him to our guest list when he is in town. He's much sought after to even out a dinner party, and dances with all of the young ladies in need of partners. Why, he danced with our sister last season, and Mother talked about it for a month."

Who would have thought. Her brother, the responsible friend and sought after guest! Emelia supposed she really didn't know much about what her brother did when he came to town to visit friends. He always just spoke of card games, boxing matches, and races. Her family seemed to be full of surprises lately.

Lady Lilly asked what Emelia had thought of the Southerland's ball, and the young people passed an agreeable quarter of an hour discussing the dances and their mutual acquaintances. Just as Emelia was beginning to think the whole room would soon hear her stomach growling, Lady Lilly announced it was time to go home for luncheon, and everyone else followed suit. Reverend

Howell blushed and stammered his goodbyes, and the Cottsworth brothers bid Emelia adieu politely and urged her to have Pierce contact them as soon as he arrived in town. Lady Lilly gave Emelia an enthusiastic hug and arranged to meet her in the park for a stroll the following week. Grinning at his sister, Lord Percy kissed Emelia's knuckles and gazed at her through heavy lids.

"I do mean *incomparable*, dear Miss Seaton, but I like and respect your brother enough not to throw my hat in the ring just yet."

He winked at her, and Emelia laughed. She could tell Lord Percy was all jest, and she was grateful for it. She needed to make up her mind about Edwin's offer of marriage before she found any more gentlemen vying for her affections. She was under no delusions of being a great beauty, and certainly not an *incomparable*. But she supposed since she was friendly, pretty enough, and—most importantly—possessing a respectable fortune, she shouldn't be surprised if she found herself with more would-be suitors.

Carter appeared again to inform Emelia that her mother and Lady R were waiting in the morning room with luncheon. Like all of the Ravenscroft Mansion, the morning room was opulent, a colorful painted fresco of nymphs and water sprites adorning the ceiling. Emelia pulled up a seat and tried not to gape at the copious amounts of food. The spread in front of them could have fed a family of ten, and was far too lavish for the three women at the table. Lady R was clearly delighting in entertaining her guests.

"Emelia, dear, I do hope you'll forgive me," Emelia's mother was saying as she filled a plate with cold cuts, cheeses, fruits, and perfectly-roasted vegetables. "Carter informed us that you had more visitors, but since it was just young people here to see you, we thought we'd let you handle it. I simply couldn't make any more small talk this morning."

"Lady Lilly is quite an interesting girl, is she not?" Lady R managed between bites of a fluffy French omelet. "She's highly intelligent, has no use for putting on airs, and I see a lot of potential in that one. And her brother is a rake, but a charming one."

"So I gathered! Don't worry, I'm not at risk for falling for his flattery."

"Of course not, love, you're far too sensible for that," confirmed Lady R. "Besides, I have a feeling the gentlemen of London have already missed out when it comes to your affections."

She waggled one eyebrow at Emelia to make her laugh.

"But still, it doesn't hurt to be too careful. There are gentlemen out there that wouldn't hesitate to put a woman in a compromising situation just to gain access to a dowry as robust as yours."

Emelia stopped mid chuckle, looking agog at Lady R and her mother.

"You can't be serious? Gentlemen would…compromise me…just for the sake of my fortune? It's not even that large!"

"Your father left you with plenty, dear, enough to live your whole life as an independent woman if you so choose. It's not inconceivable that an unscrupulous man in dire straits would find that attractive. It's one of the reasons I turned down so many offers of marriage all those years ago."

Emelia felt herself deflate a bit.

"Now I'm not sure I'll be able to take any gentleman in London seriously. At least back home no one knows or cares about my dowry. I wonder…Mother…" Emelia hesitated to even speak the thought out loud, but it had to be done. "Do you think Edwin knows about my fortune?"

Lady R and Mrs. Seaton exchanged a look that suggested they'd already been discussing that very subject.

"It's possible," Mrs. Seaton said gently. "It's not like we've been advertising it for the last nineteen years, but my fortune will pass on to you someday, and your father set aside a healthy portion of his un-entailed income for you, to be yours when you're married or when you turn twenty-five. Your father ensured you'd be taken care of nearly as well as Pierce, though he'll get the estate, of course."

"Since your father died and the details of his entailments were made public record, anyone who wants to do some simple arithmetic can figure out what you're worth, so to speak." Mrs. Seaton looked apologetic. "And since our estate and Edwin's are so close, I'm sure our servants talk to one another. There's no telling who could let a detail like that slip without meaning to."

Emelia sighed, her head beginning to pound as she processed everything. She'd known her father had left her well cared-for, but she hadn't really considered the repercussions of having such a fortune.

"So you're saying there's a good chance Edwin knows."

"There is. But Emelia, Edwin has known you his whole life, and his estate is largely the same as it was twenty years ago. There's nothing to indicate he'd offer for your hand based on money alone."

Sensing Emelia's distress, Lady R turned to Emelia and said brightly. "You know, I've been wanting to visit the British Museum again, it's been ages. Would you all like to accompany me there on Friday?

"Oh yes! Yes, of course." Emelia was grateful. She knew Lady R was simply trying to distract her, and she appreciated it, but she'd been dying to go to the museum since they arrived in London and was genuinely excited. "I am rather eager to see the Elgin Marbles. I hear they're magnificent."

Conversation happily turned to the various exhibits they could expect to see at the museum, and the three were just finishing the last bits of their luncheon when Carter appeared in the doorway bearing a calling card on a silver platter.

"Another visitor for Miss Seaton, my Lady."

"Oh no! Mother, I just don't think I can handle any more visitors today."

She plucked the calling card off of the tray reluctantly, and glanced at it.

"Oh. It's Edwin! He's arrive.!"

Emelia wasn't sure whether to be elated or nervous.

"See him in, then." Mrs. Seaton glanced at Emelia, then

nodded kindly to Carter. A few minutes later Edwin burst into the room, all smiles and excitement.

"Darling!"

He bounded across the room and took both her hands in his. His eyes shone, and he looked a bit breathless. She felt a wave of affection for her old friend, still that same dreamy-eyed boy in so many ways.

"Mrs. Seaton, always a pleasure."

Emelia's mother rose to hug Edwin, then gestured to Lady R.

"This is my oldest friend, Lady Alice Ravenscroft."

Lady Ravenscroft rose, smiling politely, but Emelia could tell she was sizing up Edwin. Lady R had a way of looking through you that made you feel as though she could see your very soul.

"Pleased to finally meet you, young man. We've heard so much about you."

After a few minutes of polite conversation, inquiring where Edwin was staying and what Emelia had been up to since she arrived in town, Edwin jumped back up out of his chair as if unable to sit still.

"Would you like to go for a walk in the gardens with me? That is, if it's okay with your mother and Lady Ravenscroft. It's such a beautiful afternoon, and we can stay in sight of the house the whole time."

Emelia looked at her mother, who nodded.

"Alice and I will sit on the back veranda with our tea, dear, just to keep everything proper."

Fetching her wrap, Emelia joined Edwin at the back door, and they strolled out hand in hand. Lady Ravenscroft's garden was a highly manicured affair, with long mazes of hedges, each ending in a picturesque statue, fountain, or ornate bench surrounded by flowers. Emelia marveled again at the vastness of the estate even in the middle of town, and wondered how many gardeners it took to keep the maze of greenery so pristine. After a few moments of walking, Edwin looked as though he would burst, and pulled her to a nearby bench.

"Emelia, I just—I couldn't wait a minute longer. You don't have to answer me today, but…but I sincerely hope you're closer to making a decision."

Turning towards her, he took both her hands in his again. A shadow passed over his eyes. Perhaps he really did love her very much. He looked truly tortured.

Emelia took a deep breath. There was no mathematical equation for love. Not for the first time, she really wished there was.

"Edwin." She stopped, uncertain how to proceed. "I'm not trying to keep you waiting a moment longer than necessary. I truly care for you, as I have since we were children. It's just that—well, the rest of our lives is a long time, and I've always had this silly notion of marrying for love, or at the very least with a deep friendship. We had that once, and I believe it's possible we could again."

Emelia saw his face light up and held up a hand.

"I just want to be absolutely sure before I say yes. Would it be possible for you to give me another week? I'm really grateful for the time here in London, I'm discovering so much about my family, and myself, and I've given myself this little quest—"

"And you could continue to do all of those things, here in London, after we're engaged as well!"

Emelia put the hand she was holding gently on his chest.

"One week. That's all I ask. I promise I won't keep you in suspense beyond that."

"Okay. One week." He gave a half-grin. "At least now I'm here to escort you around town properly. Once you're firmly off the market—"

Emelia raised an eyebrow.

"I mean, *if* you say yes, then I shall escort you to every event your heart desires, from now and eternity."

Emelia smiled.

"Deal."

She started to rise from the bench and continue down the path, but Edwin put a hand on her shoulder. She looked at him expectedly, and realized her mother and Lady R couldn't see them when they were seated. Very well, if he wanted to kiss her, she supposed she would let him. Perhaps it would be a grand revelation. He leaned forward slowly, giving her plenty of opportunity to pull away, searching her face as he brushed a light kiss across her lips. Emelia closed her eyes, and he deepened the kiss, sliding one arm gently around her waist and pulling her in closer.

Emelia waited for some bolt of lightning, some choir from heaven, some spark of attraction. He certainly was a handsome man, and although she hadn't any experience at kissing, she knew Edwin had kissed his share of girls. He certainly seemed to know what he was doing. Breaking away, he gently feathered a few kisses down her jawline before pulling away from her and offering his hand.

Rising on perfectly steady legs, Emelia took his hand and they continued their stroll through the garden.

"One week then, Emmie, my love? My lovesick heart will eagerly await your verdict."

She smiled at her old friend.

"One week. I promise."

As they made their way back towards the house and the awaiting chaperones, Emelia supposed she couldn't expect a first kiss to be magical. After all, she certainly didn't know what she was doing. But as his lips had brushed hers, her brain was sending rapid-fire messages: *this doesn't feel right, why are you kissing Edwin?* Her stomach had clenched, her palms sweaty. She supposed that *could* be what falling in love felt like. The poets all seemed to feel that way, but she didn't think so. Maybe it was because she had known Edwin so very long, but it felt rather like kissing her brother. And the oddest part? She could tell from his awkward, lopsided grin that he had felt the same way.

Why then did he still want to marry her?

Emelia's stomach fluttered more at the inevitable truth than it ever had for that ill-fated kiss.

Chapter 15

The Coast
Kent, England

How far the mighty have fallen, Henry thought with a chuckle as he wiped his sweaty brow on a tattered rag and loaded another heavy barrel onto a waiting fishing vessel. A few weeks of living as a gentleman again and he'd gone soft. Smuggling was a much more taxing profession.

Jim, his old army-buddy-turned-smuggler, had gotten Henry a job with a group of French laborers doing grunt work for Donovan Mallory's smuggling ring. Not exactly the inner circle, but it was a start. Someone in this group was bound to know something. Jim had given him a crash course in smugglers' deportment and lingo. Henry had been wearing work clothes and speaking in French for nearly a week now, and while he supposed he should be uncomfortable working amongst smugglers, it had actually been quite a relief. He'd missed honest work—well, this wasn't *honest* work, exactly, but these laborers weren't the criminal sort. They were just immigrants looking for jobs, immigrants who couldn't afford to be picky about who they were working for.

Today, they were working in broad daylight, loading smuggled goods to be shuttled further up the coast. His arm and back muscles burned in protest. It had been several months since he had done this kind of heavy lifting, and he was feeling it. All week Henry had been listening, trying not to ask too many questions about Mallory or his henchmen for fear of raising suspicions. He'd kept his head down and done the work. Their labors nearly finished for the day, Henry loaded one last barrel. Whiskey, from the smell of it. Not for the first time this week, he wondered if the whiskey shipment had been smuggled over directly, or had been stolen from other smugglers whose ships had been lost on the rocks.

An hour later, in a tiny crossroads between Collington and Aldington, Henry sat with his fellow-laborers in the dim corner of an old pub, laughing at their coarse jokes. He'd been invited to join them a few nights before, and he'd quickly accepted. He would learn far more from these men after a few drinks than he would during the workday. Henry had recounted a particularly lewd joke that had gotten his cousin Gerard assigned to clean out the stables for a week, and was rewarded with a round of raucous laughter and a few slaps on the back. He was in, and the beers and conversation flowed freely after that.

Tonight, while he appeared to be drowning his troubles in a pint and listening to some highly-embellished fishing stories, he was keeping an eye on the quiet youth at the corner of the table. The boy couldn't be more than eighteen, but he had the same calloused hands and sea legs of any of the other men. The boy—Jean, he'd heard him called—had always kept his hat pulled down, not looking anyone in the eyes, and kept to himself. Several times this week Jean had looked as if he wanted to approach Henry, but had thought better of it and turned away. This was the first night Henry had seen him at the pub. As the group milled around the table, filling drinks and switching seats, Henry finally sidled up next to the young man.

"Bonjour, Monsieur Dufort," the lad offered. Henry was using his grandmere's surname while working with the Frenchmen.

"Good evening," Henry answered in French. "Long day of lifting, eh?"

"You have questions for me, I know," the youth continued as if he hadn't spoken. "But not now. Not yet. Wait until they are all drunk, and meet me by the fire."

Henry raised his glass in a wordless salute, and the boy blended back into the crowd. An hour later Henry met Jean by the old stone fireplace, one arm propped casually on the mantelpiece and a beer in one hand, looking for all the world like they were having a casual chat by the fire's warmth.

"Monsieur, I see you," Jean began. "I know you are listening. You are discreet, but I know you are seeking answers. Please, be careful. There is a man—men—that would not hesitate to kill you if they feel you are a threat."

"Who is it, Jean? What do you know?"

Henry had decided to take a straightforward approach and tell Jean the truth.

"I'm trying to help stop these men, and I need to know how they're sabotaging ships to make them crash on the rocks. I don't want any more men to die," he added softly, hoping the boy would sense his sincerity and help him.

Jean hesitated, then nodded once.

"Two years ago, when I was but a boy, I was sailing with a group of smugglers not unlike this one. We passed through the waters close to Collington. It was a foggy night. For a moment, the lighthouse went out, and we couldn't tell which way to go. Then it illuminated again, but I could swear we had shifted somehow—the light was the right height, but it was as if it had moved up the coast. I tried to warn the captain, but he wouldn't listen to a mere cabin boy."

Jean stopped and sipped his beer, but Henry didn't miss the tremor in his voice.

"*Merde.*"

Jean drew a shaky breath.

"The captain was a good sailor, very skilled. But before the hour was up, we were being dashed upon the rocks. They appeared out of nowhere, miles from where they should have been. I don't remember much of the wreck, Monsieur, but we started taking on water. Those that could were jumping off and swimming to shore.

I could swim a bit, but I was tangled in some netting and nearly drowned. I woke up later on the beach, still wrapped in netting and half hidden behind a piece of the ship. I'd dashed my head pretty hard on a rock, and I was coming in and out of consciousness, but I was near enough to where I could hear them talking without them seeing me."

Henry fought the anger rising within him, forcing himself to appear calm to Jean and the rest of the crowded pub.

"Who was talking, Jean? Who did this?"

The boy stopped, covering his face with his free hand. Setting a comforting hand on his shoulder, Henry waited.

"I heard men screaming, it was terrible. There were a lot of good swimmers on my boat, but as they struggled to shore among the rocks and the waves, there were men waiting for them with clubs and knives. They killed them all, monsieur. Every last man. I just laid in the wreckage and pretended to be dead so they wouldn't come for me. I couldn't tell how many men there were, but one of them seemed to be in charge. He had a wooden leg and spoke with a raspy voice."

Henry's gut twisted. Donovan was definitely involved then. He'd lost the leg not in service, but in a drunken brawl. And his voice was very distinctive.

Jean continued.

"Well, the man with a wooden leg, he was arguing with a young toff, as men all around them pulled our cargo out of the water and loaded it into a wagon. They were having quite a row. The toff was carrying on about how no one was supposed to get hurt, and how he wouldn't let them use his lighthouse anymore if they were going to kill people. He sounded really angry, but the man with the wooden leg told him he couldn't afford to be picky. He threatened him with debtors' prison if he didn't cooperate."

The youth gave a shudder, and quickly took a drink to fortify himself. "Then this other man came, a huge hulking brute of a man. He got rid of the angry toff really quick—he just told him there were fates worse than debtors' prison, and he'd make sure he went missing again on one of his trips abroad and no one would ever find him. That's all I heard, because I passed out in earnest next, and woke up a few hours later when everyone was gone or dead. I knew they'd be coming to clean up the bodies soon, and I needed to disappear. I couldn't let them know there had been any survivors, or they would have tracked me down and killed me as well. I went back to France for a while, but in my village, there are no jobs. I had to come back here to work, and no one was left from my crew to recognize me anyway. I hate smuggling. I hate sailing. Luckily our team of Frenchmen mostly move goods on land during the day, anyway. We're expendable if we get caught and thrown into prison. But you won't catch me out on those rocks at night again. Even if they didn't cause us to go ashore somehow, if anyone does run ashore their life is surely forfeit. They won't leave any survivors."

Henry's chest felt heavy, his throat too tight. His heart broke for Jean and all he had been forced to endure at such a young age. And to have to return to a life he hated, just to be able to eat. Henry wished that he could help him in some way. Heaven knew Jean had certainly helped him.

What if the angry young gentleman talking about *his* lighthouse was Edwin Warwick? Henry's heart had nearly stopped when he'd heard that. But Warwick should have been abroad two years ago. Who else could have been staking a claim to the Collington lighthouse in his place? Pierce Seaton? Henry dismissed the thought as quickly as it had come. He'd only known the young man for a few weeks, but he found it hard to imagine Pierce being involved in such a scheme. Who then had confronted Donovan and his men on the beach? And how in the world did one move a lighthouse, or at least make it appear to have moved?

Perhaps it was time to have another chat with Warwick. If there was any chance he'd been back in Collington two years ago, Henry needed to know. If not, maybe he had some ideas on who had been on the beach claiming to own his lighthouse. Rogers,

Henry's eyes and ears around Collington while Henry was working with the smugglers, had reported the day before that Warwick had departed for London. Perhaps it was time for Henry to follow, both to continue the investigation and to finally see his family. He couldn't put it off much longer.

"Jean, thank you for telling me all of this. I know it's not easy, reliving it…when I left the army—" Henry broke off, struck with sudden inspiration. "If you can get back to France, you will always have a job waiting for you at my family's vineyard. It's hot, dirty, and hard work, but it's a good life, and you'd never have to sail again."

Grabbing the small notebook and pencil he always kept in his pocket, Henry scribbled out his uncle's contact information, signing his name to the bottom.

"Tell him I sent you. And Jean—" the lad looked up at him, a glimmer of hope in his eyes for the first time since Henry had met him. "You'd better go soon. If I'm successful, I hope our employer will be behind bars before long. You don't want to get caught up in that."

"Non, monsieur." Jean coughed into his elbow. "I feel I am coming down with a cold, I may not be at work for a few days."

Grabbing his coat and hat, Henry grasped Jean on the shoulder once more.

"Me too, Jean. It must be going around. Godspeed."

The British museum was everything Emelia had hoped it would be. She felt as if she could spend a week here and barely scratch the surface of the treasures within. Lady R had taken them straight to the Elgin Marbles, wandering through the crowds until they worked their way to the Egyptian antiquities. Emelia was studying a series of masks in a display case, intent on the golden and jade details, when she saw a familiar but unexpected face reflected in the glass beside her.

"Henry!" Emelia turned around in delight. "What are you doing in London?"

The relief she felt upon seeing him again was palpable, and she just refrained from throwing her arms around him in excitement. She'd expected him to be firmly entrenched within his French vineyard by now.

Henry smiled at her in a way that made her heart skip a beat.

"I had a bit of business to finish up in town, and I couldn't leave England without visiting my mother and sister."

"Is that why you're here in the museum?" Emelia craned her neck, looking around for women that could be with Henry. "Are you touring the museum with them?"

Henry grinned, and Emelia blushed at her forwardness. She smoothed her dress and tried to once again look like a proper young lady.

"No, I'm not with them today, but I will be sure to introduce you to them soon. In fact, I called at Lady Ravenscroft's, and the butler helpfully informed me that I could find you all here."

Lady Ravenscroft and Mrs. Seaton were on the other side of the room admiring a glittering case of antique jewelry. Emelia raised a hand to wave them over, but their heads were bent together conspiratorially. Lady Ravenscroft then hustled Emelia's mother around the corner into the next room. When she got to the corner, Lady Ravenscroft turned, winked at Emelia, and shooed her with an elegantly-gloved hand.

Well!

Emelia looked back up at Henry, who was watching her face curiously.

"Would you care to accompany me through the rest of the museum, Henry? It appears I have lost my party."

"I would be delighted."

―――

It had been a long time since Henry had spent such an enjoyable day. He'd toured the whole of the British Museum with Emelia on his arm, her looking as delighted at each and every artifact as if she'd been the archaeologist to personally exhume it. While most young ladies were in the museum to see and be seen, Emelia eagerly read each placard and information sheet. She had a seemingly insatiable appetite for knowledge, and Henry suspected that was the force behind her burning need to see the world. He pointed out objects from the places he'd been, mostly on the Continent, and she listened to each story as if he were the most interesting person in the world. It was enough to puff a man's ego up, and Henry found himself sharing things he hadn't told anyone in years.

By the end of the afternoon, he had told her all about the vineyard, his family, his time in the army, and even about his brother Charles. He had intended to discreetly ask Emelia if Warwick could have returned home for a visit about two years prior, or if she knew of any other gentlemen with a claim on the lighthouse, but he'd been loath to spoil her delight. He'd put it off, then he honestly lost track of time. Warwick was in meetings with his solicitor and couldn't meet with Henry today, so Rogers was keeping an eye on him from a discreet distance while Henry checked in with Emelia. He'd told himself it was to ask questions about Warwick, but he knew it was a sorry excuse. Henry realized it was nearly time for him to relieve Rogers and take the evening shift tailing Warwick, when Mrs. Seaton and Lady Ravenscroft magically reappeared.

Introductions were made, and Lady Ravenscroft's eyes sparkled.

"Ah, I have been wondering about you," she said cryptically. "Would you like to join us for dinner, Mr. Rockcliff?" She saw him hesitate and added, "I believe Lord Warwick is also planning to attend tonight."

She raised an eyebrow at Henry in challenge.

Whether she knew Henry was investigating Warwick, or just thought to inspire a bit of jealousy on Henry's part, she seemed to know more than she should. It was always an admirable quality in a woman, and he already liked her immensely.

"Well then, how am I to resist? Thank you, Lady Ravenscroft, for your kind invitation." Turning on his full English charm, Henry exaggerated his goodbyes, kissing all of the women on the hand in a way that made Emelia laugh and Lady Ravenscroft's eyes crinkle at the edges.

After hurrying back to his hotel to dress and change for dinner, Henry listened as Rogers filled him in on Warwick's schedule while helping him into his tight dinner jacket. The young Baron had spent most of the day at his father's solicitor's office, and had passed a couple of hours in the afternoon at his club. Hardly criminal behavior. Henry wished that he could have left Rogers in Collington to keep an eye on things for him there, but in addition to becoming a passable valet, Rogers had the useful ability to blend into the background life of London. He was much more likely to be unnoticed as a tail than Henry.

Looking in the mirror in his elegant hotel room, Henry was again taken aback at how quickly he could jump between worlds. He ran a hand across his freshly-shaved jaw. Rogers had done a credible job of tying his cravat tonight. Henry had caught him practicing on a bedpost one evening last week when he came in from working at the docks. He supposed it certainly beat scrubbing out Henry's fishy-smelling work clothes. When this was all over, he was going to have to burn them.

Since Warwick was also going to attend Lady Ravenscroft's dinner tonight, Rogers could have a well-deserved night off. Henry had given him a generous bonus and sent him off to the neighborhood pub, albeit reluctantly on Rogers' part. The man still wasn't keen on Warwick and was hesitant to leave Henry without backup, though Henry had assured him he was hardly in any danger at a dinner party. Even if Warwick was somehow involved in the smuggling scheme, he would hardly accost Henry in Lady Ravenscroft's drawing room. *Would he?* Donning his hat and greatcoat, Henry squared his shoulders and walked down the stairs to his awaiting carriage.

Chapter 16

Mayfair, London

The Ravenscroft Mansion was splendid any time of day, but awash in candlelight it was like something from a fairy tale. Emelia's skirts trailed slightly behind her as she walked down the front staircase. The dress her mother and Lady R had dreamed up was one of the most beautiful she'd ever seen, made of the palest blush pink with wide puffed sleeves and a delicate chiffon overlay. Lady Ravenscroft's maid had scattered tiny pink flowers throughout Emelia's hair, which was artfully gathered on top of her head. The whole effect left Emelia feeling like a bouquet of cherry blossoms, which was not her usual preference, but also not nearly as objectionable as she would have thought.

Butterflies forming in her stomach, Emelia crossed the foyer and went in search of her mother and Lady R. The guests should be arriving soon, and Edwin and Henry were both attending tonight. She'd spent a delightful afternoon with Henry at the British Museum, and she was looking forward to seeing him again. And Lady Ravenscroft was expecting a special guest, a man that might prove helpful in the quest to install Monsieur Frensel's lens in Collington and around the country.

Emelia was relieved to find her mother and Lady R waiting to receive their guests in the sitting room. They were discussing the need for a cohesive metropolitan police force, something Emelia would have normally found fascinating. Unfortunately, tonight she found herself restless, and resorted to pacing in front of the large picture window.

Edwin was the first guest to arrive. Emelia had to admit that he looked splendid in his evening wear, his brown eyes sparkling and his hair perfectly coiffed. As he bent to kiss her hand, he gave her an absent smile, and Emelia thought he seemed much less the ardent lover than he had a few days before. Perhaps he was rethinking his offer of marriage after their kiss the other day. Emelia had to admit she would be relieved if he no longer had feelings for her. While she loved Edwin dearly as a friend, she was growing more certain that her care for him could never grow beyond that. She didn't want to hurt him however, and it was taking some time to figure out the best way to tell him they just weren't going to suit. That would be much easier if it turned out he wasn't in love with her at all. Emelia suspected that Edwin had charmed many young women over the years, and perhaps his courtship was simply a passing fancy—no doubt encouraged by her ample dowry. She'd have to have a frank talk with him eventually and ask him if he needed money. Perhaps he was wanting to modernize his estate? She was sure she and her family could be of some assistance. That thought cheering her a bit, she sat in the large window seat and gestured for her friend to join her.

"How was your day, Edwin? You said you had some business to attend to in town?"

"Business? Oh yes, I had to see my father's old solicitor about some estate business, all very boring stuff."

He settled back into the plush cushions and gave her a self-deprecating grin. "I'm afraid I've never had much of a head for numbers. I'm sure my eyes glazed over after the first five minutes. My day was ghastly dull."

"Well, I quite like numbers, and even *I* am glad that mother takes care of our finances," she admitted with a smile.

"Well, when—if—we are married, I will never expect you to keep the books. I will hire a new man straightaway to take care of everything."

Emelia frowned slightly. Edwin was still pursuing her hand

then, even if it was obvious he wasn't actually as in love with her as he had claimed. Perhaps his estate really was in more trouble than it appeared. Laying a hand on his arm, she hesitated.

"Edwin, I—we—should talk about that."

"Now," Edwin continued as if he hadn't heard her, "that isn't to say you can't keep the books if that's something you fancy, being an independent woman and all that. Just that I wouldn't want you to have to worry about such things."

Emelia had a feeling Edwin knew that wasn't what she wanted to talk about, and was opening her mouth to say as much when Carter announced the arrival of a Mr. and Mrs. Hartworth and the Misses Peabody. Edwin rose politely as the guests were brought in.

The Misses Peabody were elderly spinsters who, according to Lady R, had been fast friends with Lady R's mother and were like aunts to her. Mr. Hartworth worked in the government in some capacity, and Lady R had hoped he may be of some use to Emelia and her newfound interest in lighthouse lenses. She was eager to meet him.

"Would you excuse me, Edwin? Lady Ravenscroft was eager for me to meet her friends," Emelia said, not unkindly. "May I find you again to go into dinner?"

"Of course, my love. I will see you soon."

He flashed a practiced smile that likely made most women go weak in the knees.

Crossing the room, Emelia allowed Lady R to introduce her to the newcomers. Mr. Hartworth was a jovial fellow with long, gray mustaches and a monocle that seemed genuinely needed rather than used for effect. He peered at Emelia through it for a moment, and then gestured to Mrs. Seaton.

"I dare say, you're as pretty as your mother is! If you're half as intelligent you'll be a force to be reckoned with."

Mrs. Seaton laughed, and Emelia couldn't help but smile at the old man.

"Emelia, Mr. Hartworth is a scientific enthusiast," her mother explained, "and he always used to attend readings that your father and I frequented."

"Seaton snatched you up as soon as he met you, I recall. The rest of us poor fellows never had a chance. He was a smart one, too," Mr. Hartworth said in a false whisper, winking at Emelia. She liked Mr. Hartworth, and she wasn't going to waste a moment. The dinner bell should be ringing soon.

As was so often the case, Lady Ravenscroft seemed to read Emelia's mind.

"Emelia, Mr. Hartworth is the man I was telling you about. He works for Trinity House, the government authority that deals with our nation's lighthouses. At the moment they're working on buying up as many of the privately-held lighthouses as possible, to create one cohesive, regulated entity."

"Oh! That *is* perfect." Emelia couldn't believe their good fortune. "Mr. Hartworth, there's something I very much wish to talk to you about. Are you familiar with Monsieur Fresnel's new refracting lens?"

Mr. Hartworth scratched his mustaches, considering the matter.

"Hmm…I do remember Robert Stevenson—he's head of all the lighthouses in Scotland, you see—telling me something about it last we met. He even took a prototype back to Scotland to test, I believe. But I don't think anything ever came of it. Tell me, what do you know about this lens?"

Emelia was encouraged that Mr. Hartworth didn't seem to scoff at her interest.

"A friend of mine, Mr. Rockcliff—he'll be here this evening, actually—has met Monsieur Fresnel and studied the lens apparatus. Mr. Rockcliff believes it is the key to revolutionizing the safety of our coastlines. After looking at the data myself, I believe he's right. In fact, our village is on a very dangerous stretch of coastline, and I think it would be an excellent idea to test—*ouch!*"

Emelia broke off and rubbed her arm where Edwin had

grabbed it, hard. There was sure to be a bruise there tomorrow, but what really startled Emelia was the expression on his face. He was looking at her in a dangerous way that she'd never seen before, his eyes flaming.

"Emelia, love," he muttered through clenched teeth, "I think there's something we should talk about. *Now.*"

"Edwin, I am speaking to Mr. Hartworth, and this is extremely rude! Please, can this wait?"

Without answering, Edwin began to drag her by the elbow back towards their alcove by the window. Mrs. Seaton looked as if she was about to lunge at Edwin and slap him, but Emelia held up a hand.

"Please excuse me for just a moment, Mother, Mr. Hartworth. Let me attend to Lord Warwick's obviously *very* pressing need, and I'll be right back with you."

Emelia was surprised at how calm her voice was, but there was a note of steel running through it. Her mother, recognizing her daughter would not allow herself to be manhandled, nodded brusquely.

"I'll be right here if you need me."

Emelia gave her mother a grateful look and allowed Edwin to lead her back towards the window seat. Too furious to sit, she crossed her arms and glared at him, attempting to keep her voice down.

"How *dare* you interrupt and grab my arm like that! I was speaking to Mr. Hartworth."

"Yes, I *know*, and you were about to speak to him about *my* lighthouse. You have no right to meddle in my affairs!"

"Yes! Your lighthouse. The one that you should feel some responsibility for, seeing how it's responsible for the safety of our entire community."

"Emelia, that lighthouse is on my property, and I'll outfit it however I see fit. I don't need anyone from France or—God forbid—from our very own government, coming to tell me how to run it."

Edwin's handsome eyes were sparkling with something

entirely different now, something that looked awfully like malice, and Emelia was taken aback.

"Not even if it's the right thing to do? Not even if it means saving people's lives?"

"Right now the life I'm most interested in saving is mine!"

"What in the world is *that* supposed to mean?"

"It means," said Edwin, his volume inching higher and higher and his jaw clenched, "that you should keep your nose out of my business until we are married."

Emelia's temper flared, and she felt her hands shaking with rage.

"That's another thing we should talk about, because we are certainly not going to—"

"I mean it, Emelia, I *forbid* you to talk to that man."

"You forbid me!"

Emelia, seething, clasped her shaking hands to avoid slapping the man. She had never seen such fury in Edwin's eyes. Fury, but also something that looked remarkably like fear. Emelia felt she had no idea what was really going on here.

She spat out through clenched teeth, "Edwin, I need some answers. Now."

"Excuse me, is there a problem here?" A calm voice spoke softly behind her. Releasing a breath she hadn't realized she'd been holding, Emelia felt a gentle hand at her elbow, guiding her subtly away from Edwin. She'd been inching closer and closer, and their row was about to turn to blows in the middle of Lady Ravenscroft's sitting room.

She looked up gratefully at Henry, some of her anger giving way to embarrassment at the scene they were causing. She'd been so focused on her argument with Edwin she hadn't even heard him arrive. Right on time to rescue her, once again.

"Thank you, Henry. Edwin and I were just having a bit of a disagreement."

She glared at her friend again from a safer distance.

"It was childish of me to continue here in a crowded room, I'm so sorry."

Henry still had one hand clasped gently at Emelia's elbow, as if he was afraid she might go back over to Edwin and slap him. It was still an appealing thought.

"Perhaps we should go over and talk to your mother," Henry suggested, "She looks worried."

His words were directed to Emelia, but she saw his iron gaze locked on Edwin, waiting to see if he would object.

"That's a good idea." Edwin cleared his throat. Smoothing his cravat, he looked as if he was trying to pull himself together.

"I—I'm sorry Emelia, I'm not sure what came over me."

Carter, ever perceptive, suddenly appeared at his elbow with a glass of brandy.

"Perhaps a pre-dinner drink is in order, sir?"

Edwin took it gratefully, and Henry gently steered Emelia back towards her mother and Lady Ravenscroft, both of whom were speaking softly with Mr. Hartworth and his wife.

"What on earth is going on here?" Henry asked softly as they crossed the room. "I entered just when Edwin was forbidding you to talk to someone. That someone wasn't me, by chance, was it?"

Emelia offered him a shaky smile.

"No, that someone was Mr. Hartworth." She nodded ahead of them to the gentleman in question. "He's a representative for Trinity House. They supervise the nation's lighthouses."

"Ah. Unfortunately, that could make sense." Henry sighed, running a hand through his hair and freeing a few strands from his carefully-tied ribbon. For the first time, she noticed how heart-stoppingly handsome he was in his evening wear tonight. Definitely not something she needed to be dwelling on at the moment.

"Emelia, there's something I need to talk to Warwick about, but given that little scene he just made, I'm not sure this is the time." He stopped just before they reached Lady Ravenscroft and her guests, his voice low. "Please, just for this evening, try not to talk about the lighthouse when Warwick is within earshot?"

Emelia felt herself bristle at being told again what she could and couldn't talk about.

"And why shouldn't I talk about whatever topic I want? I mean, yes, Edwin seemed angry tonight, but that's really out of character for him. I don't understand why my talking to Mr. Hartworth upset him so much."

"I think I might, but after witnessing that marvelous display of bullheadedness, it's probably best not to go into it here. Can I call on you tomorrow?"

"We're dining at Lord and Lady Drummonds in the evening, and then attending their ball."

The dinner bell rang to announce it was time for the party to move into the dining room.

"I'll come by in the morning then. Try to avoid Warwick tonight if you can, or at least stick to safer subjects. If you must talk to Mr. Hartworth, make sure I'm close by when you do. I'd like to meet him anyway; he could prove useful. I won't leave here until Warwick does, and I won't allow him to yell at you again—mostly because if he does, I'm not sure I could stop you from decking him."

Henry gave her a lopsided grin, and Emelia felt the tension in her shoulders relax a bit.

"While I admit I'd enjoy seeing that, it would be quite a stain on your reputation here in London, and we can't have that."

"Very true." She nodded with mock seriousness. "It would put quite a damper on my plans for being the season's biggest catch."

"Though, if it should happen and you need to escape to the Continent, I know of a lovely vineyard in France where you could enjoy an extended holiday."

Emelia knew Henry was just attempting to lighten the mood, but an image suddenly flashed into her mind: strolling through a lush vineyard with Henry, hand in hand under blue Provencal skies.

She swallowed hard.

"Yes," Emelia whispered, blinking the image away quickly. "If I need to flee, I'll know exactly where to go."

At that moment, Lady Ravenscroft bustled by, clapping a hand on Henry's back as she passed, and breaking the spell.

"Don't just stand there gaping at the girl, Rockcliff," her godmother boomed, "Escort her to dinner!"

She smiled as Henry offered Emelia his arm, and together they walked to the dining room. Edwin was left to follow the group sulkily, still nursing his brandy.

Emelia watched Edwin carefully all throughout dinner. Lady Ravenscroft had seated him across from Emelia, with one of the elderly Misses Peabody on either side of him. To the casual observer, he seemed his usual charming, entertaining self, but Emelia could detect a shadow behind his eyes and tension in his jaw. Something was definitely troubling him.

Henry was seated to Emelia's left, and she had to wonder if Lady R was plotting a bit of matchmaking. She remembered the way the older woman's eyes had lit up when they'd been introduced that afternoon at the museum, not to mention how quickly she'd managed to abandon Emelia when Henry had arrived. Although she couldn't deny his appeal—her heart seemed to beat a little bit faster lately whenever he was near—Emelia couldn't entertain the thought of another suitor at the moment. Not until she'd figured out what was wrong with Edwin and solved the mystery of this blasted lighthouse.

She was going over and over the last few weeks in her head, wondering if he'd said anything important that she'd overlooked. She was so lost in her thoughts, Henry had to give her foot a tap with his when Mr. Hartworth started speaking to her. Emelia blinked.

"Now, Emelia dear, what was it that you were saying about Mr. Fresnel's lens apparatus?"

Emelia held her breath, and glanced at Edwin, who had stilled. She took a moment to finish chewing a bite of pheasant, wiping her mouth delicately with her napkin, and took a deep breath.

"Just that it sounds remarkable, and it's something we certainly should pay attention to here in England, with as much dangerous coastline as we have. In fact, Mr. Hartworth, this is the Mr. Rockcliff I was telling you about. He has actually met Monsieur Fresnel and seen the lens in person, so he would be a much better source to tell you about it."

She smiled kindly at Mr. Hartworth, and clasped her now-trembling hands on her napkin in her lap. Giving her hand a reassuring squeeze under the table, Henry deftly picked up the conversation.

"Yes, Mr. Hartworth, I have seen it myself. Monsieur Fresnel is a remarkably brilliant man. I'm told you can see the light up to nine miles out to sea."

"Goodness me, that does sound impressive! Do tell me more, young man."

Henry carried on the conversation as the dessert course was served, telling Mr. Hartworth of his trip to Paris, and how he believed the lens could revolutionize the shipping industry. He did not mention Edwin's lighthouse in particular, Emelia noticed, and Edwin did not attempt to join the conversation. In fact, while Henry and Mr. Hartworth were conversing across the table, Edwin was amiably telling the elder Miss Peabody a story about his travels through Italy, though his fingers twirled on the stem of his wine glass in a way that made Emelia was sure he was following every word that was said.

"Well, I will certainly look into the matter, Mr. Rockcliff," rumbled Mr. Hartworth as he wiped the remains of dessert off his mustaches. "Thank you for the information. I may call on you later in the week to discuss this further."

"It would be my pleasure, sir."

Emelia felt a bit lighter as the ladies removed to the sitting room for tea while the gentlemen remained for their cigars and port. Her and Edwin's drawing room row notwithstanding, at least the topic had been introduced to Mr. Hartworth. Even if

Collington wasn't the first place in England to install a Fresnel lens, perhaps its widespread adoption would lead to safer waters all along the coast.

She would fill her mother and Lady R in on her argument with Edwin—what they hadn't been able to overhear from the other side of the room—after the guests had left for the night. For now, she politely answered questions from Mrs. Hartworth and the younger Miss Peabody on how she was enjoying her first London season. The elder Miss Peabody was already dozing in her armchair.

When they were rejoined by the gentlemen, Edwin was all solicitousness again. He gave Emelia such a sincere look of regret that she allowed him to join her by the fireplace.

"Please allow me to apologize again, Emmie," he said softly. "I believe the long day with my solicitor has left me a bit out of sorts. I assure you, it won't happen again."

"We all make mistakes, Edwin. But I certainly will never allow you to speak to me in such a manner again. You are a better man than that."

"If I am, it is because of you and your family."

He gazed across the room to where Henry and Mr. Hartworth were continuing their conversation.

"For a moment, when we were arguing, I heard my father talking, and it truly scared me. That's not the man I want to be—ever."

Emelia squeezed his hand.

"Then don't be that man, Edwin. You can't change the past, but you can choose who you become today."

She saw Henry looking at her questioningly, and she nodded slightly to indicate that she was fine. The danger of getting into another row had passed, at least for now.

Edwin fiddled with his pocket watch, looking uncomfortable.

"Emelia, there's something I need to talk to you about, but not tonight. There's someone I need to meet with tomorrow, and I should be able to explain the whole thing to you very soon."

Emelia sighed.

"There seems to be a rash of subjects that cannot be broached tonight. But Edwin, I need you to know, I can't—we can't—"

"Please," he interrupted, holding up a hand imploringly. "Not yet. Give me two days, and then you can make whatever decision is best for you, and I promise that—as your friend—I will support you."

His eyes flickered across the room again.

"If you don't hear from me in two days, then…well, ask Rockcliff, I expect he'll know where to find me. I suspect he knows nearly everything."

"Where to find you? Are you leaving London?" Emelia threw her hands in the air impatiently. "Edwin, why all this cloak and dagger nonsense? Why can't you just tell me what's going on?"

Edwin bowed low over her hand as he kissed it.

"Because I want to be that better man, Emelia. I owe you that, at least. Give me a chance. I'll see you in two days, okay?"

Frustrated and confused, Emelia watched as he said his goodbyes to the rest of the room and strode purposefully out the door. She had a sinking feeling that this was all far from over.

Chapter 17

Mayfair, London

Bouncing on the balls of his feet, Henry smoothed his cravat and straightened his cuffs, anticipation giving him nervous energy. In light of Warwick's behavior the previous evening, it was past time to tell Emelia everything he'd learned about the smuggling operation in Collington, and Henry had promised her he'd stop by this morning and share everything he knew. While he still wasn't sure if Warwick was the young gentleman Jean had seen on the beach two years ago, given his outburst at Lady Ravenscroft's and the information regarding his finances that Rogers had discovered by chance last night, it seemed likely he was involved in some capacity. Henry was going to have to talk to Rogers about working when he was supposed to have the night off, but in this case, Henry could have kissed him. Who knew Rogers' favorite pub was also the favorite pub of one of Warwick's accountants? And since the fellow hadn't been paid in some time, he was more than willing to share the Baron's private financial details after a few drinks.

Henry was just about to call his hired carriage to take him to the Ravenscroft Mansion once again, when Rogers came into his rented suite of rooms to inform him he had a visitor.

"'Ere's a swell of the first stare to see ye, me boy. When I asked 'im 'is name, he looked at me as iffin I was dicked in the nob!"

Henry mentally ran through the very brief list of acquaintants he still had in London, but to his knowledge, the Seatons, Warwick, and Lady Ravenscroft were the only people that knew he was in town. Henry's overactive imagination was once again whirring. Perhaps something was wrong with Emelia—had Warwick come back last night and threatened her again? He ran down the steps two at a time until he reached the sitting room reserved for his use.

A tall gentleman stood at the fireplace, one arm propped imperiously on the mantle. His hair was gray, but he stood as erect as a tin soldier and stared stoically at Henry in the doorway. Surprise rooted Henry's feet to the floor, and he stared back at the man in shock.

"Father!"

The Viscount looked much as Henry remembered him, though his hair had lost the rest of its color, and his face bore considerably more wrinkles. A million thoughts swirled through Henry's mind. While Henry's mother visited him in France every summer, his father had not even attempted to contact him in the last ten years. Somehow, Henry found his footing and crossed the room cautiously until he stood across from his father. Subconsciously he pulled his shoulders back and stood a little taller. *Old habits die hard*. Suppressing a grimace, Henry cleared his throat.

"Please, take a seat." Henry motioned for his father to sit down on one of the high-backed leather chairs near the fireplace, pleased his voice sounded somewhat steady. The Viscount looked as though he would protest, then nodded stiffly. Henry took the chair opposite him, his posture still carefully erect.

"I hope Mother is well?"

Henry's father leaned back, looking him up and down, and finally spoke.

"You could have come to see her yourself, since you've been back in the country for weeks now."

For a man who hadn't cared that he'd existed for the past ten years, his father was remarkably well-informed.

"Yes, it's true, but I've been out in the country on a business matter. I've only been back in London these past two days. I've been looking forward to visiting Mother soon."

His father was too dignified to grunt, but a sound remarkably like *harrumph* escaped his lips.

"Would you like a brandy?" Henry offered politely. "Or tea perhaps?"

"No, I won't be staying."

The Viscount studied his son's face, eyes lingering on the jagged scar and the wrinkles around his eyes from years of working in the hot Provencal sun.

"It seems France agrees with you. Henry. I..."

The Viscount trailed off, looking uncomfortable, and Henry fully expected him to say that he wished Henry would have stayed in France. Well, the old man was going to have to deal with seeing his son now and then. If things went the way Henry hoped, he'd be coming back to England a lot more in the future. He wondered at the way so much could change in a few short weeks. Grandmere always said that life had a way of surprising you.

"I'm glad you came, Father." Henry spoke to fill the void, but to his surprise, he actually felt it.

"And I...I'm glad to see you looking well, Henry. You've grown up."

The Viscount cleared his throat hurriedly.

"Your mother would like to request that you dine with us tomorrow evening. Unless you have other plans."

He raised his eyebrows as if daring Henry to be occupied elsewhere. As Henry was still shocked at the closest thing to affection his father had offered him in decades, he simply nodded dumbly.

His father stood, retrieving his beaver hat from a nearby side table.

"I was in the neighborhood, so I promised your mother I would ask you in person. I suppose we'll see you at Lord Drummond's ball tonight, then?"

Did his father know the whole of his social calendar? Henry was going to have to speak with Rogers about keeping his personal details a bit more personal.

"Um, yes sir, I'll be there."

"Perhaps we'll meet your young lady then, eh?"

Henry was still staring, stupefied, as his father chuckled his way out the door.

~

Still in shock from his father's unprecedented social call, Henry fetched his overcoat and hat and was about to depart when Rogers burst through the door once more.

"Yer to wish me at Jericho, likely, but th' lad said it was urgent from me Lord, a matter of life 'n deaf."

Again Henry strode down to the sitting room, and was only slightly less surprised to see his second visitor of the day than the first. Jean, the boy smuggler, was clean shaven, his clothes clean and nicely mended. He held his cap in his hands and stood by the window.

"Bienvenue, Monsieur!"

Henry smiled at the boy in welcome. Ever perceptive, Jean glanced at Henry's attire and apologized for catching him on his way out.

"I cannot stay," the boy said nervously in French. "No one should see me here with you. Only it was so important, and I'm leaving the country tomorrow anyway—"

Henry could see that Jean was troubled, and asked him gently what he could do to help.

"I have been—sick—all week, making plans to leave for Calais tomorrow, but one of the other men, a friend, stopped by to check on me."

He must have seen the flash of concern in Henry's eyes, for he hurried to reassure him.

"No, no, he would never tell otherwise to Monsieur Mallory, he is to be trusted. And if not, well—" Jean gave a gallic shrug. "I will not be around to find out, no? But my friend, he shares my concerns, and he told me there is a large shipment of French wine, larger than any we usually see around Collington, set to pass by within the next two days. It is rumored to be bound for a nobleman's personal collection, and the ship is to be crewed by the finest sailors France can find. Mallory has gotten too confident, and he aims to wreck this ship, steal its cargo, and murder its crew."

The young man sighed, looking far older than his years.

"I could not leave for France in good conscience without telling someone first."

Henry's mind whirled. Within the next two days. He needed to talk to Warwick, soon, and try to discover how the smugglers were making the lighthouse appear to move miles up the coast. Before a whole ship of sailors just like Charles met a gruesome end.

"Jean, thank you for the risk you took in coming here." The young man was fidgeting where he stood, obviously eager to leave. Henry crossed to the desk in the corner, and scribbled a quick note of introduction.

"Here, if you make your way down to Provence, talk to my uncle, and give this letter to my grandmere. He will make sure you have a job, and she will find you a place to live."

Henry dug into his pocket and pulled out a handful of coins.

"This should help you until you get there."

The youth's face reddened, but he did not refuse the money. He nodded, once.

"Thank you, monsieur. God willing, I will see you in Provence."

The two men shook hands, and the lad slipped out the door, fading into the busy London streets.

Henry had much to do.

∽

Hours later, Henry was alone at the edge of a ballroom awash in candlelight, watching as Emelia whirled around Lord Drummond's dance floor with a young dandy. The Drummonds had spared no expense for tonight's entertainment, and the ball was sure to be talked about as the most lavish of the season.

The ballroom glittered as the light of a thousand candles bounced off exquisite chandeliers, while countless fortunes' worth of jewels draped around the necks of society's finest added their own glow. Just outside of the open terrace, peacocks strutted through the formal gardens, while inside the ballroom champagne flowed freely from tiny fountains at each corner of the room. Closer to Henry, a group of young debutantes were wearing such lavishly beaded dresses that he was surprised they could move at all, much less dance. His eyes found their way back to Emelia on the dance floor seemingly of their own accord.

It was a strange contrast from the gravity of the afternoon. After Jean had left, Henry had reluctantly abandoned his plan to visit Emelia, and had instead attempted to track down Warwick for the remainder of the afternoon. He'd tried Warwick's townhouse, his club, even his solicitor's office. Rogers' efforts had been only marginally more profitable, as he finally learned from a servant that Warwick was "out on a matter of business" and would return shortly to ready himself for the Drummond's ball. Henry had eventually given up waiting when it was time to dress himself for the occasion, and hoped to run Warwick to ground at the ball tonight.

So far, no one had seen the young Baron. Henry was beginning to feel anxious.

The ten-piece orchestra was playing a reel, and Emelia was laughing as she worked her way through the exuberant steps. Her eyes still sparkled as brightly as they did the day he'd met her out on the fields. Henry was glad she appeared untroubled from the previous evening's quarrel with Warwick. He'd hated having to postpone his visit today, but in light of the grave timeline Jean had presented him with, he'd figured it much more important to question the Baron. If only the man hadn't vanished. Henry sighed and allowed his eyes to scan the ballroom once more, allowing them to rest again on Emelia after he determined Warwick still hadn't arrived.

He wasn't one to pay much attention to women's fashions, but even he could see that the dress Emelia was wearing was much simpler than most of the young ladies' present. The cream-colored silk hugged her figure perfectly and made her complexion glow. Her hair was bound simply at the nape of her neck, a few curls spilling artfully down her back. The whole ensemble brought to mind a Greek goddess, the lovely Persephone once more. It nearly took Henry's breath away.

She wasn't one of the ethereal, wispy beauties that was so popular when he'd been briefly in society. She was far too corporeal for that, all coiled energy ready to spring into action at a moment's notice. He wouldn't be surprised if she'd found a way to hide her quiver under that ball gown, just in case. He smothered a laugh and tried to pass it off as a cough when the dowager standing a few feet away from him sent him a glare. He supposed that laughing at the young ladies out on the dance floor was generally frowned upon.

While he waited for Emelia to finish her dance, Henry searched the ballroom for his parents. As the festivities were only now underway, it appeared they hadn't arrived yet. His mother had always enjoyed being fashionably late.

The music came to an end, and Emelia spotted him from across the ballroom. She was waving her dance card around, and mouthing what looked like "*bonne chance!*" Supposing she meant one more dance, and he smiled and nodded at her to show he understood. The dowager glared at him again, so Henry surmised that signaling to young debutantes across the ballroom was frowned upon as well. His manners were a little rusty, after all.

Walking towards the refreshment table for something to do, he busied himself by grabbing a glass of champagne while he carefully observed the room around him. Downing the champagne in one gulp, Henry cringed. If Lord Drummond had spent as lavishly on the champagne as he had on the rest of the ball, he was afraid the man had been swindled. Henry might not be any good at making wine, but he certainly could drink it. Perhaps

England was left to purchase the wine that the French couldn't bring themselves to drink.

Scanning the crowd, Henry spotted a tall blonde woman striding towards him with a determined look in her eye. He straightened his shoulders and grinned as his sister, Angelica, now Lady Haverton, strode across the room with a determined look in her eye. Clearly, she'd spotted him and was charging like Ares into battle. She'd always been a force of nature, and while he was genuinely pleased to see her, he wasn't sure if he should be opening his arms for an embrace or dodging a fierce right hook. He noticed she was wearing a gown of shimmering charcoal silk, and her smooth peaches and cream complexion could not quite hide the darker circles under her eyes. If she was in mourning clothes, but out in society, then—Henry was calculating how long he'd been away from Grandmere's, what news he'd missed.

"Henry! Do my eyes deceive me or is it really you?"

Angelica held out a trembling gray-gloved hand, and he kissed it gently. She seemed genuinely happy to see him, a broad smile across her beautiful face.

"What magic brings you back home to us?" She spoke in a half-whisper, as if afraid of scaring him away if she spoke too loudly. "I was firmly convinced I would never again see you on English soil!"

Holding him out at arms length, his sister looked him over slowly, from his calloused palms to his scarred face.

"Are you quite well?" she added in an unsteady voice, her eyes bright with unshed tears.

Henry looked down at her, the sudden lump of emotion in his throat nearly more than he could bear. This lovely young woman was so unlike the fourteen-year-old girl he'd bid adieu nearly a decade ago, her leaning out the schoolroom window waving her handkerchief as he rode down the path towards his regiment. He'd seen her a few times since then in Provence on her summer holidays from school, but it was that image that burned in his mind as he regarded her now.

"I am quite well," he replied, not letting go of her hand but keeping it within his own for a moment.

"I'm simply only old and wrinkled by the sun. But you—has Haverton—?" Henry broke off, not knowing how to ask. They'd never been especially close, but he felt like an idiot not to have known that his sister was recently widowed.

Angelica nodded sadly.

"Yes, I'm afraid Lord Haverton passed last autumn. I did write to you, but Grandmere wrote back. Apparently by the time my letter reached you, you'd already left Provence."

"I was in Paris on business for a while before I came back to England. Are you okay, you and…" Henry trailed off, realizing he didn't even remember her children's names. The oldest one was a boy, he knew that. The other? He had no idea.

"You and the children," he finished lamely. He knew their father had brokered the match between Angelica and her husband, Lord Haverton. His mother had been delighted to have an Earl in the family, but Henry had never asked his sister's sentiments on the matter.

"I'm not broken-hearted, if that's what you're referring to, *Hen-ri*." Angelica used the French pronunciation of his name with a glint in her eye. Henry knew it to be more mischievous than malicious. She sighed, her elegant posture looking suddenly weary, and gestured to a set of ornate chairs in an alcove behind them.

"We certainly weren't a love match—Lord Haverton was two decades my senior, as you know—but he was kind and generous, and he did dote upon the children, which is more than I can say for many of my friends' husbands."

She looked out at the well-dressed and glittering couples around the room, nodding politely to acquaintances and each other in the same indifferent fashion.

"Still, he took good care of us, and we'll want for nothing until little Charles comes of age and assumes the title."

Henry's breath caught in his throat. *Charles*. Angelica had named her firstborn after their younger brother. He would have been very proud. Years ago it had felt like he was the only person in the world that mourned his brother's death. But then again, it would feel that way when one was in exile, wouldn't it?

"Father may have made the match with Haverton," she said softly, correctly interpreting the emotion in Henry's eyes, "but I've never regretted it."

Henry felt a sudden wave of guilt wash over him. He'd been so preoccupied with recovering from his own trauma, he hadn't stopped to think about his sister and her experiences at all. In the last decade she'd grown up, been married, widowed, and was now raising two children alone. He could count on one hand the number of letters he'd written to her since she'd been married, and he'd never even attempted to meet her children. Perhaps his precious peace had been more costly than he'd realized.

Angelica squeezed his hand again.

"Don't beat yourself up like you do, Henry. We've all had to heal in our own way. You're here now. Let's make the most of it. You can start by introducing me to this girl of yours."

"Angie, she's not my girl, I mean, not yet—I mean, how did you?"

Henry ceased his inarticulate mumbling and sighed, running his fingers through hair that was already escaping from its respectable ties.

"Over there, dancing a quadrille in the Grecian gown."

Angelica's eyes lit up.

"Oh, she *is* lovely," she breathed. "She looks formidable, too. No wonder Lady Ravenscroft dotes on her so."

Ahh, Lady Ravenscroft. His family's sudden knowledge of his life was beginning to make sense.

"I take it Lady Ravenscroft and Mother are the best of friends, then?" Henry asked dryly.

"Oh yes, they've become quite close in recent years. I believe Lady Ravenscroft and her house guests are joining us for dinner tomorrow evening."

Well, that would speed the introductions up, at least.

"In fact," continued Angelica, "Lady Ravenscroft has been quite a good influence on Mother. She seems to have gained a bit of backbone in her old age, and rather than angering Father as you would expect, well, he seems to respect her more for it."

Henry stared at her in awe.

"Fascinating. Did you know that Father came to visit me this morning?"

"Oh yes, we all wanted to be the first to come see you, but he insisted."

"Truly? I would have thought him happy to be rid of me."

"Oh no. He could never admit it aloud, of course, but I think he's missed you, Henry. Randolph is always Randolph, you know. Dines at his club, keeps to his own business, does everything properly, that sort of thing. But you were the only one that dared challenge Father, Henry. You and Charles were the only ones of us who dared to think for yourselves. It rankled him, for sure, but I think he didn't realize what a strength that was until he'd lost you both."

Henry was still digesting all of these things as Lady Ravenscroft glided towards them, her arm looped through Emelia's. Emelia's cheeks were flushed from dancing, her eyes laughing as a few wayward curls floated around her face. As Lady Ravenscroft embraced Angelica, his sister winked at him over the older woman's shoulder and mouthed, "She's stunning!"

Henry suddenly felt the room growing very warm and pulled at his cravat.

"Angelica, may I present Miss Emelia Seaton. Emelia, this is my sister, Lady Angelica Haverton."

Her grin widening, Angelica clasped Emelia's white-gloved hand.

"If you have the admiration of my brother *and* Lady Ravenscroft, I suspect we'll become very good friends, indeed."

Emelia smiled prettily, and Henry felt his heart tighten a bit.

"Such good friends," Angelica continued, raising an eyebrow, "that I shall expect to borrow that gorgeous gown as soon as I put off mourning."

At this, Emelia laughed.

"Lady Haverton, it would be my honor. Lord knows I'll never have a chance to wear it again after we leave London. There are no occasions quite so grand in Collington."

"Do you enjoy a quiet life in the country, Miss Seaton?"

"I'm beginning to realize I'm better suited for it than a life in town, though I would also like to travel abroad someday."

Upon seeing the mischievous look on his sister's face, Henry grabbed Emelia's hand as couples began taking positions on the dancefloor.

"I believe this is my dance, Emelia. Angelica, Lady Ravenscroft, if you will excuse us."

He gave Angelica a look he hoped said, *Don't you dare. We'll talk later.*

She grinned and shooed him towards the dance floor.

A surprise visit from his father, an impending shipwreck, and now a meddling sister. This day certainly hadn't turned out to be boring.

As the musicians struck up a waltz, Emelia looked up at Henry as he took her hand in his, his other arm slipping easily around her waist.

"Your sister is quite lovely," she said, suddenly nervous as they joined the other couples gliding around the dance floor. Forcing herself to breathe, she focused on the steps of the dance.

"Lady R was explaining that Lady Haverton was recently widowed, but she was much younger than I expected her to be."

"She's not yet twenty-five," Henry confirmed. "She was still in the schoolroom when I left England. She has always been a force to be reckoned with, though, even as a girl. Kind of like you, I expect."

Henry raised a teasing eyebrow and the arm around her waist tightened.

For some reason she had not expected Henry to be such a proficient dancer, but ten years out of society hadn't seemed to affect his skills, and he was graceful and steady. The guiding hand at her back was gentle yet confident, and was sending curious little shivers up her spine.

Very curious. Curious and familiar.

Oh! Oh, dear.

Remembering the jolt of electricity she'd felt when she'd grabbed Henry's hand in the thunderstorm all those weeks ago, Emelia's stomach dropped. She'd assumed it was the charged air, but here they were, waltzing in the middle of a ballroom, and her hand was tingling in her glove from where it was clasped in his. She looked up and studied his face. His eyes were as blue as a cloudless sky, and he looked every bit a Viscount's son in his evening wear tonight, despite the scars and slightly disheveled hair.

While he was handsome enough to attract the attention of every woman in the ballroom—he received more than a few lingering glances as they waltzed around the dance floor—Emelia knew that Henry was so much more than a handsome face. He was kind and perceptive, and he'd come to her rescue more times than she cared to admit.

Her heart pounding as they stepped in time together, Emelia thought about the whole, terribly awkward situation she found herself in. She hadn't even officially rejected the proposal of another man, and it was becoming very obvious to her that she was falling in love with this one! She spared a quick glance around the crowded room, wondering if it was as glaringly obvious to everyone else as it suddenly was to her. Were matters of the heart always this irrational? It was highly inefficient.

"Are you quite alright?" Henry looked at her with concern. "You're a bit flushed, and it is rather warm in here. Should we stop dancing and find you a drink?"

"Oh no! I'm fine really." Emelia forced a smile, suddenly not able to bear the thought of stepping away from him. "Let's finish the dance first. It *is* rather warm, but one gets so few opportunities to dance in Collington, I do hate to miss out."

She looked up at him, and he grinned back, eyes twinkling, and continued to twirl them around on the dance floor. That grin was doing strange things to her insides, and she was afraid he knew she was reluctant to stop dancing because then she'd no longer be held like this in his arms.

"The waltz is really quite unexceptionable nowadays, or so I am told," he was saying. Okay, maybe he didn't know *exactly* what she was thinking, since he must have taken her inner turmoil as uncertainty about the dance. "I can't say there have been any opportunities to waltz in Provence recently. But your mother said you were cleared to waltz by the patronesses of Almack's last week, and you're doing an excellent job, so you have nothing to worry about."

Emelia smiled, relieved her feelings weren't quite so obvious, and couldn't refrain from teasing him just a little.

"I'm not *quite* a country bumpkin, you know. Despite our rather reclusive life, my father made sure we benefited from the most renowned dance instructors on their touring circuits every winter."

Emelia's eyes glittered as she remembered her father whirling around the music room with her as she practiced her steps.

"Father knew we would mingle in society one day, and wanted to make sure we were equally at home here among the *ton* as we were in the village. He was quite the progressive, my father. He firmly believed in equality among men."

She looked up at Henry thoughtfully.

"He was rather adept at making friends in every social class. I think he would have liked you."

He returned her gaze just a shade too long, which made her start to blush again, but he quickly looked away as if sensing her discomfort.

"Your mother holds quite the court." He nodded his head towards where her mother sat surrounded by fashionable ladies and gentlemen. Emelia noticed she'd been joined by Lady R and Lady Haverton.

"I've been learning a lot about my mother that I never thought to ask before we came to London," she admitted.

Henry looked at her expectantly.

"Well, apparently my mother was quite the thing in her day, if you can believe it. I always assumed that since she was older when she married my father that she wasn't popular among the *ton*, but I'm told she took the town by storm during her come-out. She even turned down an offer of marriage from an Earl!"

Emelia chuckled, still not quite able to believe it herself.

"Since she was quite wealthy she determined she wasn't going to marry except for the most profound love, and that's exactly what she did. I don't think she's missed being fawned over, but she is very glad to be back with Lady Ravenscroft."

She looked over at her mother, resplendent in her navy gown, her hair only lightly streaked with gray. Her arm was linked with Lady Ravenscroft's and they were laughing at something a dashing older gentleman was saying. For the first time, Emelia wondered if her mother would ever remarry. She was beginning to realize her mother was still quite a catch.

"My family has been full of surprises lately as well," answered Henry cryptically, shaking his head.

"But what about you, Emelia? Do you want to be the toast of the town like your mother?"

He raised an eyebrow, a twinkle in his eye.

"I assure you that you could be, and you're likely well on your way. Or are you, like your mother, content with a quiet life?"

His words were lighthearted enough, but he seemed to be waiting intently for her answer.

"Well," Emelia began, "I rather like a quiet life in the country, at least most of the time, but—" she broke off, unsure about how to explain.

Henry continued to glide her around the dance floor, patiently waiting for her to collect her thoughts.

"London is a lovely place to visit, but you'd think it was the whole world, for all that people's lives revolve around this place. But I want to go so much further—Paris, and Spain, and Rome. I'd even go to India if I could get that far. I know our little corner of the earth is just one very small part, and would very much like to see and smell and taste the rest of it. The dusty roads and the crumbling ruins seem no less glamorous to me than this ballroom."

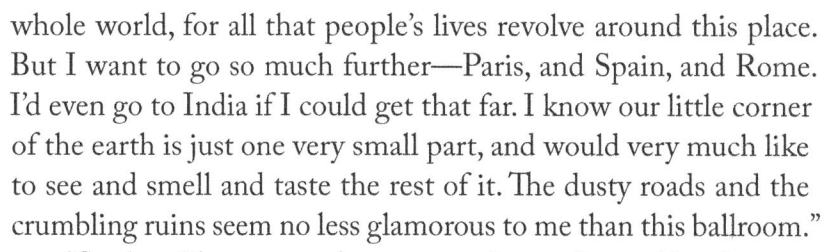

"Spoken like a true adventurer at heart. So you'd rather see than be seen?"

Emelia was relieved that he understood. Most gentlemen scoffed at a woman's desire to see the world.

"Yes, I suppose you could put it that way."

Henry's arm wrapped around her a little bit tighter, a new lightness to his steps.

"You would love my grandmere. She marches to the beat of her own drum, so to speak, and she reminds me a bit of your mother."

"Is your mother much the same, then? Lady Ravenscroft talks about her quite fondly, but I haven't yet had the honor of meeting her."

"My mother..." Henry hesitated. "She isn't as self assured as Grandmere, or you and your mother for that matter. She's always looked for someone with a stronger personality to guide her. Unfortunately, my father's harsher personality has always overshadowed her gentler one."

Emelia looked up into his handsome face, but he was miles—perhaps years—away.

"It's very important to me that, when I marry, I marry someone who knows who and what they are. Someone who's comfortable in her own skin, who won't try to shape herself to be someone that I, or anyone else, wants her to be."

His blue eyes looked suddenly serious.

"Don't ever change yourself to make someone else think better of you, Emelia. The people that matter will never ask that of you."

He looked straight into her eyes, and Emelia's heart was pounding. What if he held her in affection as well? She hadn't dared to hope, but the way he was looking at her made her wonder. Before she had time to sort her jumbled thoughts, the music ended and couples began leaving the dance floor while the musicians tuned their instruments for the next set.

"Bravo!" Henry gave her a little bow. "You can tell your mother those dance instructors did their jobs quite well. Now, I'm parched. Shall we fetch some lemonade and discuss why Warwick was acting so strangely last night? I don't have all the answers as of yet, but I think I'm getting closer. We need to include your mother and Lady Ravenscroft in this discussion as well."

Emelia took his offered hand and walked back towards where her mother was sitting. Despite the difficult conversation ahead, dancing with Henry had left her insides feeling as though she was floating on a carpet of clouds.

―

Unfortunately, those happy clouds dissipated quickly. Squirming uncomfortably in a hard-backed wing chair, her current emotional state was somewhere between shock and fury.

When they'd joined Mrs. Seaton and Lady Ravenscroft on the edge of the ballroom, Henry had requested a few words with them. Before he could go any further, Lady Ravenscroft held up a hand.

"I believe this is a conversation better held in a more private location," she said simply, and had led them to an unused parlor off the main entrance hall. There was a fire smoldering in the grate, and only a few candles lit. It gave the room a sobering, serious feel after the gaiety of the ballroom.

Once they'd settled around the fire, Henry told them the entire story about his true purpose in Collington and the real reason he wanted to introduce Monsieur Fresnel's lens. In light of Edwin's recent behavior, all the pieces seemed to be falling into place, but she still couldn't quite come to terms with it.

"You mean, Edwin *knows* about the smugglers using his lighthouse to sabotage ships, and he hasn't done anything about it?"

It was a question Emelia found herself asking more than once.

Henry grimaced, pulling his spectacles out of a little pocket in his vest, and consulted a few crumpled notes he'd pulled out of another pocket along with a small pencil.

"I don't know that for sure, but it's likely. It seems as though Warwick is in considerable debt. Rogers, my valet and assistant, had a very interesting conversation with one of Warwick's accountants last night while we were having dinner. It looks as though the estate he inherited was already badly mortgaged. Apparently Warwick's father was quite the gambler, a trait the younger Warwick unfortunately shares. Add to that his extensive travels and gambling debts from the Continent, and there is virtually no way he could ever pay off his debts with his current resources. Even if he sold the estate, it was mismanaged for so long, there's little of worth left. Anything of real value has already been mortgaged. It's possible the smugglers found out about this debt, and threatened him with debtors' prison if he didn't allow them access to his lighthouse. These men wouldn't hesitate to have him killed."

"Oh no. Poor Edwin," Mrs. Seaton murmured, a hand over her mouth. Her other hand worried the long beads around her neck.

At the moment, anger came much more readily to Emelia than sympathy.

"But he lied to us. To me! He told me he loved me, when all he really wanted was my money, to save his own neck!" Emelia shook with rage. "All it would take is one anonymous tip to the authorities, and he could have stopped this whole thing and saved countless lives!"

Henry smiled sadly. "Not everyone is as noble as you, Emelia. We need to talk to Warwick, and see if he knows how the smugglers are making the light appear up the coast. My best guess is that there's a lantern and a second reflector somewhere, but I have no idea where they're hiding it. The matter is somewhat urgent. A source of mine came to me this afternoon and informed me of the group's plans to sabotage a large shipment of French wine destined for a prominent member of the *ton*. It's due to pass by within the next two days. Rogers and I searched for Warwick all afternoon, but haven't been able to find him. I was told he had planned to be here tonight, but the evening's nearly over and he hasn't made an appearance."

Emelia groaned.

"He said he had something to take care of, something that would make him a better man."

Lady R gave a sort of *humph*, and Henry chewed on the end of his pencil.

"Perhaps he's trying to back out of his agreement, if there indeed is one. For his sake, I wish he wouldn't just yet. He's no match for Mallory, to be sure, and I hear this John Colson fellow is even worse."

"Oh, Edwin."

Emelia felt tears coming to her eyes as fury gradually gave way to concern. The man may have been a complete idiot, but she couldn't bear the thought of her childhood friend coming to such a bad end.

"Since he didn't show tonight, I will send a message once again to his London townhouse. If he's in town, I will endeavor to meet him tomorrow. Perhaps in Hyde park, at the fashionable hour when everyone is out walking. He wouldn't dare cause a stir in front of a crowd of witnesses, and if he's as desperate for a way out as he seems to be," Henry glanced at Emelia with sympathy, "we just might be able to help each other."

Lady Ravenscroft met Henry's eyes for a moment and gave a slight nod. Emelia knew what they must be thinking. They were in no physical danger from Edwin, but the smugglers were another story. Hopefully they'd also hesitate to cause a scene in a busy park.

Mrs. Seaton agreed grimly. "Do be careful, Henry. Since it *is* such a public place, surely there can't be any danger. See if you can get Edwin to come back to Lady Ravenscroft's with you after you talk. I'm sure we can figure out a solution that doesn't involve him going to prison—or marrying my daughter."

Chapter 18

It wasn't as if they were *really* trying to keep her from going, Emelia reasoned with herself as she climbed down the trellis outside the Ravenscroft's library window. Henry had sent word early this morning that he and Edwin were to meet today at the park. She'd asked again politely over breakfast for permission to join them, but both her mother and Lady R were uncharacteristically lacking in their sense of adventure today. Something about smugglers being involved—despite the fact that those smugglers were miles away in Kent—had prompted Mrs. Seaton to abandon her egalitarian tendencies and inform Emelia that this wasn't a job for a young lady. Surprisingly, Lady R had agreed.

"I'm sure Henry will bring Edwin here after he's talked some sense into him," she'd reassured Emelia, "and we can help them sort out all the details then. No need to goad Edwin into causing a scene in Hyde park."

She'd looked at Emelia pointedly, as if knowing she weren't perfectly capable of keeping her temper in check when it came to Edwin. Their noisy row in the drawing room the other night may have given her a clue.

But even despite these objections, when Emelia excused herself to the library to read after breakfast, they should have seen the bulge where she'd stuffed her reticule into her pocket. Or they should have noticed that she had a lavender wrap around her shoulders—one that perfectly matched her lavender and blue printed floral morning dress, thanks to her mother's fashion sense—while the library was already perfectly warm with a comfortable fire crackling in the grate.

A Brilliant Convergence

No, her mother and Lady R were both highly intelligent, observant individuals. So if they'd really wanted her to stay home instead of sneaking out to meet Henry and Edwin, they would have stopped her, right? Emelia comforted herself with these thoughts while she jumped the last two feet down to the ground, brushed herself off, and walked calmly out the side gate in the direction of Hyde Park.

Henry strolled through Hyde park with Emelia on his arm, his clenched jaw the only indication this wasn't a friendly social outing. He was still furious that she'd shown up at the park, and without a chaperone or her mother's permission. It was just like something Angelica would have done, he thought grimly. Hopefully Mrs. Seaton had been right, and there would be no danger in meeting Warwick in a very public place.

His aching head told him otherwise.

Warwick had responded to his note first thing this morning, admitting nothing but that he was in a jam and could use Henry's help. Henry glanced around the park vigilantly, trying to look for all the world like another nob out for an afternoon stroll. Rogers trailed along behind at a respectful distance, ostensibly as chaperone, but more importantly to watch Henry's back.

Emelia, a smile pasted on her face as she nodded to fashionably dressed men and women strolling through the park, rested a gloved hand at his elbow. He could feel the tension in her fingers, so he knew she shared some of his apprehension.

Henry tried to think of another way to convince her to go home and wait for him there. His last attempt had been futile, Emelia glaring at him while he insisted he would have to bodily remove her and carry her away. As distracting as that particular image was, he didn't have the time for such antics, nor did he want to make a scene. So he was forced to reluctantly agree to her involvement. He comforted himself with the fact that, as much as an unconscionable rogue as Warwick might be, he seemed to truly care for Emelia and would not do her harm. He hoped.

He was scheduled to meet Warwick at a bench near the Serpentine in about ten minutes, and Henry rubbed the back of his neck again.

"Why do you that?" Emelia's soft voice was curious.

"Do what?"

"Rub that one spot at the base of your skill. I've seen you do it several times this morning, but I seem to remember you rubbing that same spot that day we went sailing. Do you get headaches?"

Henry took a deep breath. This wasn't a topic he had planned to broach right now.

"I…well."

She was going to have to know sooner or later. Henry sighed in resignation.

"Yes, I do get headaches, but not the usual kind. These are more of a sense. A feeling that warns me when danger is near, or that I should be careful of something. I've had them ever since I was a kid, but it wasn't until I was in the army that I figured out it only happened right before something bad was about to happen, when someone's safety was in jeopardy. It wasn't just an anxious headache like I'd always assumed."

He'd only ever told his mother and family in Provence, and more recently, Emelia's brother, about his *gift*. His cousin Maurice had laughed and teased him for a whole summer until Henry saved him from what could have been a deadly fall from a ladder in the vineyards, before anyone else even knew he was in peril. He'd never laughed at Henry after that.

Emelia looked at Henry closely, and he held his breath. He knew a sixth sense sounded crazy. She had every right to turn around and walk the other direction as fast as she could. In fact, he hoped she would. He looked down at her, hoping she'd come to her senses and decide to return to Lady Ravenscroft's. Though it might not bode well for his future hopes, at least it would keep her safe for today.

Henry saw a dimple appear on the side of her cheek. The wretch was trying not to smile. Henry didn't know whether to hug her or wring her neck.

"So, you knew I was in danger before anyone else on the boat didn't you?"

Henry swallowed. He'd never been more grateful for his gift than that day.

"Yes. I jumped in just after you'd hit the water."

"I wondered, that long week I was sick in bed, how you managed to be the first one to me when you were on the opposite side of the boat."

Henry raised his eyebrows.

"You're very perceptive."

"Oh!" Emelia put a hand to her mouth. "That's why you said you ducked because you knew my arrow was coming! I thought your brain had been truly addled by the shock."

"So you don't think me addled now? You probably should, you know."

"Not at all. As a scientist of sorts, I must allow that we do not know everything about the universe, or the human body. There could very well be some sort of inherited trait for your special gift. A genetic anomaly, if you will."

Henry looked at her sharply.

"As I don't want to be studied as an anomaly, you can see why it's important that this isn't general public knowledge."

Emelia's eyes grew wide.

"Oh! Oh course. I promise I won't tell a soul. It really does explain so much. I've always felt that you were quite a safe person to be with, despite your roguishly handsome exterior—oh!"

Emelia bit her lip, her cheeks bright red, and despite his nervousness, Henry felt his heart lighten a bit.

"Roguishly handsome, huh?"

"I am so sorry, that was terribly forward of me. I mean, you *are* roguishly handsome, of course—it's not like you don't have a mirror, you know this—but polite ladies don't go around saying such things."

Henry couldn't help but smile slightly at her flustered rambling and raised her hand to his lips.

"You, Emelia, are delightfully refreshing, not to mention good for my ego."

He found it hard to stay cross with Emelia for long. Tucking her hand gently back into the crook of his arm, he turned to look her in the eye.

"There's much more I'd like to discuss with you, and I still wish you hadn't come today, but we must focus on the task at hand. Perhaps Warwick will open up to you more freely than he would to me on my own."

As the words left his mouth, Rogers cleared his throat a few feet behind him.

"The leery 'toff is 'ere, me Lord. And 'e's sportin' a shiner."

Sure enough, Henry looked towards the bench where they were supposed to meet Warwick. He was standing there, dressed in his afternoon best, a blackened eye and cheek visible despite a beaver hat perched at a rakish ankle.

"Edwin!"

Emelia called out in alarm, then remembering she was in a public place, allowed Henry to lead her casually to Warwick's side, saying in a normal voice in full earshot of a pair of dowagers strolling by, "Edwin, how nice to run into you this morning."

Edwin smiled and bowed, seemingly at ease, and gave a self-deprecating grimace.

"Please, excuse me, Emelia, dear, for my appearance. I'm afraid I had a bit of an accident with a borrowed horse. He took a dislike to me."

"Oh, that's terrible, I do hope you learned your lesson and won't ride the horse again."

She looked at him pointedly.

"Certainly, madam, it will never enter my mind."

"Would you care to walk with us, Lord Warwick?" Henry

pointed towards a manicured floral path, still in full view of the park but out of earshot of the now-curious dowagers.

Edwin fell lazily into step beside them, and they strolled down the path three-abreast.

"I believe I've met your man before," said Edwin cheerfully, tilting his head slightly to where Rogers still walked dutifully behind.

"Ah, yes, he's been your shadow the last few days in London. Well, until you disappeared on us."

"How long have you known, old chap? And who are you really?"

"I've debated your involvement for some time, but I only learned about your, um, financial difficulties by chance two days ago."

"And are you some sort of government tool then, an undercover excise man?"

"Not at all, I am merely who I say I am—a former army officer and Provencal farmer with a vested interest in making the English coastline a safer place. I do not work for the government. I take little issue with smuggling, but I do have a problem with murder."

Warwick had the grace to look abashed.

"I *did* meet with Monsieur Fresnel," Henry continued, "and I *am* a proponent of his lens, but I came to Collington specifically at the behest of a friend in the army. He had his suspicions about the number of shipwrecks, and he needed someone who wasn't known in the area, someone who could easily blend in to the smuggler's world, or to yours, to come investigate."

"And you played the part admirably. Was it all a game?" Warwick glanced briefly at Emelia, who still strolled uncharacteristically quietly on Henry's other side.

"In the important things, I've been quite truthful."

Warwick nodded.

"Good."

"Edwin." Emelia's voice sounded strangled, and she cleared her throat and tried again, stronger this time. "Edwin, if you are involved in all of this, please, how are the smugglers signaling the ships aground?"

Well, Henry supposed they could get right to it. They were well out of earshot now.

Warwick sighed, running a hand raggedly over his bruised face and suddenly looking far older than his years.

"I'd best tell you the whole wretched story. A few years ago, shortly after my father died, I was hanging about in Calais in some of France's best gaming hells. I was running a bit short on blunt and a fellow approached me and said he'd known my father. He said he'd had a deal with him, but my old man had passed away before he could make good on it. Apparently, in addition to being a wretch, my father shared my penchant for gambling. The estate I had just inherited was mortgaged to the hilt, and I had not a feather to fly with. The man—his name was Mallory—was quite a seedy character, and that should have warned me off from the start, but it seemed like a simple enough proposition. Let them use the lighthouse on my land. He said something about misdirecting smuggling ships, and re-purposing the goods. He said since the goods were already being smuggled illegally, it wasn't stealing really, and that no one would get hurt. He promised to pay all of my debts and keep me afloat until the estate was back on its feet. Since I was young and scared, I was naive enough to believe him."

"Oh, Edwin."

"I didn't even have to come home. It was more than a year before I did, mostly because what little cash I had left ran out and I needed to know how much work it would take for the estate to become profitable again. The night I came back to Collington, I happened upon a terrible shipwreck. Mallory and his men were there, but rather than helping the survivors, and merely claiming the goods, he was—" Warwick's voice broke.

"He was killing them," Emelia finished grimly.

Warwick nodded.

"I was so shocked, so outraged, so…ashamed. I yelled at Mallory, and planned to go to the authorities, but then his muscle, a brute named Colson—I'll never forget his eyes. It's like they were completely empty. To him these sailors were simply parcels to be disposed of. He reminded me that this deal was the only thing standing between me and debtors' prison. And if that wasn't enough of a threat, he told me that he had ways of making me disappear on my next trip abroad. If you saw him, you'd know it wasn't an idle threat."

"I didn't have any family, and your father, Emelia…" Warwick stopped, collecting himself. "Your father had just died a few weeks before, and he was the only one I knew I could trust. I didn't want to burden you and Pierce or your mother, so I took the coward's way out. I ran. I never even made it home. I just got on my horse, rode to Dover, and took the next boat back to France."

"Word of your family reached me a few months ago, quite by accident, in the form of an old school fellow and his father touring the Continent. I asked after you and Pierce, wondering how you were doing, and they mentioned you were both well and still living in Collington. The schoolfellow was quite drunk and rambling on about things I won't mention in polite company, but he said that Pierce's younger sister had turned into quite the catch and had an impressive fortune. Turns out his old man was involved in the reading of the will, and he'd let slip the extent of your inheritance."

"Oh, dear." Emelia looked quite pale, and Henry squeezed the hand on his arm in encouragement as Warwick continued.

"I landed him a facer for some of his more—*erm*, colorful comments, Emelia, and my blood was nearing boiling at the thought of all those young bucks vying for your fortune. At first, I wanted to come home and fight them off and defend your honor myself, like the second brother you always saw me as."

Warwick smiled sadly.

"And then, I had the wretched thought, *if some young buck was going to benefit from your fortune, why not me?* I was scraping by with what I could make at the gaming tables, but it wasn't a pretty existence. At least I would love you and protect you like family, because that is what you are, Emelia. I don't love you in the way you deserve, not like—" his eyes flicked briefly to Henry—"a better man could, but I thought maybe this could be a way I could save you from these fortune-hungry grovelers, as well as extract myself from Colson's clutches."

Warwick sighed. "As if I were any better than them."

Henry rubbed the prickling at the base of his skill, glancing around them once more, but he saw only peaceful hedges and well-dressed members of the *ton* walking and rowing along the river.

"Warwick, I hate to interrupt, but I really need to know if I'm to alert the authorities in time. Where is the second light?"

The Baron sighed again, sounding exhausted.

"Mallory said they have a second reflector, hidden high on the cliffs just down from Old Man Anderson's cabin. It's a treacherous climb to get up to it from the beach. From what Mallory said, they lower a man on a rope from the top to light it. "

Henry nodded.

"I can have Captain Phillips and his men help search the area. But, Warwick, I have to know." Henry gestured to the other man's face. "How did this happen? Are there any new developments that I need to be aware of?"

Henry felt a sudden panic, stopping in his tracks and looking intently at Warwick.

"Are Mallory and his men here in London?"

Warwick grimaced.

"Not Mallory or Colson, no, but I knew that one of his underlings had been following me since I'd come back to London. Someone other than your Rogers, that is. I suspect Mallory is wary that I'll be backing out of our agreement, since I'm sure word has gotten around that I'm courting a lovely heiress—sorry, Emmie, love—and soon might not need their financial assistance as badly as before."

"When I left Lady Ravenscroft's two nights ago, I managed to run Mallory's man to ground outside my townhouse. I demanded an audience with Mallory outside of Collington tomorrow. I didn't tell him I wanted out of our agreement, simply said I had some information he might want. My plan is to have the authorities waiting quietly to arrest him, then come clean on the whole thing."

Henry heard Emelia gasp softly at his side.

"I know, love," Warwick consoled, "but maybe your mother's right. Maybe there's another way to keep me out of debtors' prison that I haven't yet thought about. At any rate, I can't keep living like this. I've no doubt the thug will relay my message to Mallory, but he roughed me up just a bit to show me who was still in charge."

Henry found it hard to feel sorry for the young man considering he'd known about the smugglers' crimes for years now and was just now attempting to involve the authorities. They would alert Colonel Phillips of course, and arrange for his men to be waiting when Warwick met with Mallory. With any luck, they could intervene before the wine shipment was sabotaged, and this whole mess would be at an end by tomorrow. He gave a sigh of relief.

"I wonder if Rogers saw the man who was tailing you. If we could find out where Colson is, maybe have another group move in on him while you're meeting with Mallory, it would simplify things a bit."

He turned back to ask Rogers, and his heart dropped down to his shoes.

Rogers was gone.

∽

Emelia looked around in confusion. Henry had suddenly gone completely still, his eyes scanning the park all around them.

"What's wrong, Henry?" She spoke softly, not wanting to disturb his concentration.

"Rogers is gone."

Edwin slowed, too, looking around them.

"Perhaps he's…*erm*…relieving himself, old chap?"

"No," Henry growled. "Rogers is a soldier, first and foremost. He would never abandon his post. Something is wrong."

Emelia shared a worried look with Edwin. She was still furious at him, but for a few moments there, she'd become hopeful that they could find a solution if they could just work together.

"Perhaps we could walk back towards the river." Emelia looked around, noticing their surroundings for the first time in a while. The rose-lined path they had strolled down had wound slowly away from the river—and the crowded portion of the park. From here, Emelia could see plenty of people in the distance, but they would likely not be able to hear her even if she shouted for help.

"Yes, Emelia," agreed Henry. "Let's walk that way."

Henry grabbed her hand this time instead of her elbow, and the three began to stroll quickly in the other direction.

"I say, old chap," Edwin was saying, "I'm sure Rogers is quite well, let's just retrace—"

They hadn't made it fifty feet when Emelia heard a slight rustle in the bushes and Henry pushed her down to the ground—hard.

She heard a whistle of air, then saw a flash of rough, brown clothing as someone charged at Henry. At the same time, a flash of blue came out of the bushes from the other side, and began fighting with Edwin.

Fighting the urge to scream, Emelia looked around in panic for anything that could be used as a weapon. If only it was acceptable to carry one's bow and quiver around in town!

"Run…for…help!" Henry managed to gasp while dodging blows from the roughest looking man Emelia had ever seen. Of course! They were still in a crowded park, surely she could reach a few people that could be of assistance.

Emelia picked herself off up the ground and ran as fast as she could, not daring to look back, grateful for all those years of practice running out on the farm. Her sides stitched from the lack of air—*Blasted corset!*—as she ran down the path towards the large open field to her right. She could see crowds of people milling around and chatting politely. Surely some of these gentlemen would render assistance to Henry and Edwin! She had nearly reached the opening in the rose hedges that would take her into the open field, when she felt herself stop suddenly, the wind leaving her lungs in a whoosh as she was caught bruisingly in a pair of strong arms.

Struggling to draw a breath, she shouted for all her lungs were worth.

"No! No No No No No!"

Emelia kicked her heels in vain at the kneecaps of the man behind her, but he had to be taller than Henry and twice as broad. Emelia should have been terrified, but fury outweighed any other emotions at the moment.

"Let me down, you brute! Help!"

She screamed out and saw a few heads turn her way just as a meaty hand clamped over her mouth. Emelia squirmed and kicked, but the man held a handkerchief soaked with some sort of foul-smelling substance over her nose and mouth. *Blast and wretch!*

Still struggling, she felt her limbs growing weak. Suddenly, she had a vague memory of floating on the sea as a child, her father floating alongside her, as they looked up at the cloudless blue sky above them.

And then the world went black.

Chapter 19

Breathing in dust and an acrid, metallic smell, Emelia rolled over, then groaned and wished she hadn't. Her head pounding and her limbs stiff and heavy, she tried to open her eyes and was met with darkness. Blinking rapidly, Emelia realized her eyes seemed to work fine, but she was peering into a dark piece of cloth. When she started to raise a hand to remove it, she discovered to her dismay that her hands were bound.

Biting back a curse, Emelia forced herself to breathe normally. If only she'd listened to Henry and went back to Lady Ravenscroft's! That wouldn't have saved her friends from being ambushed, but perhaps she would be in a better position to rescue them.

Emelia choked down a sob, desperately hoping Henry and Edwin were still alive. She had to get out of these bindings and find help. Her dry mouth and empty stomach told her she'd likely been out for several hours. With much effort, she rolled over on her side and felt the ground with her bound hands. Thankfully her captors had tied them in front of her.

The dirt beneath her was packed hard. She ran her hands over the ground around her, but couldn't feel anything that might aid her in cutting the ropes from her hands. She sniffed again. Something was…familiar. Emelia winced at her aching head. Whatever they'd knocked her out with certainly came with quite the hangover. She was struggling to think straight. There was something important about the smell here. Something she would have known right away if her head wasn't so muddled.

Emelia decided to try to sit up, and after a few tries, managed without falling over. She ran her hands down the front of her dress. The intricate lace was tattered and there was a large tear in the outer lining of her bodice, but she seemed largely un-injured on her person. She was grateful for that at least. As the feeling slowly crept back into her limbs, she wiggled her hands and her feet, tentatively testing her muscles. Nothing seemed broken. It was time to get out of here—wherever *here* was.

Just…a few inches…to the left. Emelia ignored her aching head and continued feeling around for something to cut her bonds or use as a weapon in case, God forbid, someone came back. Emelia stopped to listen again. She could hear something a few feet to her right. It sounded like…breathing. She felt a frisson of fear. Could it be a captor? Or perhaps her friends were also here!

Pushing her fear aside, she continued scooting along in the dirt, feeling with her hands. She bumped into a boot. Then a leg. The man wasn't moving so she was going to assume it belonged to a captee, not a captor.

"Henry! Edwin!"

She whispered softly, not wanting to alert any nearby henchmen that she was awake. Feeling slowly up the leg of the man until she came to a greatcoat, she pressed her hands to the man's chest. It rose and fell steadily with the reassuring movement of steady breathing. He was alive, at least. Trembling now, she continued her gentle movement until her fingers brushed a firm jaw with a raised scar running down it. *Henry!* She almost cried in relief.

Henry. Burying her head on his chest, she listened to him breathe. It was soothing, and Emelia decided to rest her heavy limbs for just a moment. Perhaps she fell asleep, or passed out again, but Emelia was dimly aware that some time had passed when she heard a cough. There was a soft rumble, and a quiet voice called out, "Emelia. Emelia, are you unharmed?"

"Henry!"

Emelia heard her own voice call out hoarsely.

"I seem to have no major injuries, but my hands are bound. And my eyes, too, I can't see you."

Then, to her shame, Emelia couldn't hold back the tears any longer, and she broke down into wracking sobs, her body curling up involuntarily on his chest.

"I'm so—*sob*—grateful—*sob*—you're here—*sob*—and you're safe. But where is Edwin? Do you think they—"

Emelia felt Henry wiggling around a bit, heard a rustle and snap, and then strong arms encircled her.

"Emelia, we will find him. His instinct for self preservation is remarkably high."

Emelia chuckled through her tears.

"You're right." She pulled in vain with her bound hands at the now-soaked fabric still covering her eyes.

"I'm so sorry he hurt you," Henry continued. "I know you love him. I'm so sorry I didn't find out the truth sooner."

"I don't love him!" Emelia abandoned her task, suddenly intent on Henry knowing the truth. "I mean, I do, but not in that way. He is like family to me, but I realized weeks ago that I could never marry him."

As Emelia was still processing everything in her foggy brain, she suddenly realized she was being held. Which required the use of two arms.

"Wait, how did you get free?"

"I don't think those men are very used to taking hostages." Henry began to gently loosen the knots of fabric tangled up in Emelia's hair. "My ropes were tied with simple sailors' knots. Easy to loosen if you know what you're doing. The fact they left us alive at all is a very good thing. I don't think they mean to leave us wherever we are forever."

Emelia shuddered at the thought of those men coming back.

Henry was quiet for a moment, then the fabric covering her eyes finally fell away and Emelia blinked in the dim light. Wherever they were, little daylight reached them here. Or perhaps night had already fallen.

Blinking back in Henry's direction, she found him methodically looking her up and down.

"Did they hurt you?" he asked again, running a finger gently down her cheek over an injury she could tell had the makings of a fantastically colorful bruise.

Emelia shook her head, grimacing.

"Not much. Just a couple of bruises, really."

She hoped the man who had grabbed her sported a few fantastic bruises of his own. Emelia had kicked her hardest. She shivered again, involuntarily, and Henry drew her to his chest once more, running his hands gently over her arms to warm her. She looked up into his face, and all of a sudden, nothing outside of this dusty room seemed quite so urgent.

Henry looked to be in much worse shape than she. He had a nasty-looking cut on his chin, his lip had broken open, and his left eye was swollen and blackening. Reaching out, she gently touched his broken lip.

"I'm so sorry they hurt you."

"What, this? This is nothing." Henry chuckled then clutched at a rib with a grimace. "Why, I came much closer to death when a beautiful young lady with riotous curls nearly shot me clean through with an arrow."

He grinned at her, but the intense gaze that accompanied it warmed her cheeks.

Without a word Henry picked her up from her dusty spot on the ground next to him and set her in his lap. Taking her still-bound hands in his, he kissed them softly, then set to work untying the ropes. Her traitorous, still-muddled brain found it hard to think about the danger they were in, about the ship that could even now be sailing to its doom. All she could think about was how close Henry was, how comforting it was to be held like this, and why couldn't she have realized weeks ago how very much she loved him.

She loved him! The thought should have surprised Emelia, but it didn't. Watching him untie her hands in his calm, methodical way, she wondered if she'd loved him since that day he'd been standing by her fireplace, calmly bleeding on her mother's best carpet, heedless to the ruined cravat in his hand.

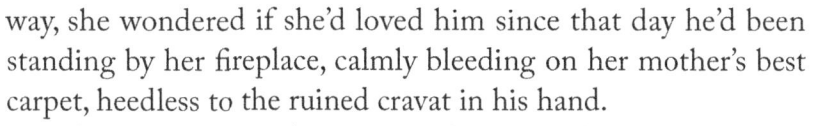

Once Henry set the ropes aside, he gently massaged some life back into Emelia's hands.

"It will likely tingle for a bit, just move them around slowly," he advised, as though discussing something they did every day.

Circling her wrists around experimentally, Emelia could easily forget the burning by looking back at Henry. She looped both hands around the back of his neck and snuggled in closer.

"I think I'll just leave them here for a bit."

"An excellent idea."

She looked back up at his blackening eye and boldly feathered a kiss on his cheekbone. Now free from the confines of the blindfold, her hair straggled down over her shoulders and into her face. Henry grabbed a wayward curl and gently tucked it behind her ear, then cupped her face with bruised and bloodied hands. He must have gotten in more than a few punches before he'd been overpowered.

Resting her hands on his shoulders, she reached up and softly kissed Henry's busted lip, attempting to be as gentle as possible. Henry, however, seemed to have other plans. His arms circled tighter around her, pulling her closer to him as he kissed her properly. Emelia's stomach dropped down to her toes, and her limbs tingled in ways that had nothing to do with having been bound. *What a difference from my first kiss,* Emelia thought with an inconvenient bubble of laughter. This was perhaps the best feeling she'd ever experienced.

A few rather breathless minutes later, she pulled away reluctantly.

"I…we…should probably," she stammered and blushed.

"You're quite right." Henry was apparently struggling to catch his own breath. "As much as I would enjoy continuing in this manner for as long as possible—and fully plan to as soon as circumstances allow—we should see to getting out of here and getting back to Collington to warn that ship."

Suddenly, all the pieces clicked into place, and Emelia smacked her forehead with the palm of her hand.

"We're here! Collington, I mean. I've known where we were since I woke up but my muddled brain couldn't quite relay the message."

Excited now, Emelia jumped up and slowly helped Henry to his feet. He was certainly worse off than she was, and he seemed to be favoring the ribs on his left side. But he straightened easily enough and took a few cautious steps forward in the tight space.

"Lead the way, Emelia. Let's go save some sailors."

Henry watched as Emelia felt her away around the walls of the small, empty room, his heart feeling much lighter than it should under the circumstances. Their prison was little bigger than a closet, with a packed dirt floor and stone walls, but high ceilings. A dim twilight filtered in from a sizable hole in the roof several stories above them. As a prison, it was effective, but Emelia seemed unperturbed. Finally, she stopped at what looked like just another section of wall. Moving closer, Henry realized that what had looked like a shadow was actually a door made of thick wood. He watched Emelia running her hands down one side of it, presumably looking for a latch of some kind, and did the same to the other side.

"It should be right around here somewhere," she huffed, biting her lip in concentration. Her face was scratched and her hair matted, but Henry had never seen a more beautiful sight.

"Pierce and Edwin locked me in here once when I was a little girl. My father was so mad when he found out that Pierce lost riding privileges for a month! He had a secret release installed on this side of the door so they wouldn't be able to lock anyone in again. We haven't used this closet in years, since the roof leaks like a sieve whenever it rains. I suspect Edwin told the smugglers about the hiding place but not the secret latch, and I'm so grateful I could kiss him."

Henry felt his jaw clench involuntarily.

"N-not that I will," she stammered, nose wrinkling. "That's not an experience I ever want to repeat again, and I expect he feels the same."

Henry comforted himself with the fact that while she'd apparently kissed Edwin during their brief courtship, it was not something she wanted to do again. And she'd seemed very happy to be kissing *him*. As if she could read his mind she suddenly abandoned her task, threw her arms around him, and kissed him thoroughly. Life was never going to be dull with this woman. Henry couldn't believe his good luck.

As Emelia turned back to her task, Henry attempted to make himself useful by searching the room for anything that could possibly serve as a weapon. Other than a few piles of dust and a moldy burlap sack, the space was truly empty.

"There's nothing in here, Henry, but don't worry, we'll have everything we need in just a moment." Emelia seemed to read his mind once again.

"Aha!"

Henry heard a soft click, and the door moved ajar, just a crack. Emelia pushed with both hands flat on the door, her fingers and knuckles scratched and bloodied from her efforts, but the door moved barely an inch.

Finally, it was Henry's turn to be useful.

"Allow, me, my lady." He gave her a mock bow, and Emelia stepped aside so he could push hard on the door.

"They must have tried to block the door with something, usually it just swings open."

With a good bit of effort, Henry got the door open wide enough to squeeze himself through, and held up a hand to stop Emelia. He held a finger to his lips in the dim light and hoped she understood his need to make sure they were safe before she followed. Henry was sure if there was anyone in the immediate vicinity, their escape would have been discovered by now. And while he sensed no immediate danger, after that last debacle in the park, Henry wasn't too keen to trust his extra sense at the moment. Looking quickly around the larger room to confirm they were alone, he was surprised to see a blacksmith iron, stove, workbench, and tall baskets of arrows. Several bows were hanging on the wall. No wonder she knew where they were by smell. They were being held captive in Emelia's own workshop!

A soft moan heightened Henry's senses and drew his attention to the floor behind the door. Leaning down as quickly as his sore ribs would allow, he assessed the injured man that had been blocking their way out.

"Emelia, you can come out now. Warwick is alive, but I think he is going to need our help."

༺༻

A half hour later, Henry, Emelia, and Edwin were in the Seaton's drawing room, a now-conscious Warwick lying on the sofa. Emelia was holding a towel to a particularly large gash on his head, and a shocked-looking Davis was pouring hot water into a basin for her. Henry was surprised to see that anything could ruffle the stoic butler. He supposed that seeing his beloved Emelia in such a disheveled state—her cheek turning purple, hands bloodied, clothes torn, and flowing hair matted into a rat's nest on the back of her head—was too much for the old man.

It was certainly too much for Henry.

Leaning over the sofa, Henry examined Warwick's head wound again. Since he'd stopped to vomit into the grass a few times as they carried him to the house, Emelia under one arm and Henry propping up the other, it was likely Warwick had a concussion. One of his eyes was already swollen shut and dark purple, and the cut on his head had reopened on their walk to the house and was now bleeding profusely. The man was extremely lucky he hadn't bled out in the workshop.

"That gash is going to need stitches," Henry said, looking

over Emelia's shoulder as she wet a clean towel Davis had handed her.

"Grab mother's sewing kit," Emelia instructed. "It's in a basket next to the green armchair."

"Emelia, forget me, I'm not worth the time," croaked Warwick pathetically. "Go get the magistrate and alert him before Mallory and his men realize we've escaped. We've got to stop them from wrecking that ship."

"This will take me two minutes, and then we'll be off. I have to say, it's going to hurt, and I'm not really sorry about it. You really have made quite the mess of things."

Emelia glared at her friend as she threaded the needle. Warwick had the decency to look abashed, and Emelia started to sew up the gash on her friend's face.

If Warwick hadn't been so remorseful, Henry would have been tempted to blacken his other eye for everything the blackguard had put Emelia through. For her sake, he was glad Mallory's men had left Warwick alive—though judging from the amount of dried blood on Edwin's clothes, and the fact that he wasn't locked in the closet with them, they'd probably just left him for dead.

"Zounds, Emmie!" A loud voice came from the doorway just as Emelia finished sewing the last stitch. Davis handed a pale and shaking Warwick a generous glass of brandy.

"Does mother's best rug mean nothing to you, or must you use every man we know as a pincushion?"

Pierce stood just inside the room, his mouth agog at the scene before him. Henry nodded gratefully at Davis as the butler offered him a glass of brandy, then handed one each to Emelia and a very confused Pierce before carrying the bloodied towels out of the room. Henry put a hand on the young man's shoulder.

"You might want to sit down, Pierce. It's a long story."

Before Henry could tell a word of it, however, there was a great commotion in the hallway. Henry grabbed the nearest weapon he could find—the fireplace poker—pushed a bewildered Pierce behind him, and stood between Emelia and the doorway just as the door burst open again.

"Merciful heavens! Thank goodness you all are okay! Henry darling, you can put down the poker, I'm not going to attack you."

This time it was Henry's turn to be confused as he stared at an out-of-breath Lady Ravenscroft, Mrs. Seaton rushing into the room on her heels. Mrs. Seaton looking shaken, rushing immediately to her daughter's side and embracing her. Lady Ravenscroft had a fiery glint in her eye, and not for the first time he was glad she was on his side.

"Oh, Mother! I'm so, so sorry that I snuck out to join Henry and Edwin." Emelia sobbed into her mother's arms. "I was so angry at Edwin, and I thought maybe I could talk some sense into him—but how in the world did you know we were here?"

"Mr. Arbuckle had just arrived in town, and was out walking with Lady Lilly and her brother and a few other young people in the park today." Mrs. Seaton stood with an arm still around her daughter's shoulders, as if afraid to let her out of her sight again. "They saw you all being attacked, but by the time they could reach you, you were already being stuffed into a carriage. Mr. Arbuckle punched one of the remaining ruffians in the nose, and Lord Percy held him down while Lady Lilly alerted us and the authorities."

"We would have been hot on your heels if we hadn't had to squabble with that constable to speak with the prisoner," huffed Lady Ravenscroft. "Seriously, the police are such *amateurs*. Once I threatened that smuggler with the names of a few of my husband's old contacts, the man spoke quite freely and told us you were here."

"What *did* you say your husband used to do, exactly, Lady Ravenscroft?" Henry stared at her in wonder.

"I didn't. Say." Lady Ravenscroft smiled sweetly.

"'Pon rep, doesn't explain a thing," Pierce said wearily, taking off his hat and rubbing his eyes. "Been out at the new granary, tinkering on the steam engine. Get home to find my best friend 'n sister in tatters, and you telling me Mr. Arbuckle, the most proper gentleman I know, mind you, punched a fellow in the middle of the park. Henry, old chap, do help a fellow out."

The room suddenly went quiet and everyone looked at Henry.

"There are some smugglers using Warwick's lighthouse and a spare reflector up the coast to send ships to their doom on the rocks. They then kill the crew and steal the goods. We found out about their plans, and they didn't like it. Now, we need to alert the authorities, break into the lighthouse and see that the light remains burning, and take out the spare reflector up the coast before a large ship is due to sail through later tonight. All will be heavily guarded, and the smugglers are desperate enough they won't hesitate to kill anyone in their way."

All eyes were turned on him, solemn, and Pierce's brow wrinkled as he processed the news.

"Oh, and when this is all over, I'd like to marry your sister."

CHAPTER 20

SEATON HOUSE

The noise level in the small parlor was deafening as everyone started talking at once.

Emelia sat, mouth hanging open, while her mother, Lady R, and Pierce all attempted to speak over one another. Patting her hand, Edwin gave Emelia a sad smile. He tried to sit up, winced, and shrunk back down into the sofa.

"You could do much worse, Emmie—and, in fact, you would have if you'd stuck with me."

He gave her a lopsided grin, his bloodied lip only moving halfway.

"I am so sorry for misleading you, and for all the pain I've caused you."

While she was still furious at Edwin for being such an idiot, Emelia couldn't help but feel a little bit sorry for her old friend.

"Even though you don't love me and I *certainly* don't want to marry you, I'm grateful you came back into my life."

Tears came to her eyes.

"You made some terrible mistakes, but you are still my friend, and we will find a way to keep you out of debtors' prison. I promise. Besides, without this mess, I would have never met Henry, and I'm thinking that would have been quite the tragedy."

She grinned at Edwin through her tears, and Mrs. Seaton cleared her throat.

"As overjoyed as I am to discuss this intriguing development further, it is nearly ten o'clock. There are still some brutal smugglers on the loose, so we should probably make a plan. But, first, I do have one more question."

Solemn once more, everyone glanced at her expectantly.

"Pierce, what in the *world* have you been doing the last four weeks?"

She turned to her surprised son, who seemed to struggle a bit for words.

"Is it...*erm*, quite the time for that?"

"Give me the summary, then."

She leveled a look at Pierce that Emelia took to mean no one was leaving this room until she got her answer.

"Well...I...became responsible, I guess."

Emelia listened with delight and, frankly, astonishment as her brother quickly explained how he had taken a shine to running their estate and helping the tenants increase their farming yields. Together with Mr. Appleton, Pierce had converted the village mill to run on steam power, helped an elderly tenant repair his roof, leased a vacant farm to an enterprising young farmer with progressive views on crop rotation, and—apparently—even trained Emelia's beast of a dog!

"Oh, Cerus. Where is he?!" Emelia exclaimed, looking around. She was ashamed to admit she'd forgotten about her pet in all of the excitement.

"With Clara, at the moment. Taken quite a shine to her. She taught him to leave birds alone, so he's not terrorizing chickens anymore."

"Brilliant, she is," Pierce added rather proudly. "In fact, well, we've been spending quite a bit of time together, what with me working with her father, and you in London the last few weeks... why....she..." Pierce trailed off, and Emelia could have sworn that was a blush on her very suave, sophisticated brother.

"She's become quite important to me," he finished hurriedly.

At this Edwin laughed and let out a whoop, seeming for a

moment like his old self, and Emelia's mother and Lady R smiled as they bent their heads together, whispering. As for Emelia, she couldn't imagine a more perfect outcome for her brother and best friend. She wondered why she didn't think of it sooner.

"Pierce! That's wonderful, truly. She couldn't ask for a better suitor." She crossed the room to give him a big hug, and stood next to him with a goofy grin on her face. Her brother and Clara would be perfect for each other. Henry winked at her, and Emelia was so happy she almost forgot the trials of the day. Almost.

"As much as I can't wait to tease you endlessly about this," she said, playfully pushing her brother on the shoulder, "we have a band of smugglers to stop."

Taking his cue, Henry spoke up.

"I believe this task is going to take all of us. I've known Mallory for years. From what I've learned of him and his men, they're brutal. They've killed survivors from dozens of ships. He's smart, and since they know that we know what he's doing now, they'll be expecting some sort of interference."

"But Henry, darling," said Lady Ravenscroft wryly, "They certainly won't be expecting us."

Emelia looked around at the rag-tag group—Edwin with his pale, bloody face; her mother, looking fierce and determined; Pierce, now pacing the floor; Lady Ravenscroft, looking for all the world like she was enjoying herself immensely; and Henry, serious, but quietly confident. Lady Ravenscroft was right; the smugglers certainly wouldn't be expecting *this* group.

And they just might be able to use that to their advantage.

Over a plate of hastily-prepared sandwiches, the group formed a plan. Or rather, it seemed to Emelia that Henry and Lady Ravenscroft made a plan while the rest of them ate quickly and washed it down with a bracingly strong cup of tea. In the end, it was decided that as the fastest rider, Pierce would ride to alert the authorities and fetch Colonel Phillips and his men. Lady Ravenscroft and Mrs. Seaton would gain entry into the lighthouse to stop the light from being extinguished, while Henry and Emelia would head to the cliffs to disable the extra reflector, along with Rogers, the newest addition to their strange little party.

The poor valet-turned bodyguard-turned-spy—Emelia couldn't keep up with exactly what roles the man played—had burst through the door a few moments earlier sporting a black eye and a few scrapes, but thankfully alive and well. He had woken up behind a hedge in Hyde Park and hobbled his way to Lady Ravenscroft's. When her staff had informed him the Lady in question had raced to Collington, he borrowed a horse and followed at top speed, knowing her to be a "rum mort," which Emelia gathered meant that Lady Ravenscroft knew what she was doing. Rogers had stopped only to grab a few "barking irons"— which Pierce explained meant he'd stocked up on firearms—and now sat working his way through a rather large plate of sandwiches as plans were finalized, washing it down with a fine claret right from the bottle.

Emelia thought it a sign of the importance of the situation that none of the ladies in the room so much as batted an eye.

Through many protests, Edwin was ordered to stay at Seaton House, since he still couldn't stand without falling over.

"It would hardly do to get yourself killed—or one of us, for that matter." Lady Ravenscroft admonished him with a frown when he began to protest. "I think you've caused enough trouble already."

Edwin had the grace to look abashed. Davis was going to look after him, and Marietta had been sent to summon the village doctor to tend to his wounds properly. The groom, the gardener, and a stable hand had been armed and posted around the house in case someone discovered Edwin wasn't dead after all and came looking for him. Emelia also noticed Pierce quietly lay a pistol down on the side table next to the settee, just in case. She shivered involuntarily and sincerely hoped Edwin wouldn't have to use it.

After managing to choke down a few bites of sandwich,

Emelia had quickly washed her face and hands and changed into the thick linen dress she normally used for archery practice. Her hair, too matted to comb through completely, was gathered in a hasty braid down her back, and she ran back into the sitting room to find the others quietly discussing how to get to the second reflector.

"I snuck down there one night after I came home," Edwin was explaining, "knowing what Colson and his men were really up to that night on the beach a couple of years ago, I had to see if I could do something. I went down when I knew the men were elsewhere and tried to see if I could disable the reflector somehow."

Her friend rested his battered head in his hand, winced, and continued.

"It's tucked into a hollow in the cliffs, the kind the birds usually build nests in. There's no way to reach it from the beach below. It's just too high. They must lower a man from above, but it must be terribly dangerous. There's a narrow pathway, if you can call it that, that winds itself through the cliffs to the beach below, but it would be foolish to attempt in broad daylight, and madness in the dark. You would surely fall to your death. The only other way to access the beach there is by rowboat. Perhaps if we can make our way to the beach by boat, we can throw something up at the reflector and break it, as Pierce and I would try to hit the birds nested in the cliffs with rocks when we were children."

"Pierce!" Mrs. Seaton admonished her son as if he were a lad just returned from that very activity.

Pierce rolled his eyes.

"We never actually hit any of them, mother. The clefts in the rock are just too high up. Even a firearm of the highest quality would be..." Pierce trailed off, a sudden gleam in his eyes.

He looked Emelia directly in the eye.

"Emelia can do it."

Everyone looked at him, surprised.

"If you stand on that rocky bit of beach below, you could take out the reflector with an arrow. You've done it in these conditions before. I know you can do it."

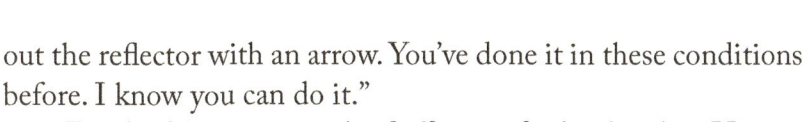

Emelia felt a warm rush of affection for her brother. He was right. She was the only one that could reach it from below.

Mrs. Seaton pursed her mouth, but nodded her assent.

"Yes, I think it's our best option. I'm not sure we'll reach it in time otherwise."

"It will likely be heavily guarded from above," added Henry. "But if Rogers and I distract them at the top of the cliffs, you might just have a chance on the beach."

He stopped, head cocked to one side as if listening, though they were miles away from the cliffs at the moment. Emelia wondered curiously if he was listening to his second sense. He seemed to come to some sort of decision, and nodded.

Henry looked at Emelia with concern in his eyes.

"It'll mean getting back out on the water, alone and in the dark. It's a short row from the harbor, but I can't ask you to do that unless you're very sure."

Emelia squared her shoulders, an idea forming in her mind already. "I can do it. And I know exactly who can get me there."

⁓

Barely an hour later, Emelia was listening to the quiet slosh of rowboat oars dipping into the water. The fog was so thick that the muffled sound barely reached her ears, though she was merely a few feet away. The cold seeped through her clothing as she crouched on the floor of the narrow fishing boat, a thick wool blanket concealing her from any watchful eyes that might happen to spot the boat through the fog. At the helm sat Mr. Aveyard, his weathered face alight with excitement for their secret mission. Mr. Barlow, who'd insisted on joining them despite the late hour, sat in the middle of the boat near Emelia, his head nodding now and then towards his chest. Rowing opposite Mr. Aveyard was Mr. Coffery, posture as straight as ever, strong arms pulling confidently at the oars. Despite their advanced age, the men navigated the ship through the fog with the precision borne of a lifetime on the water.

Emelia felt her stomach clenching as they neared the rocky beach in the darkness. Running her hands along the quiver tucked in beside her, she comforted herself by counting the arrows inside. She knew each one by feel, the weight of each material and its thickness, knew which one to use for every distance and condition. Suddenly all those hours of practicing in every possible condition didn't seem so crazy.

She hoped tonight it would be enough.

They'd chosen the easiest route to the rocky little beach, staying close to the shore to avoid the dangerous rocks, hoping the darkness and growing fog would cover their approach. Mr. Aveyard had insisted Emelia stay covered in case anyone should spot them, reasoning that the three older gentlemen were known around town for their odd antics and wouldn't be seen as suspicious, but Emelia suspected Mr. Aveyard just had a flair for the dramatic. Mallory's men were likely to take anyone seen approaching the area as a threat, elderly or otherwise. She prayed the fog would hold.

Emelia forced down her growing panic by shifting her focus to Henry's rash announcement back in her sitting room. Did he truly want to marry her? Or was he just offering because they'd been locked up alone together in a compromising situation, and he was an honorable man? Thinking of the warm twinkle of his eyes whenever he looked at her tonight, she thought he was at least rather fond of her. Most marriages in her day and age were built on far less affection. Like was a far cry from love, however, and recent events had proven her judgment in this matter less than sound. As she listened to the quiet swoosh of the oars through the water, she wondered idly if Henry would attempt to force her to give up archery or reading scientific journals. That could be a good litmus test. He hadn't protested a bit at her involvement in this dangerous escapade, so she knew he respected her skills as an archer. Or perhaps he simply knew it wasn't in his power to control her.

Emelia exhaled into the darkness. Life was so much simpler when she thought she never wanted to marry. Thinking of their kiss while locked in the tower room, and the electricity she'd felt when they'd waltzed the other night—well, marrying this particular gentleman didn't seem so bad.

A whisper in the darkness broke through her muddled thoughts.

"Just up ahead, lass. We'll come back for ye after the ship 'as passed, as planned."

Emelia nodded, though she knew Mr. Aveyard couldn't see her, and eased the blanket off of her head as the boat scraped quietly onto the rocky beach. The fishermen had chosen to pull up just behind a large cluster of rocks, so Emelia could scramble out of the boat without attracting attention. Then it was just a matter of waiting for the smugglers to light the lantern, so she could get a clear shot at it before the ship came through.

Feeling a bony hand on her shoulder, she turned and looked in surprise at Mr. Coffery, as strong and straight as ever. To her utter astonishment, he was speaking to her.

"Be mindful of the tide," he whispered. "In another three hours, most of this beach will be underwater. The ship won't risk sailing through here in the daylight with so much valuable cargo just waiting to be taken, so I'd say it'll be here in the next two hours, before the first light of dawn. If it doesn't come before the tide comes in, don't risk it. We want to save these sailors' lives, but not at the cost of your own. We'll be back for you."

Emelia nodded, awestruck at the first words she'd ever heard the old man speak. She'd been so certain he was mute.

"Thank you, Mr. Coffery," she whispered, "I will be watchful for the tide."

Mr. Coffery offered her his hand, and gripping it she scrambled out of the boat, taking care to make as little noise as possible. While it may prove deadly to the sailors soon to come, Emelia was grateful for the fog. The filtered moonlight created long shadows behind the boulders on the beach for her to hide behind. Mr.

Aveyard's boat glided back out into the water with only a few quiet scrapes on the rocks around them, and then they were gone into the fog, and Emelia was alone. She prayed silently that the elderly men would make it back to shore safely.

Taking quiet steps along the rocky shore, Emelia wrapped her heavy woolen cape around her tightly and crouched behind a few large boulders jutting out of the sand. She could just make out the faint outline of the chalky white cliffs above her, but she heard no sound or movement coming from above. The cold and damp was already seeping through her clothes and the adrenaline of the evening was starting to wear off. Emelia was suddenly exhausted.

All she could do at this point was wait, so she leaned back against the cold boulder, sliding her quiver down silently beside her. With the sound of the waves lapping onto shore only a few feet away, she felt her eyes growing heavy. She wondered how her mother and Lady Ravenscroft were faring at the lighthouse, and hoped Henry and Rogers were safe as they staked out a hiding spot only a few hundred yards above her. She allowed herself a few minutes to close her eyes, and feeling a cold breeze blowing gently on her cheek, comforted herself with equations of distance and wind speed.

◆

Lady Alice Ravenscroft had seen a thing or two in her day. But that day had been a very, very long time ago, and as she and her dear friend Elizabeth pulled up to the Collington lighthouse in the Seatons' carriage, she felt a shiver of excitement run through her. Oh, how she missed the game! The driver—his livery straining at the seams and a cap pulled down low over his face—offered her his hand. Alice disembarked, Elizabeth close behind her. Despite the fact that it was nearly midnight, the two ladies looked for all the world as if they were on a little pleasure jaunt to the coast. Nodding at the women, the driver took his place back on the carriage and scratched one cauliflower-shaped ear in signal. Very good, it was time to begin.

They'd agreed on the direct approach, and walked right up to the front door of the lighthouse. It was a stout old brick thing, and Alice thought idly that it was fortunate it wasn't one of the taller, more modern structures. This one would be much easier to scale if need be. But she was quite out of practice, so hopefully it wouldn't come to that.

Arm in arm with her friend, Alice knocked briskly on the door. There was a long pause, and she felt Elizabeth shift nervously by her side.

"Don't worry, love, he's just assessing if we're a threat. Just smile and look like the genteel matron you are."

Elizabeth smiled and nodded in return. *Good girl.* She'd always been a plucky one.

After several minutes, they could hear a scraping sound as the door was unbarred, and a weathered, toothless old sailor stuck his head out the door.

"Meh? What er ye wantin'?" he grunted rudely.

"Hello, good Keeper," Alice boomed warmly. "We just finished the most delightful dinner party, and my friend Mrs. Seaton here was just gushing about how charming the town lighthouse was, and I simply couldn't wait to see it! Do let us in for a little tour."

"It's thuh confounded middle of night, woman!" the old man mumbled. "Tourist hours er over. Come back 'n eh mornin'."

"Well, my good Keeper," Alice went on, still smiling, "I'm afraid I have to go home in the morning, and being a city-dweller and all, can you believe I've never seen the inside of a lighthouse? And I simply *must* see it before I go, think of all the stories I can tell the ladies over tea! Oh, do be a dear and let us in."

The old man *harrumphed*, looked Alice and Elizabeth up and down, and slammed the door firmly in their faces. She could hear the scrape of wood on wood as he barred the door back in place.

"Oh dear," murmured Elizabeth. "Now what?"

A Brilliant Convergence

Her friend looked up, no doubt calculating the distance to the large windows at the top of the structure.

"Oh, don't worry, Elizabeth, dear, we've only begun."

She knocked loudly on the door again. The scraping began almost immediately, telling Alice the man was still standing at the door. She was smiling broadly as the door opened.

"Now, Keeper, sir, may I ask your name?"

"Smiff."

"Ah now, Mr., *erm*, Smith, I know you are so very good at your job, so it would only take a brief moment to show us around, and I promise we will let you get back to your very important work."

The man's chest puffed up a bit at the praise, but he simply shook his head and said, "Tomorreee."

Alice then held out a few gold sovereigns in her palm, letting the money jingle around and catch in the lantern light.

"Mr. Smith, I know you're very busy running the lighthouse, but perhaps if we compensate you for your time, we could just—"

The door slammed in their faces again.

"Ah, good."

Alice pocketed the gold sovereigns again.

"Just a moment, I must answer nature's call, I'm afraid. I'll be right over there."

Elizabeth's mouth dropped open as Alice pointed to a rusty old shed in the shadows just beyond the lighthouse.

"Do be a dear and knock once more and ask the gentleman what time we should be 'round in the morning?"

Incredulously, Elizabeth knocked again, stepping back from the door a couple of feet as Alice disappeared around the corner.

"Tarnation!" Mr. Smith was sputtering and cursing up a storm Alice could have heard for miles. "I don't give a tinker's dam 'bout a couple of lady-bird swells out for sightseein' in the middle of the night! I don't care how much blunt ye have t' bribe me, it ain't worth me life!"

He stepped through the doorway for the first time, rubbing his wrinkled hands together menacingly.

"I've half a mind t' teach ye bluestockings a lesson 'bout trampin' round in the middle of th' night, why—"

The old Keeper's diatribe came to a screeching halt as Alice hit him squarely on the back of the head with a large shovel. He slumped down to the ground, out cold.

"Oh heavens! Alice, did you kill him?"

Elizabeth knelt quickly and felt for a pulse on Smith's dirty neck.

"Nonsense! It would take a far harder blow to kill a man," Alice dismissed, returning the shovel to its home beside the shed. "I simply rendered him unconscious. He'll have a nasty headache, but no lasting damage. Now, we have a light to keep burning."

She motioned to their driver, who slipped down from his perch without a sound, holding a coil of rope.

"Do take care of this one, Carter, if you please. I'll check upstairs for any compatriots."

"Yes ma'am." The stout butler nodded politely, as if discussing taking the tea seat away. Alice saw Elizabeth's mouth fall open once again.

"But Carter—your butler—how did he? I mean, when?"

"Oh, I never travel without Carter, dear. He's proven himself handy in all kinds of situations. He ties an excellent knot, so I know we won't have to worry about our friend Mr. Smith again tonight."

Pulling a slender pistol out from a specially-designed pocket in her skirt, Alice motioned towards the still-open door.

"Now, let's go keep that light burning, shall we?"

Chapter 21

The Cliffs of Kent

The fog had started to lift, and Henry watched a weak beam of moonlight dance on the water stretching out in front of him. Even at night, the sea was beautiful. Rogers stirred beside him, watching and waiting. The two men were tucked up behind a farm cart full of hay, conveniently left in a field near the cliffs. He thought of Emelia, cold and alone on the beach just below them, and his heart clenched. Had he really declared he wanted to marry her in front of a room full of people only a couple of hours earlier? What a wretched idiot he was!

While he was incredibly sure he wanted to spend the rest of his life with this woman, that was hardly the time to declare himself. Young ladies needed wooing, romancing—he could have at least told her he loved her first. And Emelia was still sorting through the complicated feelings attached to her last, rather disastrous marriage proposal. Henry exhaled as loudly as he dared. Not for the first time, he wished his sixth sense included some sort of social faux pas warning system along with the danger.

Speaking of danger, surely they would see some signs of Mallory or his men here soon. Scanning the area around them, Henry let his eyes wander down the rocky cliffs. If he had the right equipment and experience, a man could climb down, but it would be a long and tedious process. The beach below, where Emelia was waiting, was just a small, rocky inlet, no more than fifty yards across. The clearing fog allowed a few glints of moonlight to sparkle against the stones, and Henry wasn't sure if it was a blessing or a curse. It could allow them to be more easily seen by the smugglers, but could also prevent the French ship from meeting its end on the rocks. He sincerely hoped Mallory's men wouldn't be examining the beach too closely just yet.

From his position behind the farm wagon, Henry saw a faint light in the distance and heard the rumble of wagon wheels. The smugglers must be arriving. From the sound of the men's voices approaching, they were talking and laughing in normal voices, not hushed tones. This far out of town, they must not be worried about being overheard. Or any nearby locals were paid well for their silence.

The voices stopped moving somewhere near the cliffs, and Henry suspected they were congregating just above where the second reflector was located. The question was, how did they light it without scaling the cliffs? Henry waited quietly as cold from the ground seeped in through his pants, chilling him to the core. Rogers was a bundle of coiled energy next to him. They had waited out many battles together, but Henry had never expected to be this close to one on the coast of Kent.

After what felt like an eternity, but couldn't have been more than half an hour, the men stopped laughing and chattering.

"It's out!" someone hollered.

Henry tried to peer around the farm cart, his heart sinking. *Of course! The men had been waiting for the lighthouse to extinguish its light before they could light their reflector.* Henry wondered grimly if that meant Mrs. Seaton and Lady Ravenscroft hadn't been successful in gaining entrance to the lighthouse. He hoped they were safe. It was up to Emelia now, and it was his job to keep the smugglers busy so she could succeed.

The sound of grunting and scraping echoed across the rocks. The moonlight was stronger now. Henry dared not move yet to get a better look, but from his little viewpoint between wagon wheels, he could just see a cluster of men gathered around a heavy coil of rope, lowering it down the cliffs. Whatever was on that rope must be quite heavy, for it took three grunting and cursing men, muscles straining, to hold it. Henry heard a faint clink of glass, the lantern being lit somehow, then the whole cliffside was ablaze with light. He listened this time—listened to his sixth sense instead of waiting for it to interrupt him like it usually did. It was time.

∽

Emelia crouched further down behind her boulder as the whole cliff lit up, the light of a strong lantern bouncing against a metal reflector. She'd seen the shape being lowered down in the semi-darkness, but when the shape moved to light the lantern, she'd had to stifle a gasp. It was a man, dangling from a harness fashioned out of rope. He must certainly trust his comrades—one slip of the rope and he would fall to his death.

The reflector's light wasn't quite as bright as the village light-house, but she could see how a ship looking to steer from the position of the lighthouse could mistake the two lights, particularly if the lighthouse was extinguished. From her position down on the beach, she couldn't tell if her mother and Lady Ravenscroft had been successful in keeping the lighthouse burning, but even if they had been, she still needed to take this reflector out. The men shouting and cheering above, she quietly drew out her bow, watching the man on the rope slowly ascend as the others pulled him up with grunts and groans.

She wondered if this man, Mallory, was among them, or if he left the men to do his dirty work for him. Remembering Henry's account of Mallory killing men on the beach, she suppressed a shiver. It seemed that Mallory enjoyed doing his own dirty work.

Waiting for the man to reach the top of the cliffs, Emelia briefly tried to calculate where the ship would end up if they did crash along the coastline. Perhaps Mallory and a greater group of men were gathered there. She hoped so, if it meant there were fewer smugglers here for Henry and Rogers to deal with. She knew they were waiting quietly somewhere up above.

The reflector burning brightly, it was time to act. Her chance of being spotted had risen dramatically with the light, and she wouldn't put it past these men to lower themselves down the rocks one by one to see her dealt with. Not to mention that every minute the fake light was lit increased the chances of shipwreck. Closing her eyes, Emelia felt wind against the back of her neck, heard the waves crash a few feet to her right. She took a deep breath, willing her pulse to slow. Blocking out everything but wind speed and trajectory and target.

Tossing her cloak behind one shoulder, Emelia raised her bow and let an arrow fly towards the reflector. What followed was an explosion of sorts, but not the explosion of breaking glass that she'd hoped for. No, it was an explosion of fury as her arrow fell short and bounced harmlessly off the cliffs. The smugglers had suddenly become aware of her meddling presence.

Men shouted and hollered in the pre-dawn light, and she was vaguely aware of the man in the harness being hauled over the top of the cliff as she withdrew another arrow from her quiver. Taking a deep breath to still her shaking hands, Emelia closed her eyes and pictured herself a few miles away in the field behind Seaton House. She felt the ocean breeze stirring at her cheek, pictured the lantern and reflector in her mind's eye, and drew back her bow. She opened her eyes at the last possible second before releasing the arrow into the air, and was rewarded for her decade of archery practice with the satisfying sound of shattering glass. A small fireball roared up the cliffs as the lantern's oil combusted, and she blinked as her eyes adjusted once again to the dim light. She'd done it!

There was no time to celebrate her success, however, as she heard a small explosion and something ricochet off the rocks in front of her. She'd known it was well within the realm of possibility that the smugglers would have firearms, had known going into this that there was a high degree of danger involved, but for some reason, she stared at the rock with eyes wide in surprise. Not over the fact that someone was actually shooting at her, but at the fact that their firearms could actually reach her from that distance, why, they must be—

Her stomach filled with dread as she saw shapes picking their way down the jagged rocks on the other side of the beach. *Drats. The smugglers must know the path very well—or they simply valued their jobs more than their lives.* She shivered involuntarily. Judging from their location and the surprising speed at which they were proceeding, they would be at her position in less than ten minutes. And Mr. Aveyard's boat wasn't due to return for at least an hour.

She waited until another shot bounced harmlessly off the sand a few feet in front of her, then pulled back her bow and leaned out from the cover of the rock. It was a good thing she'd packed all of her arrows, just in case.

∼

As the lantern exploded and extinguished, Henry launched himself out from the cover of the farm wagon and began to fire his musket in the general direction of the smugglers. An early, pre-dawn light crept across the landscape, but from this distance his enemy was still difficult to spot among the shadows. He was going to have to move closer, but there was no more cover. He ducked back under the cover of the farm cart as a flurry of the smugglers' bullets began to fly in his direction.

"We're going to have to leave our cover," he shouted to Rogers, who was ducking and firing in a similar dance.

"For a corky cove, ye can sure be beetle-headed at times," Rogers shouted back, causing Henry to cease firing for a moment and blink back at him. It'd been ten years since his military service, after all, and his cant was a little rusty.

Rogers rolled his eyes and nodded his head toward the farm cart.

"Your cover has wheels, me Lord."

Understanding dawned, and Henry quickly shuffled with

Rogers to the back of the cart and put his shoulder to it. Slowly, the heavy wheels rocked out of their grooves in the mud, and they began to inch forward.

"It's a regular Trojan horse, Rogers!" Henry grinned as he ducked another shot bouncing off the top of the wagon.

"If wishes were horses, lad, we'd 'ave the run on them."

Shaking his head, Henry realized the amount of shots being fired wasn't slowing, but the number hitting his wagon had diminished considerably. He risked a glance over the top, and saw the smugglers firing over the edge of the cliff—right at Emelia. He wasn't sure if they could reach her from this angle, but judging from the smugglers beginning to pick their way down the cliff, and the fact that there were already fewer there than there had been a minute ago—they were heading in her direction. Even with a quiver full of arrows, she wouldn't last long against half a dozen men. It was time for more drastic action. Henry noticed the wagon was rolling easier now, the ground sloping downhill slightly towards the cliff.

"Rogers, how are you at jumping?" Henry asked the older man as they pushed, still gaining speed.

"Spryer than a har-toofed hare me lord!"

Henry hoped that was sufficient.

"Our chariot awaits!" Henry hopped into the back of the rolling wagon, Rogers jumping in behind him.

"Let them fly like at Salamanca, my good man!"

"Ye were yet a lad in knickers for that one, me lord."

"Just shoot at anything that moves."

As the wagon picked up speed, Henry and Rogers paused their barrage of bullets only long enough to reload. Henry saw with satisfaction that the smugglers began climbing back up the cliffs towards the melee. Henry estimated they'd killed or injured several men, which left maybe an additional eight.

That's when he saw him, standing alone at a distance, hands on his hips. A cigar dangled from his mouth, smoldering like a pinpoint. Even at this distance, Henry could clearly see the man's wooden leg and imagine the sick grin of pleasure on his face. Mallory had always liked a skirmish.

"Okay, Rogers, time to jump."

And with the wagon hurtling towards the edge of the cliff, Henry and his valet executed their best tuck and roll onto the rocky grass. A few moments later, the wagon flew off the edge of the cliff, thankfully far away from the rocks behind which he knew Emelia was taking cover. If she'd followed instructions, she'd be fine.

His jaw clenched.

She never followed instructions.

⁓

It was amazing how calming firing arrows into the pre-dawn light could be. Emelia had advanced considerably across the beach, which was shrinking by two feet every 6.2 minutes with the incoming tide. It was all math, really—glorious calculations. She'd deal with the emotions of injuring or possibly killing these smugglers later. After all, she hadn't planned on shooting arrows at anything but the lantern until the men had started shooting at her.

The barrage of bullets from above had slowed considerably. Emelia could only make out one man firing at her from the side of the cliffs, and he'd stopped to reload. From the trajectory of the men who'd been slowly picking their way down the rocks, the path wasn't quite as steep as Edwin had thought. Then again, she'd always left Edwin and Pierce behind when they were scrambling around on the rocks as children. Climbing was simply a matter of physics, something neither of them had ever understood as well as she.

And it was a good thing, because the speed of the incoming tide told Emelia that either Mr Coffery's estimate was off, or something had delayed the men in returning. If she didn't get off this beach soon, she was going to be swimming. Which meant… it was probably time to put those climbing skills to good use. Not for the first time, she was glad she'd been an odd child. She ducked as a bullet soared past her right ear. Time to take care of her last opponent, and then it looked like the only way to go was—

Emelia heard shouts and cries from above, and glanced up just in time to see a large, dark shape hurtling over the cliff—right towards her. Picking up her skirts, she ran towards the cliff as fast as she could, heedless of any bullets in an effort to get out of the path of whatever was falling towards her at an alarming rate. Trajectory, gravity, mass, all swirled unbidden through her brain as she threw herself onto the ground at the foot of the rocky path winding up the cliff. The world exploding behind her in a crash of splintering wood, Emelia adjusted her leather quiver to cover her head as debris rained around her, thankfully bouncing harmlessly off the quiver.

When the commotion stopped, she spared a brief glance at the remains of what appeared to be an old farm cart, noting gratefully that it seemed to have been unoccupied. Then she glanced up the path in the growing pre-dawn light. The smuggler who'd most recently been shooting at her was lying unconscious on a small ledge a few meters up. From the large gash on his forehead and the chunks of wood laying around him, he appeared to have been knocked out by a piece of splintered farm cart. That left the path ahead clear for the moment. Glancing once more at the shrinking sliver of beach behind her, Emelia adjusted her quiver, tied her skirts up on the special loop sewn into her archery dress for that very purpose, and began to climb.

She was about halfway up the cliff, grateful for the growing light on the horizon, when the path grew from tricky to treacherous. Her arms shook with fatigue, and the cries and grunts from above told her there were still smugglers up ahead. Stomach growling, she wished she'd had time to eat more than a few bites of sandwich within the last twenty-four hours. Still, she'd made it this far up the cliff, and there was still no sign of Mr. Aveyard's boat below, so up she would go. Using her legs to push her weight up instead of trying to pull up with her arms—a mistake Pierce always made when they were children—she managed to heave herself up onto a small ledge to catch her breath for a moment. Looking up at the sharply turning path, Emelia was calculating her next few moves when she heard scraping and grunting coming from just around the bend. Someone was coming.

Chances were, since she couldn't see them past the sharp bend and rise in the path—if you could even call it a path at this point—he couldn't see her either. Could she draw her bow while perched on this ledge? Likely, but it would be little use at close range. If she stayed on the ledge, she'd be spotted as soon as the smuggler rounded the bend. The pistol he likely carried would be much more useful in close combat. Emelia closed her eyes, willing her brain to work quickly. She could hear the scraping sounds almost directly above her now. Above! She looked up, the ledge ending in a sharp wall of rock jutting out above her, the path directly above that.

Looking at the smooth wall, she searched for handholds in the rock. If she could make herself even a foot taller, she could reach up the rock to the path above and... *And what?* She ran her hands along the arrows in her quiver, picking out the longest and sharpest one. It would have to do. Wedging the toes of her right boot into an indention in the rock, she pushed her weight up the ledge. Almost! Her left foot slipping as it searched for purchase, Emelia grabbed hold of a sturdy looking scrub brush growing out of the rock and pulled herself up. Gaining a foothold, she listened to the crunch of footsteps on the rocks above, then silently as she could heaved the top half of her body over the rock ledge, an arrow clutched securely in her right hand.

A howl of rage pierced the air as her arrow buried deep into a very rough looking smuggler's calf. She'd been aiming for the knee, but this man was much taller than the average and her estimate was off. His roar of fury echoing in her ears, Emelia suddenly felt herself weightless as the man lifted her up over the ledge, two meaty hands clutching her cloak and dress.

"Such a dainty thing, causing us so much trouble," he growled, barely seeming to notice the arrow embedded in his leg. "Shall I throw you over the edge and be done now? Or perhaps I should drag you to the top and let the lads have a little fun first, eh?"

Suspended off her feet, her arms bound within the heavy cloak by the man's vice-like grip, Emelia kicked hard with her boots, the blows bouncing harmlessly off his tree trunk legs.

"It takes more than a little arrow to take down the mighty John Colson," her captor chuckled darkly. "Struggle, little lady, struggle. It'll make it so much more fun for me when we reach the top."

Colson! Emelia stilled for half a second as she remembered the name of Mallory's second in command. She had no doubt this brute was personally responsible for the death of many sailors. She closed her eyes and went limp, as in surrender, and Colson laughed again.

"Not so tough now, are you little one?"

When he turned to look back up the path, Emelia kicked hard at the arrow still embedded in his shin. He roared with fury, and pain shot through Emelia's scalp as he grabbed a huge handful of her hair, long escaped from its braid, and began dragging her up the path behind him. Her head hit the rocks, hard, as she fell to the ground. Tasting blood, she felt rocks scraping against her cheek, and struggled to push herself up with her arms. Perhaps this way she'd at least make it to the top, she thought grimly, but chances of sustaining a serious head injury before then were high.

Her cloak tore and her palms shredded as she tried in vain to push herself off the ground. Still, Colson held fast to her hair and a handful of her cloak, and dragged her mercilessly upwards. She was just beginning to think perhaps unconscious would be a mercy when the sound of gunfire rang out a few yards above her. The unbearable pain in her scalp suddenly ceased. Struggling to push her head up off the rocky path, she heard the quick scratching and sliding of someone coming down towards her. Since they'd obviously taken out her assailant, the odds were high that it was a friend, but she wasn't about to stake her life on it. Drawing an arrow out of her quiver with her right hand and wiping blood out of her eyes with her left, she managed a half-sitting position just as her rescuer scrambled carefully down to her side.

"Emelia, my darling, I know you were always a bit of a show-off when it came to climbing the rocks, but that was certainly not part of the plan. Do you know what a ghastly mess you've made of your beautiful face?"

Edwin. Smiling through her tears, she'd never been happier to see him.

"You're still looking pale, Eddie," she countered. "You ought to be lying down."

"Just wait until you see a mirror, love. Now, your beau and his valet," Edwin shook his head, as if still mystified by the odd pair, "are engaged in a rousing bout of fisticuffs with a few ruffians up top, so I figured it was up to me to play the hero for a change."

Pulling a clean handkerchief out of his pocket, he began to gently wipe the blood off her face with one hand, the other still clutching firmly to the side of the cliff in front of him.

"I'd say we wait down here until things die down, but I don't love hanging onto this cliff. I nearly died three times on the way down, and I'd hate for Goliath down there to regain consciousness and seek his revenge." He grimaced, gesturing with the bloody handkerchief to the ledge that Emelia had occupied only a few minutes earlier.

She gasped as she saw Colson balanced precariously on the ledge, a gunshot wound to the shoulder. If any man could survive an arrow to the shin, a gunshot wound, and a fall of several yards, she wouldn't put it past this one. It was likely wise not to wait around to find out.

"He's Colson," Emelia explained, wiping her bloody hands on the handkerchief as best she could and stuffing it into a torn pocket of her cloak. "He's the muscle behind Mallory's operation, I think."

"Well, then, let's hope that muscle stays down here on the ledge, at least until the authorities arrive."

Extending a hand, Edwin pulled her to her feet.

"Since I have the pistol, it's best I go first. That way, you can catch me if I fall," he added with a wink.

Emelia breathed deeply, willing herself to ignore the pain of her cuts and bruises and focus on the path ahead.

"Just like old times, then. Let's go."

༄

They were rushed by several men as soon as they hit the ground, so Henry hadn't been able to spare a glance back at Mallory. One smuggler he disarmed by shooting the pistol out of his hand, and as the man rushed at him, Henry realized grimly that he would have no time to reload his own weapon. Instead he used it as a club to deflect a rather nasty-looking fishing knife. Before long, the only sounds on the cliff were the grunts and cries of a proper brawl. Since he hadn't yet been shot, Henry realized the remaining men must be out of ammunition as well. Unless they were waiting for something. Or someone.

He knocked one smuggler out with a right hook he was particularly proud of, and brandished a knife he'd managed to wrestle from another's grasp. He longed to look over the edge of the cliff and check on Emelia's welfare, but for now he just had to stay alive. Sensing each blow a second before it came, Henry ducked as a gap-toothed, grizzled old sailor swung a heavy cutlass right over his head. Rogers was close by his side, and managed to fire his pistol at the old man's hand. The cutlass clattered to the ground ,and Henry raced to pick it up just as another smuggler scrambled over the top of the cliffs again and headed toward Henry.

The man carried an enormous club in his hand, which would easily deflect a cutlass blow. He backed up a few steps and charged at Henry, the club held sideways like a battering ram. In some recess of Henry's mind he remembered Jean's story, how the smugglers used clubs to beat any survivors to death. His stomach churning, Henry swiveled to the right, deflecting some of the blow with the cutlass, but the handle of the club caught him hard against the temple. Staggering back towards the cliff, pain exploded down one side of his face. He wiped at the blood coming from his nose and a sizable cut above his ear and realized his spectacles were gone, lost in a shattering of glass and metal somewhere at his feet.

Grinning, the man stepped back a few more paces and charged again. If he made contact, he would push Henry right over the edge of the cliff. Henry closed his eyes for a split second, took a deep breath, and dropped his cutlass to the ground beside him. Surprised, the man slowed slightly, and Henry dropped quickly to his knees, pushing up with all his might just as the club reached him. The man, carried by his own momentum, swung up and over Henry's head, scrambled for purchase on the loose rocks behind him, and with a piercing cry, went over the edge of the cliff.

As Henry stopped to catch his breath, Rogers, his right eye swollen shut and blood pouring from his lip, crouched a few feet away from him, arm around a wiry-looking man's neck. Henry turned suddenly as he heard the chilling sound of crazed laughter. Donovan Mallory was standing thirty feet away, a large rifle aimed right at Henry.

"Who would have thought, Rockcliff," the other man rasped. "You and your uncanny ability to cheat death. Me and my uncanny ability to orchestrate it. It makes so much sense that you've been the one throwing a wrench in my plan. You may have stopped us from taking that ship tonight, but you and your lap dog there won't be around for the next one. And putting your pretty little archer friend down there on the beach? Well, brilliant idea, as always, but the beach is certainly underwater by now, and there's nowhere to go but up. Shall I kill you first, and then tend to her? Or perhaps I'll take care of her first so you can watch."

"Why did you do it, Mallory?" Henry bit out, his jaw clenched in anger. He was still bent over, hands on his knees, breathing in great gasps. "Why kill all those men? You had the goods, you didn't need to resort to murder."

"And let them spill the beans about our second light? Hardly. They were mostly *Frenchmen*, Rockcliff," the man spat. "Miserable frogs from that blasted miserable country took everything from me."

He nodded down at his leg.

"And they were French *smugglers*. It's not as though anyone was going to miss them."

"They were men, Mallory. Men just like you and me. Former soldiers that just did what they had to do to eat."

Mallory laughed again, and Henry shivered involuntarily.

"You always were a feely sop, with your spectacles and your books. Hands up, you and your lapdog. I don't want any heroics."

Rogers had rendered the wiry man unconscious, dropping him unceremoniously onto the dirt, but Henry knew Rogers' pistol to be as empty as his own. He had the cutlass at his feet, but if he tried to charge Mallory with it, he'd be dead before he could set one foot in front of the other. Slowly raising his arms, Henry nodded to Rogers to do the same.

"Let's see if my men on the cliff have retrieved your pretty little archer yet. Then, I'll be rid of the whole lot of you and back to business."

Every fiber of Henry's being begged him to jump into action, but he shook his head ever so slightly at Rogers' questioning look. Pierce was coming with Captain Phillips from the north. Emelia could be working her way up the side of the cliffs even now. All they could do was wait.

Chapter 22

Emelia and Edwin were nearly to the top of the path when he motioned for her to stop. As his footing was less certain than hers, she'd let him go first. Once, he'd slipped and would have fallen down the cliff if not for her strong grip on a tree root, the other hand pushing at his back until he found his footing. It had taken several minutes for her heartbeat to settle enough to continue. But the stitches on his head wound seemed to be holding, they were still alive, and they had nearly reached the top.

Stopping at Edwin's upraised hand, Emelia heard muffled voices from above. One was Henry, and her heart soared. At the very least, he was still alive. But the other voice was pure evil and sent chills down her spine. That must be Mallory.

From their position on the path, a few scrubby trees and bushes would hide them from view once they reached the edge of the cliff. As quietly as he could manage, Edwin picked his way gingerly up the last few feet. Emelia scrambled behind him, her movements quicker and more assured than they had been the entire climb. This was not an experience Emelia ever wished to repeat, but she'd managed with only a few close brushes with death. The blood on her face had long since dried, and though the cuts and scrapes stung, and her lip was swollen, she would heal.

Instead of taking the path directly back to the cliff, Emelia pointed to a steeper climb just to their right. If they scrambled over a small boulder and around a tree growing out of the side of the cliff, they could pop up closer to Henry—and not at the expected top of the path. Safely around their obstacles a few moments later, they crouched behind a scrubby bush at the top of the cliff.

She could see Henry and Rogers, hands lifted, a few yards to her left, their backs to the cliff. A man with a wooden leg and a nasty sneer on his face was an additional thirty feet away, closer to the main road. In his hands was a long rifle, pointed directly at Henry's heart. He was cataloging all of the ways Henry had managed to spoil his fun in the army, and why it was going to be such a pleasure to kill him. Emelia hoped his list of grievances were long, perhaps it would buy them a few precious seconds. Reaching her hand back into her quiver, her stomach dropped when it grasped only air. She must have lost her last few precious arrows when Colson attacked her.

"Do you still have ammunition in your pistol?" Emelia whispered as quietly as possible next to Edwin's ear.

"Yes, but we're out of range."

He held up a hand before Emelia could interject.

"And even if we tossed it to Rockcliff, there's no way he could hit him accurately from this distance. It would take an expert marksman, not a man who…wears spectacles."

Emelia blinked at her friend for a minute, then rolled her eyes.

"Is it loaded or is it not?"

"Yes, it is! The only shot I fired was at the man who was dragging you. You're welcome for coming to your rescue, by the way."

She leaned over and gave him a quick kiss on the cheek.

"I never really expected you to stay at the house for long. You are a better man than you think you are. Now, give me that pistol."

Eyes still full of doubt, Edwin handed it over.

"How are we going to get in range without getting shot?"

Emelia's eyes glittered.

"It's time for you to revisit your role from Tuscany."

Henry's arms were growing heavy as Mallory rattled on about the times that Henry had prevented him from committing unspeakable acts, or as he put it, "having a bit of fun with the frogs." His jaw clenching, Henry forced himself to breathe slowly. This man was unconscionable. He knew he was just buying time, waiting for one of his men, or heaven forbid, Emelia, to come up the path, but the airing of grievances was oddly encouraging to Henry—how many people would Mallory have hurt or killed if Henry hadn't been there to stop him? He tuned out the madman for a moment and tried to listen to his sixth sense. Everything in him told him to wait. *But wait for what?*

A few moments later, Henry's heart dropped as he heard a crunching noise drawing nearer. A high pitched voice called out, "I'm coming over and I'm unarmed, don't shoot!" A bow and empty quiver was tossed over the edge, and then a cloaked figure followed, ragged hood pulled low over her face.

Henry's eyes drifted to his right, and just as the figure doubled over, gasping for breath and drawing Mallory's attention, Henry dropped his right arm to catch the pistol that was sailing towards him. It was over in two shots, fired in quick succession. The first hit Mallory square in the shoulder, causing him to drop the rifle, the second buried in his good leg, bringing him to the ground. As the man writhed and hollered in pain, Henry and Rogers quickly closed the gap between them. Rogers grabbed the rifle, while Henry took a handkerchief from his pocket and stuffed it in Mallory's shoulder wound none too gently.

"Unfortunately, Mallory, you're likely to live," Henry said grimly. "At least until you make it to the hangman's noose."

Mallory cursed at him once more through clenched teeth, then passed out cold.

Henry turned to see Emelia and Warwick behind him, Warwick still wearing Emelia's cloak. The young Baron had an astonished look on his face.

"But Rockcliff, how in creation did you make that shot? Would have been challenging for even the best marksman I know, and I thought you were, well…" he trailed off, looking confused.

"Edwin," Emelia said patiently, as if talking to a small child.

"Henry obviously wears spectacles to see things up close. Which means he has hyperopia—he can see far off just fine. How I thought you and I could ever suit is beyond me."

She shook her head in dismay, and Henry couldn't help but laugh. He quickly closed the distance between them, enveloping her in a gentle hug.

"I'm very grateful for that beautiful brain of yours," he said with a grin. "And also your excellent pistol-tossing skills."

His grin faded quickly as he noticed her injuries.

"Where does it hurt?"

He checked the gash at her temple, which had bled profusely but appeared to have clotted. Then he ran his hands gently down her arms, moving to her sides. She sucked in a breath sharply when he passed over a rib, and Henry frowned.

"Does it hurt when you breathe?"

"I don't believe I've punctured a lung, if that's what you mean, but I do think my sixth rib is cracked and my seventh is bruised."

Henry closed his eyes, bending down and touching his forehead to hers. She would be in a lot of pain when the adrenaline wore off.

"And the man who did this?" He asked in a whisper.

"It was Colson. Edwin shot him, and he fell a ways onto a ledge. It's possible he survived."

Henry raised his head sharply.

"Rogers, take Mallory's rifle and stand guard at the top of the path, just in case any of the smugglers recover enough to climb back up. Warwick, can you watch Mallory for a moment until Pierce and Phillips find us?"

"With pleasure." Edwin took the pistol back from Henry as he looked in disgust at the man laying in the dirt.

"What are we going to do?" Emelia looked bewildered as Henry took her gently by the hand and led her a few steps away.

"Something I should have done weeks ago."

A Brilliant Convergence

Tired, hungry, and confused, Emelia eyed Henry warily as he led her a few paces away towards the main road, and grasped both her hands in his.

"Emelia, about what I said last night in the sitting room, I'm so sorry…"

Her heart dropped. Here it was then. He didn't really want to marry her, he didn't love her after all, he'd just been trying to do the honorable thing. Maybe now that this was all over, he was ready to head back to France—without her. Couldn't it have waited until she'd at least had a meal and a bath? She felt tears starting to form in her eyes.

"I'm so sorry for blurting out that I wanted to marry you in a room full of your family."

"It's okay," Emelia found herself saying, "it was the heat of a stressful situation, they will understand about you changing your mind—"

"Oh darling, no." Henry looked suddenly anguished

Emelia's heart lifted. Maybe he wasn't trying to back out. While she'd always said she wouldn't settle for anything less than a love match, if Henry even liked her enough to marry her, that would have to be enough for her. Because she loved him, heart and soul, and couldn't imagine being parted from him. The tears started flowing in earnest now, mingling with the dried blood on her face, stinging her cuts. Her sleeves were so torn and dirty, she couldn't even use one to wipe her face. She knew she was a frightful mess, and for some reason that made her cry even harder.

"Emelia," Henry said softly, "look at me."

Emelia looked up, and saw such tenderness and concern in his face that her heart swelled. You couldn't look at someone you didn't at least care about like that, could you?

"Emelia." Henry gently cupped her filthy chin in a bruised and battered hand. "I love you, and want nothing more than to spend the rest of my life with you. My only regret is that I announced that fact imperiously in front of your family before I ever asked you if you could bring yourself to feel the same about me."

Stifling a sob, a happy one this time, she smiled at him through her tears as he gently wiped her face with his equally bruised and dirty hand.

"I'm not always good at expressing myself, and I'm terrible at flattery," he continued. "I cannot write you poems or sonnets, but know that my heart is yours and will always be—and it has been for some time. Since the day I saw you tearing across the field with your skirts flowing behind you, I believe."

He gave her a lopsided grin that made Emelia's heart want to burst with happiness.

"I should have told you weeks ago, but I wanted you to make your own decision regarding Warwick first without me complicating things. But believe me, if I'd known earlier that he wasn't worthy of you, if I'd know what he'd drag you into here—"

Henry broke off, tears in his own eyes now, and held her bruised face in his palms. She rested her cheek in his hand for just a moment, closing her eyes.

"You couldn't have known. None of us knew—though I should have suspected something. I thought I knew him better than anyone."

"Emelia, my life has been anything but peaceful and quiet since you've been in it, but I find all that peace and quiet seems impossibly dull now. I know that you're still recovering from a shocking betrayal, and you might not trust me just yet, but perhaps in time you could even grow to…well, to love me, too."

He looked at her carefully, gently, as if she were a thing to be treasured. Not because she was fragile or incapable, but valuable.

"But I do—love you, too, you know," she whispered when she finally broke away and looked into his battered face. "I realized weeks ago that I could never marry Edwin, because it was you I loved. I will live as quiet or as exciting a life as you desire, anywhere you want to be—as long as you are there."

"I've given my word to Colonel Phillips to see this through, and we're nearly there. When we get back to your family, I will ask their permission to court you properly, like I should have done before."

"Oh, please don't."

Emelia blushed beneath all the blood and dirt.

"I mean, you can ask my mother, of course, but I don't need a long courtship. I realize now that I needed time to decide with Edwin because I knew right away that I couldn't marry him. But I cared for him deeply and didn't want to hurt him. I don't need time to know if I want to marry you. I just know. Just like I know the square root of two hundred and twenty-five is fifteen. It's not debatable. It just is. It's not as if the square root of two hundred and twenty-five could be sixteen—"

Emelia broke off as Henry pressed a tender kiss to her lips.

"You're perfect. And you can recite all of your favorite square roots to me long into the night, very soon. But now—"

Henry gestured with his head to his right, and Emelia heard the rumble of many horses' hoofbeats approaching. She shielded her eyes against the rising sun on the horizon.

"Better late than never, I suppose."

It took Colonel Phillips and his men less than five minutes to take all the living smugglers into custody. Three had perished on the cliffs, eight more were wounded. Having regained consciousness, John Colson had to be hauled off by four soldiers, cursing and bellowing at the top of his lungs all the way. Emelia shuddered and was glad to see the back of him.

Donovan Mallory was quiet as he was led away, his good leg dragging behind his wooden one. He simply looked at Henry, malice in his eyes, and nodded.

"You win this one, Rockcliff," he ground out between clenched teeth. "But you haven't seen the last of me."

Henry knew that was likely true, as there would be a trial to testify at, if Mallory lived that long. As soldiers milled around them, Pierce jumped gracefully off his horse and ran to embrace his sister, looking around in dismay when he realized the fight was over.

"Can't believe we missed it! Took me a devilish long time to find your Colonel, Rockcliff."

Grabbing a blanket off the back of his horse, he wrapped it around his sister's shoulders and held her close to warm her.

"Emelia, you don't want for pluck, I'll give you that, but if you go running off to battle again without me—" Pierce, broke off, looking unusually pale.

"I'm okay, Pierce," Emelia reassured, patting his arm as her brother whipped a pristine handkerchief out of his pocket and began to gently clean her face. The blood was largely dried now, and the effort was of little use. But it obviously made her brother feel useful, so Emelia just smiled at Henry and let Pierce give the job his best effort. Henry left the siblings to tend to each other, joining Colonel Phillips and Warwick.

Warwick seemed to have given the Colonel the whole story, and was listing the names of all of the men he could remember.

"I only met a few of them, Mallory and whoever was with him at the time. The big ugly man that was attacking Emelia, that was Colson, Mallory's muscle. Heard, Temple, and Jones—they were the only others I met. I heard them referring to another man by the name of Petters."

Colonel Phillips, the instigator of Henry's involvement in this entire adventure, nodded at Henry as he approached, casual as if they met regularly for afternoon tea. He wanted to both hug the man and deck him. Henry settled for wiping his lip—which had taken to bleeding again after kissing Emelia—on a tattered corner of his sleeve as he waited for the Colonel to finish writing his notes.

"Ah, there you are, Rockcliff," Colonel Phillips said as he finished, as if Henry were a tardy young sergeant in the inspection line. "My hunch was right, eh? I always could count on you to ferret out the truth. You're drawn to it. Young Mr. Seaton filled me in on the whole story during the ride over. I knew you could handle yourself, but I'm sorry your young lady was dragged into it. Ladies just aren't cut out for this nasty business."

Henry looked over at Emelia, smiling and laughing with her brother, and couldn't suppress a grin.

"Well, that's where you're wrong, sir. Emelia handled herself quite well. We could never have disabled the other reflector without her. And she took down at least as many smugglers as I did."

Colonel Phillips looked at Emelia again with new respect in his eyes.

"Well, then, Rockcliff, you seem to have met your match. Now, we have a few more details to work out here, and then you're a free man. But I promised Mr. Seaton I'd wait until we got back to his house. It seems he's eager to keep his friend out of prison—debtors' or otherwise. Let's go see what we can do for this young idiot, eh?"

∽

Emelia felt as if at least a week had passed since they'd last assembled in this drawing room, but it had been merely hours. As the adrenaline of the night wore off, she was increasingly aware of how much she hurt all over. More than anything, she wanted a hot bath, a cup of tea, and to climb in her bed and sleep for days.

The drawing room was fuller than it had ever been. Emelia was tucked up under Henry's arm on the sofa and Clara, who had been at the house when they all returned, sat clutching Emelia's hand on her other side. She clucked and fussed over Emelia, and not for the first time Emelia thought her friend was quite the most beautiful crier she'd ever seen. Her cheeks were rosy, and there were tears running down her face as she alternately wept and laughed over the whole harrowing tale. Since she'd missed out on all the excitement, Emelia indulged her, and let her friend gently clean her wounds and rub salve over them.

Mrs. Seaton and Lady Ravenscroft sat in the armchairs

opposite them, and Edwin and Colonel Phillips had pulled two chairs over from the card table. Pierce sat unceremoniously on the rug at Emelia's feet, unwilling to let her out of his sight again. No one protested this breach of social etiquette, and he balanced his tea saucer on one knee.

Lady Ravenscroft and Emelia's mother had been recounting their adventure in gaining entrance to the lighthouse. At her mother's astonishment at the driver turning out to be Lady R's prizefighter-turned-butler, and Lady R rendering the Keeper unconscious with a shovel, Emelia laughed so hard she sucked in a painful breath, her cracked ribs throbbing.

Frowning, Henry rubbed the back of her hand with his thumb gently. They were all going to have to tend to their wounds soon, but gathered here in front of the blazing fire and sipping hot tea after such a harrowing night felt so comforting, no one wanted to be the first to break the spell.

"But please, explain to me," Henry was asking, "how did the lighthouse go out if you'd already gained entry?"

"Well, Alice and I surmised that the smugglers wouldn't light the second lantern until they knew the one in the lighthouse was extinguished. As the Keeper was already out cold and tied up, we weren't sure exactly what time that was supposed to be. We just waited until we were sure you were all in place, turned off the lantern for a few minutes, and then lit it back again so no ships would be in danger."

"But how did you know how to work it?" Pierce asked, shoving a huge piece of buttered bread into his mouth. The cook was busy coming up with a hearty breakfast for everyone, but she'd insisted they have something with their tea to hold them over.

"Darling," Lady R began gently, "your mother is a highly qualified scientist, and I am—well, let's just say I'm highly experienced and very capable. I think we can handle a measly lantern and a reflector."

Colonel Phillips finished his tea, set his cup aside, and cleared his throat. The man was older than Emelia had expected, his hair white around the temples, and deep lines across his face from years of the pressures and sun exposure of the military. He looked to be a bit older than her mother and Lady Ravenscroft, and Emelia understood as soon as she'd seen him why he'd needed Henry to investigate the smugglers. The Colonel wore a dark eyepatch over one eye, and walked with a cane. Smuggling favored the young, and after years of service in this part of England, he would have been far too recognizable.

"Well, Lord Warwick and I were talking on the ride over," Colonel Phillips began, "and while I cannot condone his actions in allowing the smugglers to continue their operation without going to the authorities, I don't think the Crown will want to press charges in the matter. That means if he can find a *legal* way to settle his debts, he's a free man."

Emelia felt tears of joy come to her eyes, and she slumped against Henry in relief as she let out a breath she didn't know she'd been holding.

"Capital, Colonel!" Pierce beamed as he nearly overturned his teacup onto the rug.

"You're forgetting one important thing, old friend." Edwin looked grim. "The only reason I let those fools rope me into this scheme is because I'm completely in the basket—even if I sell my crumbling estate, there's no way that's enough to cover the entirety of my father's debts."

"Ah, but that all depends on what someone is willing to pay for it, no?" Lady Ravenscroft smiled slyly. "As it turns out, I've been hunting for properties in the country for quite some time. My son, you see, inherited our estate in Essex, but rusticating in the dower house just isn't my style. Up until now, I've never found a property that suited me, but I find myself growing quite attached to Collington, and I would love a summer home here."

She squeezed Emelia's mother's hand, and the two friends smiled at each other.

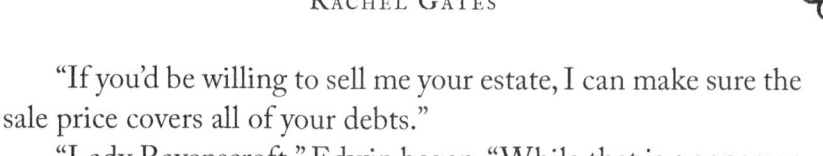

"If you'd be willing to sell me your estate, I can make sure the sale price covers all of your debts."

"Lady Ravenscroft," Edwin began, "While that is a generous offer, I cannot allow you to pay me more than the property is worth. It would be a terrible investment."

"Son, it is worth a lot to me to live near my dear friends. I have far more money than I will be able to spend in the remainder of my lifetime, and if a small portion of that money can buy me more time with the people I care about, well, then I think that's a very good investment, don't you agree?"

Emelia struggled to comprehend the vastness of Lady R's wealth, if she could buy Edwin's entire estate with a small portion of her income.

"Besides," Lady R continued, "I think putting the property to rights would be a fun challenge. I've been haunting my drafty townhouse alone for far too long. And I was hoping, Elizabeth dear," she turned to Emelia's mother, "that you might consider coming to live with me eventually. Why, you could have your own wing!"

Lady R gave a sly glance to Clara, who was still holding Emelia's hand and listening to the entire conversation with undisguised awe, and added, "Besides, young Mr. Seaton will want to settle down…eventually…and raise his own family in this beautiful house of yours. We could all be neighbors."

Emelia swallowed a happy lump in her throat at the thought of her family, her beloved Clara, and Lady Ravenscroft all living together as neighbors. She noticed that Lady Ravenscroft hadn't mentioned her, since there was little doubt that she was going to marry Henry. And Henry lived in France. She was already looking forward to seeing his family's vineyard, and especially to meeting his grandmother. Her heart would just have to learn to be in two places at once.

As if reading her thoughts, Henry slid an arm around her waist and snuggled her up closer to his side.

"Since that's settled, my man of business will be contacting you shortly, Lord Warwick," Lady R informed a still-stunned looking Edwin, "I will ensure you have enough funds after paying your debts to get to wherever you want to go."

"About that." Colonel Phillips eyed Lady Ravenscroft with respect. "While we seem to have apprehended most of the smuggling group, I was going to suggest you make yourself scarce for a while, Warwick. If there are a few rogue actors out there looking for revenge, it's possible you could become a target. It might be wise to consider returning to the Continent for a while."

Edwin grinned, looking for a moment like his old self, despite the bruises beginning to darken on his face and the bandage still around his head.

"It's funny you should say that. Now that it's clear that Emelia and I will never suit," he gave Emelia and Henry a wink and a wicked grin, "I've been thinking about finding this beautiful Italian girl I met a few months ago. It might be time for a return trip to the Riviera."

Emelia laughed. Only Edwin could barely escape death and debtors' prison and be planning a romantic escapade by the Mediterranean all in the span of a few hours.

"I truly wish you the best of luck," she assured her old friend.

"And once we're sure that there are no smugglers bent on settling the score, you always have a place to stay with us when you return home," Lady Ravenscroft added warmly.

There was a soft knock on the door, and Davis entered the room.

"Excuse me, madam, the doctor has returned, and brought two assistants. I told him there were quite a few cuts and bruises in need of attention."

Dr. Eldermeyer entered, then looked around the room.

"Since I've already assessed that young man," he said bemusedly, nodding towards Edwin, "and he has obviously *not* been following my instructions, we'll start with the others first."

In the end, Henry only needed a few stitches above his right eye, a nasty gash in his left thigh cleaned and dressed, and a collarbone popped back into place. He'd rarely gotten through a battle so unscathed. Rogers fared a bit worse, having still been sore and bruised from his initial beating at the hands of Mallory's men. He suffered a broken wrist, two cracked ribs, and a fortunately shallow knife wound in his side. With proper care, the doctor expected him to make a full recovery, and Henry was grateful.

After dressing gingerly—the bruises on his torso were already beginning to color spectacularly—Henry waited outside Emelia's bedroom door. She was inside with the doctor, and it was all he could do to prevent himself from breaking down the door and ensure she was being treated properly. Broken ribs were nothing to scoff at, and if she'd punctured a lung—Henry couldn't bear to think about it.

In lieu of breaking down the door, Henry settled for pacing the hall while wondering where they would go when Emelia recovered. Would she want to stay here with her family? They seemed so close, and he couldn't bear to make her unhappy by tearing her away to live in France. Yet, she longed for adventure, so perhaps she would welcome her new country with open arms?

For a decade Henry hadn't imagined ever stepping foot in England again, but with this strange new truce between him and his father, and a chance to see his mother and sister more often—staying in England a little longer didn't seem so bad. In France they could have a home, an occupation—but going back to the vineyards indefinitely felt a little like running away all over again. Perhaps there was some sort of compromise, where he could maintain his peaceful life in France part of the year, but live in England the rest. But what would he do? Henry hadn't spent a dime of his military pay in the last ten years—there had been no need for income living on the family farm—and he had invested some of that income wisely over the years. He wasn't a rich man, exactly, but he and Emelia could live comfortably anywhere they chose.

He'd been pacing for about ten minutes, wondering if the length of time the doctor had been examining Emelia was a bad sign, when Colonel Phillips approached him.

"Rockcliff, son, you're going to wear a hole in that carpet. I'm sure Miss Seaton will be just fine. Come with me for a moment, I want to have a word with you."

As if he were still a fresh recruit, Henry followed him obediently down the stairs to Mrs. Seaton's study and took a chair by a roaring fire. With so many extra people in the house at the moment, every room had been prepared for guests.

"You handled yourself admirably these last few months, Rockcliff. You did everything I would have done if I were a younger man—well, if I were a younger man who happened to speak French and was a bit more inconspicuous."

Phillips pointed to his eyepatch with a grin that belied his years.

"Since I've been commanding the troops in this part of the country, I've become too recognizable. And Mallory always hated my guts; he would have sniffed out my involvement within a day. Thanks to you, we'll be back to dealing with the usual smugglers and tariff-dodgers—not these murdering scumbags. I'll take a rowdy band of Frenchmen over that loose screw Mallory any day."

"Sir, you remember what happened to my brother," Henry began. He'd written to Colonel Phillips after Charles had died. The man had even gone to Charles' funeral in his stead. Henry swallowed a wave of guilt and continued.

"If my work here prevented even one sailor from ending up in a watery grave—smuggler or otherwise—it was completely worth it. Honestly, it seemed like a daunting task at first, but over the last few weeks—well, to be honest, I haven't felt this useful in years."

"How would you like to feel useful from now on?"

Henry's heart gave a little leap, which surprised him.

"I must confess, first, Colonel, that I'm not sure where I'll be living after this. I plan to make Emelia my wife, and, well, with everything going on here, we haven't had a chance to speak about where we'll live."

"Well, Rockcliff, I may have a solution for you. I'm not getting any younger, and neither are my colleagues. There are too many old men with one foot still firmly planted in a war that has been over for a decade. It will take young men like you to move this country forward. I've been speaking with Mr. Hartworth of Trinity House, who I believe you've met recently. He was quite taken by his conversation with you, and he recommended to me that we offer you a job."

"We, sir? I'm not interested in a military post."

"I don't mean the military. Now that the war's over, I serve in a different capacity. I oversee the troops in this area, yes, but only so I can have my eyes—well, eye," he chuckled, "on what goes on right over the Channel. It's more military intelligence than military. I report directly to the Crown."

Henry wasn't terribly surprised. Colonel Phillips had always seemed to be more informed than your average military officer.

"We want you to be the scientific liaison between England and France," Phillips continued. "Most of the time, you can continue your quiet life, making wine, reading books, taking care of your very pretty and courageous little wife. But whatever you choose to do, you will keep abreast of any new scientific developments coming out of France, and keep us informed. A week in Paris here and there, attending the scientific conventions and meeting with the sharpest minds. We're very interested in this new lens as a matter of national security. We're on an island for God's sake. Making the sea safer makes us all safer. But it's even more than that. From what we've heard, there's a brilliant community of scientific minds that go from London to Paris and back. These scientists are very…fluid in their loyalties. Truth before country and all that. We want you to get to know these men. You're very perceptive, son. You always were able to see through to the heart of the matter."

Colonel Phillips paused, waiting for Henry's reaction.

Henry wasn't quite sure what to say.

"Colonel, I'm a soldier, not a detective, and you know I won't spy against the French."

"No, no, it's nothing like that. I think in the future our countries could be allies. Friends, even. We merely want you to be our inside man among the scientific community. Monsieur Fresnel's lens…it has the potential to change the world, you know. And it's the tip of the iceberg! More change is coming. It's going to be a new kind of revolution—a revolution of science and technology. It's time for our country to decide whether we'll be active participants or merely observers."

Henry found himself warming to the idea despite his hesitations. He'd felt more alive over the past few months than he had in years. To associate with some of these brilliant scientists, to learn from them—Henry had to admit the idea was appealing.

Colonel Phillips had years of experience reading Henry, and the older man smiled, assured of his success. Henry realized Phillips truly wanted him to take this job. The fact that his old commander had so much faith in him was encouraging.

"You're very good at blending in and listening," the Colonel continued, driving his point home. "You don't have to decide what to do with the information, although you are an intelligent man. You and I both know your military file paints far too modest a picture of your true skills—talents, gifts—whatever you want to call them. But the war is over, and our countries are going to have to figure out how to coexist as peacefully as possible from here on out. It's technology, not military strength, that will determine who stays on top in the future. We think you can be of service to *both* your countries."

Colonel Phillips stood, and Henry followed him into the front hall, thoughtful.

"Rockcliff, I have to go ensure some particularly evil, murdering louts are safely in jail to await their trials. Think about the job offer, talk it over with your intended. I'd be lying if I said you're the only man for the job. But you're certainly the best one."

"Thank you, sir. I'll let you know soon."

"I'll be seeing you again in London in a few days, I'm sure. Oh, and Henry?"

"Yes, sir?"

"Take good care of that horse. He's yours now."

Henry watched as Colonel Phillips donned his hat, limped to his horse, and mounted deftly despite his injury.

He was still standing on the front steps, staring out at a beautiful early June morning, when he felt a presence at his side. He turned to find Emelia, freshly stitched up and clean, wearing a lovely marigold yellow morning gown. She laid a hand on his arm and smiled. Despite her injuries, she looked like spring itself. It reminded Henry of the day he met her, and that gave him an idea.

"How are you feeling?" He took her hand in his and threaded their fingers together. His knuckles were raw and bruised, and one of her palms was bandaged.

"Good news. I'll be sore for weeks, I'm sure, but Dr. Eldermeyer thinks my ribs are merely bruised, not broken. I only needed a few stitches on my scalp—fortunately above the hairline, so I won't be too disfigured."

She grinned at him. He knew she would need time to heal from this ordeal mentally as well as physically, but she seemed to be handling it well.

"C'mon, then," Henry grinned back at her, pulling her by the hand down the steps and towards the stables. "I have a quick errand for us before breakfast."

∽

Henry rode on his horse, Gideon, with Emelia tucked up in front of him. Apparently Lady Ravenscroft already had Gideon brought back from London. The woman missed nothing, and he was grateful. He'd climbed up in the saddle and lifted Emelia up ever-so-gently, careful not to touch her bruised ribs. She looked exhausted after their long night, but she didn't protest their outing, and Henry was determined not to waste a minute.

She looked at him, puzzled, when they came to a stop at the edge of the field, near the road that led to the village. There was no one else around, but the warm sun rising overhead and a gentle breeze promised a spectacular day to come. Henry dismounted, then lowered Emelia down gently and tied Gideon to the fence post.

"Do you know why we're here?" A smile played at the corner of his mouth.

"I believe this is where we first met, not so long ago."

"Where I met you and promptly fell in love with you," Henry amended. "Emelia, I've spent my whole life running away. First from my father, then from the war, then from Charles' death. Since I've been here in England, since I've met you, I've realized it's time for me to stop running. You've seen me for who I truly am—scars, bizarre gifts, and anxieties included—and you loved me anyway."

Henry pulled a small cloth bag out of his vest pocket, and slowly and stiffly bent down onto one knee. Laughing through the tears that instantly sprang to her eyes, Emelia covered her mouth in shock as he pulled an amber and gold ring out of the bag.

"But where did you—how did you—" Emelia, for once, seemed speechless, and Henry grinned.

"Apparently my sister gave this to Lady Ravenscroft in case she saw me before Angelica did. It was once Grandmere's, and Angelica wanted me to give it to you. Lady Ravenscroft, your mother, and Pierce presented it to me while you were in with the doctor, with their enthusiastic blessing."

"But please," Henry became serious once more, "I did a terrible job of stating my intentions last night; please allow me to try again. There's so much about you I love. I love how brave you are, I love that you care well for others, I love that you read Physics books for entertainment and that you know more about mathematics than I could ever learn. I love that you're an amazing archer and that you can scale rocks, but you can waltz with the grace of a Greek goddess. I love that your best friends are farmers' daughters, widows, and elderly fisherman, and that you can hold your own in a ballroom of London's finest. I love that your hair will never stay bound and that you can't keep from running when you see an open field. I hope to spend the rest of our lives learning from each other. I need you to be the courage to my caution, the liveliness to my reserved nature..."

Henry broke off, chuckling, and gently wiped the tears now flowing in earnest down Emelia's cheeks.

"I was going to write all of this down, but my spectacles were broken in the fight this morning, and I can't see a blasted thing. So suffice it to say, Emelia, I love you, I need you, and I wish never to be parted from you. Please say you'll do me the honor of becoming my wife."

Emelia nodded, and for a moment she seemed too overcome to speak.

"Yes," she finally managed to whisper, a hand to her throat. "Nothing would make me happier."

At that Henry slid the lovely ring on her finger, then picked her up off her feet as gently as he was able and twirled her around, brushing her rogue curls away from her face and kissing her soundly.

After a long moment, Emelia looked around them at the early summer day, her eyes sparkling. Henry imagined she was committing this special moment in one of her favorite places to memory.

"There's more you should know. Colonel Phillips has just given me a unique opportunity to become a scientific liaison between France and England, which would require us to split our time between both countries. I want you to know that while I'm not a wealthy man by any stretch of the imagination, I've done well for myself. I have enough that we could live comfortably anywhere we choose—France, England, or otherwise. But the last few months working for Phillips, even before I met you, I felt alive again, as if I had a purpose once more."

Henry ran a hand through his windblown hair. He hadn't even attempted to tie it back, and it swirled around his head in the breeze. He imagined he looked more the pirate than ever.

"I need you by my side," he continued, "and if I take this job from Colonel Phillips, it'll be as much your job as mine. How would you feel about meeting with scientists like Monsieur Fresnel and learning about the latest technologies? The advancements that made it possible to manufacture Fresnel's lens, the ones that have revolutionized the textiles industry here in England, this is only the beginning. The world is changing, and we have the opportunity to help both of our countries work together towards a common goal."

Emelia tilted her head to the side for a moment, thinking, but there was a sparkle in her eyes that filled Henry with joy.

"Honestly, I can't imagine anything more wonderful." When she finally answered, her voice was thick with emotion. "It sounds like the best possible fit for both of us. To not only continue my scientific studies but to actually meet with and learn from the best scientific minds of the day—well, I don't have to tell you that it's an opportunity not afforded to many women. And to get to see your home in Provence, and your grandmere, but also spend time with my family, well it's a dream I never could have thought of dreaming."

Her voice cracked a little on the last few words, and Henry drew her close, kissing the top of her head.

"As soon as we're able, I'd like for us to go back to London so you can meet my family. My sister adores you already, and I know my mother will, too. And from what I've heard about my father lately, I think you will have his respect, which is about the closest thing to affection he can give. We can get married, here, there, in Provence—wherever you'd like."

"What about right here, in this field?"

Henry looked around and grinned.

"It's perfect. We can let your mother and Lady Ravenscroft host the reception in your garden. Planning that should keep them busy for at least a few days, and give me more time to do this."

Henry kissed her once more, then tucked her up gently against his side as they both leaned on the fence. Smiling, Emelia wiped away happy tears as Henry saw three dots appear on the horizon moving towards them. As they came closer, he could see Pierce and Clara, hand in hand, with Cerus darting around them in canine joy.

"Oh, Cerus!"

Emelia bent down, favoring her bruised ribs as Cerus bounded towards her and covered her face with kisses. He seemed to realize his mistress was hurt, or maybe it was just Clara's excellent training, because he was polite and gentle, his massive paws never leaving the ground. She gave his ears a thorough scratching.

"Good, boy, Cerus. Surprisingly, I have missed you. I'm told Pierce and Clara taught you some manners while I was away."

He also appeared to have had a bath and a haircut, and was looking nearly respectable. Having said his hellos to Emelia, Cerus bounded over to Henry, sitting on his foot and leaning affectionately against his legs.

"There, you are, old boy," Henry said fondly, scratching the mutt's ears. "How do you feel about accompanying your mistress on a few adventures?"

The dog barked in acknowledgement and leaned in closer in a furry embrace.

"Sorted everything to your satisfaction, Rockcliff?" Pierce asked with a knowing grin, as Clara spotted the ring on Emelia's finger and squealed with joy, throwing herself in her arms.

Henry steadied Emelia with a hand on her back as Clara sobbed with happiness.

"Quite. We even have a bit of a plan for the future."

"Capital!" Pierce grabbed the three of them in a giant hug, and Henry smiled. He was grateful for his future brother-in-law's enthusiastic acceptance.

"Which really only leaves one question, I think," Emelia added with a sparkle in her eye as Cerus planted himself at her side once more with a look of adoration.

"And what is that, my love?"

"How attached do you think your grandmother is to her chickens?"

Cerus woofed, his love of poultry apparently not forgotten, and Gideon neighed in response.

"Realize you have to take us to Provence, too, eh Rockcliff? Clara's all agog to paint your vineyard and meet this grandmother of yours," Pierce explained, linking one arm in Clara's and the other in Emelia's and setting off back towards the house. "Of course, not so bird-witted as to crash your honeymoon, mind you, and we've plans of our own to make. Beginning with breakfast. Cook sent us to fetch you, there's a feast spread out in the morning room…"

Pierce continued as he guided the two women carefully towards home, pausing to check on Emelia's injuries every few steps. After assuring her brother that she would be fine as long as she went slowly, Emelia winked back at Henry over her shoulder as her brother waxed poetic about the kippers and roasted ham awaiting them.

Releasing Gideon's reins from the fence post, Henry followed on foot. For the first time since he could remember, Henry's anticipation for the future was just that—anticipation. Excitement even. Not dread. There was no tingling at the base of his skull, no warning of danger. Henry was—relaxed. Happy. After the war, he felt as if he'd be given a second chance at life in Provence, but lately he'd come to realize he'd only been half-living. There might not be any risk in a cautious life, the way he'd be living in Provence. But to love was to risk. And this woman, these people, had taught him that the risk was worth it.

They'd be taking quite the entourage with them back to Provence this summer.

Grandmere was going to be delighted.

Epilogue

Seaton House
Collington

August 1825

Fanning herself with a large, colorful brocade fan, Alice Ravenscroft used the other hand to lift a dainty glass to her mouth and take a sip of cold coffee. She raised an eyebrow, considering the concoction. An idea of Davis'—truly, Elizabeth's butler was worth his weight in gold—the coffee had been brewed, cooled, then mixed with sugar and cool milk from the larder before being pressed into service as the household's morning beverage. With the oppressive late summer heat wave they were having, it was simply too warm for hot coffee or tea, and Alice found lemonade with breakfast rather unappetizing. Lord knew that she'd drunk many cold cups of tea in her life, and it couldn't be called a hardship, but this felt somewhat like a treat. She'd have to remember the trick for when she took up residence at Ernside Manor in a few weeks.

Alice was in no hurry to leave the hospitality of her friend, but the manor's renovations were finally coming along to her satisfaction. Together with Clara's natural eye for beauty, she and Elizabeth had been able to turn the rather depressing old pile into a much lighter and airier dwelling with the careful use of paint and furnishings. After Emelia and Henry's wedding in July, the young couple had left for their honeymoon tour of the Continent, and Alice and Elizabeth had thrown themselves wholeheartedly into the renovations.

The wedding had been a simple but lovely affair, Emelia wearing her mother's wedding gown and a crown of flowers specially designed by Clara. Alice had advocated for a bit more pomp and circumstance—Emelia was her goddaughter, after all, and Lord knows her son would likely never get around to marrying—but Emelia and Henry had overruled her, and for once, Elizabeth had agreed. The couple was married in the front field under a simple arch made of driftwood and yellow wildflowers, followed by tea and cake in the Seaton's back garden.

Alice had worked a little of her magic, however, and had managed to get not only Henry's parents and sister to attend—the miserable old Viscount put on a show of reluctance, but Alice knew it was all an act—but also Henry's grandmother, uncle, and cousins. The latter was quite the feat, given the short window for planning and the distance to be traveled from Provence to Kent, but Alice was nothing if not resourceful. A wealthy steamship captain that owed her more than one favor made the trip down to Provence himself to summon Henry's relatives, oversaw their travel to the coast, and made the sea journey in record time.

Counting the many Appletons, the elder and younger Arbuckles, plus Lady Lilly and Lord Percy from London, Emelia's elderly fishermen friends, and an enchanting matron from town called Mrs. Oaks, the assembled guests made quite the merry party. Alice was delighted to read in the *London Times* that the wedding was recounted (by an unnamed but clever source that could have only been Lady Lilly) as one of the most exclusive and tasteful events of the season, thus ensuring a lavish welcome for the young newlyweds amongst the *ton* if they should ever decide to return to London society.

Adjusting the outlandish dressing gown she was wearing, a startling combination of jonquil and vermilion florals from Sicily, Alice twirled her coffee glass thoughtfully and turned to her friend.

"Elizabeth, dear, what would you think if we had the entire ceiling of the great room at Ernside painted a light blue? It would lend quite an air of sophistication to the place, don't you think? I remember this one room with a blue ceiling in the Palace of Versailles that was absolutely stunning."

Elizabeth, in her own colorful dressing gown of lavender and blue patchwork (Alice couldn't remember from whence it hailed, but it appeared vaguely North African in origin), looked up over a letter she'd been reading and blinked over her spectacles.

"You've been in the Palace of Versailles, Alice?"

"Oh, yes, of course, official business of Albion's and all that," Alice dismissed airily with a wave of her hand, the wide bell sleeves of her dressing gown flapping like a bird's wing.

The friends had taken to wearing Mr. Seaton's old dressing gowns instead of their own over the summer. They were made of the lightest, finest silks, and proved much cooler in the summer heat. And as Elizabeth pulled a new one out of storage every few days and recounted the travels her husband had acquired it on and what he'd loved about it, it had proven therapeutic for her as well. Alice had begun telling stories from her own marriage to Albion (the ones that weren't state secrets, of course), and the exercise was a balm to them both.

"Oh. How fascinating. Well then, yes, dear, I think blue is an excellent idea. Perhaps we should get Clara to paint another fresco on that wall opposite the great fireplace. That wall does look rather bare now that the rotten paneling has been taken out and the entire room whitewashed."

Alice grimaced. They'd discovered a leak in the room that had gone untended for years, and it had turned into quite a lengthy and expensive repair. Not that she minded the expense—to be honest it was a relief to have somewhere productive to put her extensive funds after all these years—but she was hoping to have the house finished by harvest time, and the project had set them back weeks. She had plenty of places to live, mind you, but she liked to have her hands in a project, and wanted to have it completed before they left for Provence in September.

The whole entourage was going: Alice, Elizabeth, Pierce, Clara, and even the shaggy mutt of a beast that had taken to following Clara around all day in the absence of his beloved Emelia. Cerus, that was, not Pierce. Pierce was anything but shaggy, and lately, not nearly as glued to the girl's side as the dog had been. Alice wondered if he was having second thoughts about their courtship. She was determined to get to the bottom of the matter soon, lest he lead Clara on and hurt the poor girl. She'd enjoyed getting to know Clara over the last few weeks as they worked on projects for the manor together, and had become quite fond of the lovely thing. It had been so long since Alice had had a protegee. Since her son, Andrew, now Lord Ravenscroft, was abroad with the state department more often than he was home, the last five years since Albion died had been dreadfully lonely.

Having Emelia and Elizabeth breeze back into her life had saved it, really. That nasty business with the murdering smugglers had shown her that there was still work to be done, work that even a middle-aged has-been such as herself could participate in. From her friend's delightful country home, Alice had slowly opened some old lines of communication, just to dip her toes into the water and see what was going on in the world.

Colonel Phillips had been of great help. She'd known he was a part of the War Office, of course—he'd joined that department shortly after the war, while Albion had still been alive. Back when Alice hadn't been entirely out of touch with her former colleagues. When he'd learned of her background, Phillips had been happy to keep Alice informed of anything that might be of interest—strictly in an advisory role of course—and suddenly, it was as if no time at all had passed, though the world had certainly changed since Alice had last been in the game.

England and France were at peace now, if not quite friendly. Phillips was right in that it was technological strength, not military might, that would determine world leaders in the future, and Alice hoped the civil relations would continue for some time. But there were whispers in the intelligence world of those who wanted to use the rapidly changing environment to their own advantage, those that weren't too wary of collateral damage. Henry, Emelia, Clara, even Pierce—these young people were the future. It was time to equip them for such, whatever it held.

So she'd begun with Clara. The girl had great talent, a natural artistic bent with a good eye for detail. She'd proven invaluable in Alice's work on the manor, but as they were designing draperies and painting frescoes, Alice was watching Clara, testing her memory, her knowledge of patterns. There was a little errand she hoped to send the girl on in Provence. Hopefully young Pierce would be an asset and not a distraction.

Alice and Elizabeth had encouraged Pierce in his suit of Clara, of whom they knew him to be genuinely fond. The girl seemed amiable about the connection, but the whole thing was moving rather slowly. Pierce certainly didn't seem in a rush to give up his dashing bachelor lifestyle. Perhaps the upcoming trip to Provence would prove a catalyst for the young people, one way or another. Getting outside of one's comfort zone would be the making—or the dismantling—of young love. At least that was how it had always been in Alice's experience.

"Speaking of young people," Alice said, fully realizing she hadn't actually been speaking any of her thoughts aloud but not caring, "how are Henry and Emelia?"

She nodded her head towards the letter her friend had returned to perusing.

"Oh, they seem to be getting along famously," Elizabeth answered, smiling contentedly. "They're working their way through the Alps before the weather turns, and plan to spend a fortnight in Italy before joining us in Provence."

"Ah, splendid," murmured Alice, remembering fondly one particular sojourn in the Alps with Albion. In addition to being quite romantic, it had saved the life of a vital Austrian dignitary. Ah, those were the days.

"It will be delightful to have everyone together again soon," mused Elizabeth as she sipped her coffee, swapping Emelia's letter for her usual morning newspaper.

It would be delightful, Alice thought warmly. She still had a few tricks up her sleeve, and she'd take care of these young people as if they were her own.

She couldn't wait to see where they were headed.

About the Author

Rachel Gates is a writer, entrepreneur, and life-long Francophile. She spends her time writing historical fiction set in France and England, planning trips to Europe (both real and aspirational), and curating vintage fashion. She lives in Chattanooga, Tennessee with her husband, two boys, and Murphy the big red dog. You can find her online at:

https://thefauxfrenchgirl.com

Also available from

WordCrafts Press

Paint Me Fearless
by Hallie Lee

The House on Maple Street
by Marian Rizzo

Providence
by Gail Kittleson

Maggie's Song
by Marcia Ware-Wilder

Beauty Unveiled
by Paula K. Parker

www.WordCrafts.net

Made in the USA
Coppell, TX
22 January 2025

44840111R00163